Guy,
Food for thought
Cheers,
Tom

Our Great Society

Thomas J. Reynolds, Ph.D.

D0089933

Dedication

One's path in life is to a great part determined by the instructive guideposts along the way. These guideposts are teachers and mentors who pointed the way to opportunities and painted a vision of the future. In my case, there were many such instructors, but three mentors stand out as truly visionary: Ara Parseghian, Norman Cliff and Clarke Nelson. It is with my most sincere gratitude that I thank them for sharing with me their intellect and inspiration, which has provided me the motivational fuel for my life quest.

Prologue

Washington D.C.—August 6, 1965, just before noon

Outside, by 10:00 a.m., the temperature already hovered near 90 degrees. Inside the Capitol Dome, over 100 dignitaries and invited guests arrived early not only to escape the notorious Capitol Hill heat but to ensure their place near the signing desk, where at noon President Lyndon Baines Johnson would sign his anticipated "greatest legislation" in a nationally televised address. Everyone who was anyone in the cause of civil rights was desperate for permanent, filmed proof of participation. The president had made attendance available only to a select and privileged few, those who had most supported him and those who had made the greatest contributions that would make his legislative legacy. As a result, the everyone-who-was-anyone attending the signing that day would owe him plenty . . . in "spades," he joked.

The Voting Rights Act of 1965 came little more than a year after his truly momentous Civil Rights Act of 1964, at which the president had handed out 75 pens to supporters of the bill present at the signing. Perhaps his true feelings were evidenced by his presentation of six pens to Bobby Kennedy and one to Dr. Martin Luther King Jr., where LBJ had reached awkwardly and noticeably very uncomfortably over his left shoulder to hand the deservedly celebrated Civil Rights leader his keepsake pen.

Senior staff assistants Rufus MacIntosh and Sam Brown had been tasked to assemble the pens the president would gift later that day for the Voting Rights Act, as they had for the Civil Rights Act a year earlier, symbolically guaranteeing each of them would receive a pen for their service in drafting and shepherding this keystone legislation through the political land mines in Congress.

It was known by all in the White House and left side of the aisle in Congress that Rufus and Sam were LBJ's most inner circle of advisors. They had open access to all White House formal briefings and meetings.

On this momentous day, they had both overheard Martin Luther King congratulating the president while shaking his hand, speaking slightly louder than a whisper directly in his ear, "Mr. President, you have created a second emancipation." The president immediately responding to Dr. King that "the real hero is the American Negro." Both Rufus and Sam knew LBJ's definition of hero was not in the Oxford Dictionary, unless it was printed in Mississippi.

LBJ was almost giddy this day. One could almost realize his state of mind by the look in his eyes, the way he talked and spoke. His ultimate strategic goal had formally become a reality. LBJ and his core inner circle were walking down the hallway, immediately following that comment to Dr. King, on the way to a private commemorative gathering, when both Rufus and Sam witnessed LBJ turn to Bill Moyers, his White House press secretary, and heard him defensively express, "Bill, we just delivered the south to the Republican Party for a long time to come." This seemingly astute comment was based upon the simple fact that Democrats had tried to block the Civil Rights legislation with a filibuster and in the final vote the Republicans had overwhelmingly voted Aye in both the House and Senate, to defeat the Democrats. Sam knew the truth. The passage of this bill under a Democratic presidency would supplant these vote-determining party negatives; in fact, resulting from its passage would become the most voter-stable strategic cornerstone upon which the party's future success would rest. This was LBJ's true strategic keystone.

Of course, neither Rufus nor Sam had been surprised by either of the president's remarks. What LBJ said and what he thought were often times diametrically opposed. Both had known him since their days at San Marcus College, where the three had become close friends, graduating together in the summer of 1930. Both had been on LBJ's payroll since he began his formal political career. Being part of the president's brain trust, both having earned their doctorates prior to entering the political arena, they were well aware of the Democratic Civil Rights strategy executed by LBJ. Rufus had drafted it, Sam had explained it, and LBJ had sold it, for what Lyndon knew was longtime political gain.

They had often witnessed their friend Lyndon bend with the winds of political change, believing, he told them, that "the best politicians were the quickest to sense change." Thus, for a man they knew firsthand to be a dedicated racist, who, as a Senate candidate had virtually endorsed white supremacy, this seemingly new direction came as no surprise, since they both understood that LBJ, their college pal, never did anything that was not part of achieving a political goal. And, given that LBJ laid out the goal, Rufus provided him the game plan.

Rufus and Sam were well acquainted with their friend's peculiar persuasion, knowing his political disposition could be summarized in LBJ's own words by the following quote: "It is the melancholy law of human societies to be compelled sometimes to choose a great evil in order to ward off an even greater evil." Such "LBJ-speak" had become second nature to him. Sam described it as "a perfect example of obtuse, scholarly rhetoric that elevated the perception of the speaker, while obfuscating his true meaning and intention. The correct interpretation is actually quite simple, namely, think ahead and sacrifice what and who you need to in the short term to assure your long-term political success."

"Evil," in Lyndon Baines Johnson's opinion, was anything that opposed his own current political point of view, and thus his long-term political interest. LBJ's driving force had always been power, as evidenced by his mastery of the Senate. He knew better than anyone during his time in office how to think and strategize four steps ahead of the folks on the other side of the aisle. The Civil Rights legislation, he was sure, would be his greatest accomplishment.

His dear friends had never shied away from their boss's Machiavellian behavior, which many described, often only privately, using mostly nonflattering personal descriptors ranging from "altruistic and petty, to manipulating and crude, to generous and petulant, bluntly honest, and always calculatingly devious." Uniquely, LBJ could exhibit virtually all of these traits within a few minutes.

Rufus and Sam had often helped their friend, who began his political career as an editor on the *College Star* newspaper at San Marcos, to accomplish what he termed "necessary tasks." In their first exposure to LBJ's shrewdness, they accomplished an impossible outcome, at least at that time: they wrested political control of the campus from the historical student-athlete coalition to a bunch of campus nerds, led by their political mentor. LBJ's purpose? To gain control of the student fees to fund his own personal political agenda. Over subsequent decades, Rufus and Sam often reflected on how their boss's sleight of hand in achieving this campus takeover was simply evidence of a master political strategist in training.

Such "necessary tasks" had been behind LBJ's Senate victory in 1948 and had proven one of their first major-stage accomplishments. They had both served as assistants to John B. Connally, Johnson's campaign manager in that first Senate race, in which Lyndon had proudly earned the moniker "Landslide Lyndon" after winning the election by 87 votes of 988,295 cast. So what was behind their first grand-slam victory? What was the "necessary task" to succeed in pulling out this incredibly slim victory? Rufus and Sam had worked in Precinct 13, where 202 ballots arrived just at the close of polling. Rather amazingly, all the votes were for Lyndon and were, perhaps even more interestingly, listed in alphabetical order, written with the same pen and in the same handwriting. This was an oversight Sam often raised with Rufus on private occasions, especially when fueled by vintage bourbon.

Through the years, from college, in his political races, during the White House years, and for years after, Sam and Rufus were often at their friend's side, endorsing whichever position he currently supported. Even in the president's final, melancholy years when his favorite, self-reflecting song was "Bridge over Troubled Waters," they helped him make things happen that he believed should happen. They were truly lifelong friends, with no hidden agendas.

LBJ was always loyal to his San Marcos classmates whom he had recruited to be his behind-the-scenes political partners. And when he made the decision not to run for a second presidential term in 1968, Lyndon took care of his friends, immediately gaining them both full professorships in the Department of Government at the University of Texas at Austin. In the years following, Lyndon often attended football games with them. LBJ was an ardent fan, frequently yelling so loud that, at the last game he attended, he had almost worked himself up into a heart attack. In fact, he died only weeks later, having screamed his last curse word at the season's final home game, a one-sided victory most Longhorn fans described as an ass kicking of their archrival Aggies.

The spirit of LBJ's political genius inspired the academic agenda at UT Austin and was always faithfully delivered by Rufus and Sam. They carried on his legacy and the true Democratic Party legacy that he envisioned.

Chapter One

University of Texas at Austin, September 29, 1980, Monday, 9:00 a.m.

A brand-new champagne-colored Mercedes Benz 450 SL pulls up to the LBJ Presidential Library and into a preferred parking spot near the entrance. Two graduate students, both studying for their PhDs in political science, which provided them this highly preferential parking, decide to stay inside the air-conditioned car a bit longer to avoid facing the stifling heat of Austin in late September. Even though it is only 9:30 a.m., the temperature has already surpassed 90 degrees and is more than likely going to exceed 100 as it has for 67 out of the last 70 days.

"It's hotter here than in Kuwait," Aga Khan, 26 and a native Kuwaiti, comments to Richard, his head resting back on the brown leather seat. "It's always this hot in Kuwait," Aga notes, "but everything there is air-conditioned. It would be nice if all the buildings here were as modern as ours."

Richard Rucker, a 31-year-old African American, smirks, "I'm sure there is air-conditioning in the palace." He then more lightheartedly adds, "I don't know what I hate to give up more, exiting your car and the air-conditioning or losing that new car smell. It's addictive! I swear it's addictive."

Looking directly at Richard, Aga says, "You'll be able to afford it for yourself, once you are successful in your current task."

Richard comes back, "I suppose that's true, especially coming from a royal who can afford anything. And I do mean anything."

Not flustered at all by the dig, Aga points out, "Look, I have given you a great opportunity. I have paid you for almost three years, with the guarantee of a big bonus if you find what I

9

know is there. You'll be able to buy a new car every year, like I do."

Richard points at the library building in front of them. "I know, searching the files in this fucking library three nights a week is more than a full-time job," he says. "I review maybe 90 to 95 files per night, meaning I have to scan more than a 1,000 pages. Given you grace me occasionally with some help one night a week, to complete our review of the 31 million documents, even after we initially sort for only those of Dr. Sam, Dr. MacIntosh, and LBJ, which are roughly 11 percent, will take . . ."

While Richard pauses to do the math in his head, Aga says, "To search all 31 million, with roughly 3.3 million after the sort, would take the two of us at 4,000 pages per week about 16 or so years. I know. But it only takes finding one key document. It is an investment I am more than willing to make. And you are paid well for your time. Did you find anything noteworthy last week?"

Richard laughs, "Noteworthy? It depends what you mean. I did find LBJ's memo ordering a three-console set of televisions for the Oval Office, so he could watch all the network news at the same time." Before Aga is able to comment, Richard continues, "And, perhaps even more noteworthy was his memo ordering 29 push-button phones for the White House, just for his private use. Maybe most noteworthy was that he had one installed on the bathroom wall adjacent to the shitter next to his bedroom and the one next to the Oval Office."

Chuckling, "No shit?" Aga then reaches across Richard into the glove box and hands an envelope to Richard, saying "This is for last week's work." Richard looks into the envelope, then sticks it into the back pocket of his jeans. Aga reaches for the key to turn off the car. Richard opens his door, and as he steps out he comments, "Seriously, the extra income has allowed me to pay my bills; it has really saved my ass. Thanks." Richard grabs a small stack of papers he had stored just behind his seat, and both men begin to step out into the Austin sauna but hesitate, again avoiding the outside heat.

Aga looks across at Richard and both men laugh.

"By the way," Aga says, "I have to thank you again for coming to my aid last night. I never expected to add bodyguard to your duties, but it came in handy."

Richard smiles, looking in the rearview mirror at the slight dark coloration of his right eye.

"He was lucky to get a shot in on me. I must be slipping."

"Slipping?" Aga asks.

Richard hesitates uncomfortably, as if having said something he regrets.

"Oh, they were just locals, good old boys with a few too many Lone Stars in them."

Aga, a sincere look on his face, comments on the previous night's altercation at one of Austin's night spots.

"You responded so fast. I know you said you played football, so I figured you were tough, but you moved like you really knew what you were doing. You knocked both of them down . . . and out," Aga laughs. "I mean, they were unconscious! I never saw anyone do anything like that before . . . except in a movie, maybe."

Richard laughs.

"Yeah," he says. "I should have let them walk away, but calling you a 'camel jockey' and employing the n-word to my face was more than I could handle. But I was a bit overserved. I shouldn't have let them get to me." Realizing a clarifying rationale was needed, Richard adds "I wouldn't want to get in trouble with school after all the work I have completed and how close I am to finishing."

Aga nods and opens his door.

"Well, I'm glad you took care of them. They had it coming, and it's good to know you can handle yourself that way. I had no idea. Really, and those guys had to be surprised. I mean, they won't ever be bothering us again . . . not as long as you're around, anyway."

Richard and Aga step out of the car and, immediately after exiting the car, they start walking across campus toward their graduate student offices. As they are leaving the parking lot, their graduate school colleague Roger pulls up in his baby-blue 1974 Corvette convertible.

While Aga and Richard wait for Roger to park and catch up, Aga mutters quietly to Richard, "Our doofus academic pretender is making an early appearance today."

Richard affirms, "Doofus is right. Who the fuck would have their top down in this heat?" Richard smiles, then addresses Aga's observation, "Yeah, he must want to scout the new targets in residence here this fall. School has been in session for more than a month, and he's still on point." Aga and Richard look at each other and shake their heads.

Roger Forsell, 27, also a graduate student in the Department of Government, known to the students as Political Science, steps out and joins Aga and Richard, carrying his ever-present briefcase, which is only for creating an academic effect. "Hottest part of the day," Roger comments, "and we're going to school, one that has barely any air-conditioning at all. Just how sick are we, really? We could be drinking beer in an air-conditioned saloon."

It had been an incredibly hot summer in Austin, with temperatures in late August exceeding 110 degrees. Students slogged from classroom to classroom in an attempt to escape the heat on the cross path campus walk below. Unfortunately the cool classes they were escaping to were rarely lower than the high 80s, due to very inefficient air-conditioning. Sweating profusely in class did not provide, to say the least, a very conducive educational environment.

The three political science graduate students walked side by side. Aga did not appear to be affected to any significant degree by the heat, looking almost comfortable, in his neatly starched white shirt and pressed khaki pants. Richard, dressed as always in faded blue jeans and a long-sleeved shirt, had a confident stride, with apparent purpose, almost defiantly in an attempt to ignore the heat and with an erect and military quick step. His standard long-sleeved shirt occasionally drew questioning looks from passersby in this oven-like heat. The third, Roger, appeared slope-shouldered, wearing a worn straw Stetson and battered jeans, his curly dark hair hung to his shoulders. He was going for an "I'm cool" look, which was hard to pull off on such a day as this, especially when he was clearly struggling to keep up with the other two.

The campus grass along the walkways was dappled with dead spots, due to the unmerciful heat and a poorly designed sprinkler system. This was overlooked, for the most part, due to the rise in the football polls of the Longhorns, who had just won their third straight game the previous Saturday against the Oregon State Beavers. There were still signs hanging out of the men's dorm rooms with the most popular Longhorn motivational phrase for this opponent, "Gore the Beavers."

These three men, all candidates Sam and Rufus were considering for the final stage of the doctoral program at UT, spoke casually, occasionally challenging each other, discussing potential question topics for the upcoming PhD qualifying exam. They were all aware that it was improbable for all three to be accepted to the Political Science Doctoral Program at the university. Richard and Aga believed that Roger was more than likely going to fail this career-determining final exam.

They had all attended the same graduate seminar classes. Everyone, especially the professors, knew who was likely to pass or fail. The senior political science faculty was consistent in their assessment of Richard Rucker as a serious student with high potential. This was always somewhat of a conundrum to them, given the fact that he had enrolled at UT after several years of "blue-collar" employment. Though he was never explicit about his jobs during this period, Richard often described how he came home every night with his hands dirty. In his admissions interview, Richard said his primary motive for going to grad school was to find a job where he would never come home with dirty hands, with dirty finger nails. Although it was not scholarly, this rationale played well with Rufus and Sam, who clearly understood this mentality. It was in their DNA as well.

Richard had rationalized to them his time away from academics as necessary for him to obtain funds necessary for his continuing education. Again, Rufus and Sam understood, having gone through the same situation when going for their PhDs.

During his time at UT, Richard was recognized by the faculty as a hard worker, dedicated to achieving his academic goal, their supposition being that, as a Black man, he knew he always had to work harder than his white rivals for attention, recognition, and advancement.

The common view of Aga, held both by the faculty and his fellow grad students, was that he was exceptionally bright, this being reinforced by his undergrad perfect 4.0 grade point from the London School of Economics. That he had a new car in each of his three years in grad school was solid evidence that he was from a wealthy Kuwaiti family. Aga's choice to go to UT, when he could have gone to any grad school, was accepted by the faculty as validation of their composite academic reputations. Ego is never in short supply within academic circles.

Roger lagged behind the other two, as usual. But he was keenly aware of his good looks and charming appeal to young coeds on campus. He was suave and easygoing with a laid-back style and attitude. But this laid-back style, unfortunately, carried over to his academics. He frequently took educational shortcuts. Roger had graduated from the University of Southern California with very mediocre grades but had scored high on the Graduate Record Exams, which was the basis for his gaining admission to grad school. Roger's roving eye was usually focused on Amy, 25, who was a doctoral candidate in economics. Roger's choice of his primary girlfriend, his fellow students thought, was not random. Her grandfather was Dr. Sam Brown, chairman of the Government

Department, who had the ultimate determination of whether Roger succeeded or failed.

As the three grad students walked together toward their offices, Richard and Aga were aware that any sign of interest from one of the passing coeds could draw Roger away from their conversation, so they typically only shared their thoughts with one another, excluding Roger.

"Exam questions are key," Richard loudly announced, and Aga responded.

"Yes, to everything. We must anticipate."

Cutting Aga off, Richard speculated, "Two, maybe even three of us, if the doofus finds some magical elixir, will pass the last exam all of us will ever take, and those who pass will be assigned an advisor, their dissertation chair. Then the final phase, selecting the topic and completing the dissertation. We are down to the short strokes, my man. This is the end game."

"I hope for Dr. MacIntosh to chair my committee," Aga responds. "I would love to get into his head and learn how and why he thinks the way he does. His seminars were too cut and dried, too factual. I need to better understand his process of political strategy development."

Richard queries, "So, you are really hoping he will share his insights, providing some directional guidance for our library research?" Aga nods in the affirmative.

Smiling and aware of Aga's honesty, Richard confidently quips, "Yup. Dr. Mac is your choice, and either he or Dr. Sam would be key to me gaining insight into their political inner workings. The added benefit could assure an academic position, which is my real goal. Dr. Sam, though, would be my first choice. I believe he would allow me to explore any dissertation area I would choose. He is a doer, he knows how to get things done in the political arena, and I know that I must develop that skill set."

Catching up to his friends as Richard was talking, after having fallen behind while connecting with a very beautiful blonde intent on hurrying to her next class, Roger animatedly chimes in on his friends' conversation: "Given I am low man on the totem pole, that just leaves Dr. Bowman for me." And at this point, Roger audaciously begins singing the lyrics from the song in the movie *Grease*.

"She's the one that I want any . . . wayaaaye! Whoop de whoop de do!"

Richard and Aga, both frustrated with Roger, the "constantly on-point doofus," exchange anguished looks, and Richard almost drops his armful of papers as he attempts to wave his arms in the air, in obvious frustration with Roger's antics.

"Of course," Richard responds. "A woman! It's always a woman! Won't you ever grow up?"

"Oh, fuck you," Roger responds. "But she does have a great ass, for an older woman. Dr. Bowman has a great, pump-in ass. You know what I mean?"

Aga, obviously confused, apparently not affecting a clear translation, responds.

"A pumpkin ass?"

"No," Roger responds, while coordinating his pelvic thrusts with his extending arms, "Pump-in, not pumpkin."

Eyes wide, Aga looks to Roger. "May Allah forgive you."

Smiling as though to himself, Richard comments, "This is most likely the last go-around for Dr. Sam and Dr. Mac, you know. We, or the candidates they select, will be their last shot, their last opportunity to develop doctoral candidates who can pass on their firsthand knowledge of the well-practiced and highly successful mechanics of political strategy."

Richard adds, "We all know their backgrounds, their accomplishments. We certainly know their political orientations inside and out. It's the test questions that are at issue here. We must focus on passing our exams so we can move on to our dissertations."

The three men begin walking quicker, not even realizing their nervous frustration has propelled them into a faster pace, despite the extreme heat.

Roger, deciding in a rare moment to take a serious tack, says, "This will be our opportunity to learn about legislation that has changed the course of American society, from the men who helped change it!"

Richard responds, "True! And each of them has his personal favorite stories of their ol' drinking buddy's Great Society programs. Such stories to share! Such personal connections to history! We have the last chance to gain what they know."

"Yes, and to discover their untold secrets?" Aga adds, glancing to Richard for support.

They walk silently for several moments until Roger again attempts to contribute. "They each have their own priorities, scholarly lessons they want to share, to serve as a basis for their legacy. And each of them, as we have learned in their classes, has a different perspective on the stories and subjects they have created, been a part of, and experienced."

Richard appears surprised at Roger's realization that Rufus and Sam actually did have different perspectives; as such insight required actually listening carefully to what they were saying.

Aga interjects, "Look, dissertation topics are guided if not totally determined by the chair, and these men certainly are not going to work on something they are not personally vested or at least very interested in pursuing for themselves. Given this will be the last one they will orchestrate, I think they will want to make one final, definitive mark. I considered this when I decided to come to UT. I knew I would be watching the passing of an era in American politics."

Before Aga is finished speaking, Roger's attention is diverted to another passing coed. Ignoring Richard's hand gesture, beseeching him to leave the girl alone, he laughs and turns to follow the young girl, who had simply returned his smile in a polite attempt to wish him a good morning.

Richard and Aga have often suffered through Roger's forceful alignment into their group. Though neither ever say so, it is clear to both that their association with Roger could lead them to a more successful set of skills when dealing with the opposite sex.

As Roger makes his way back to the group after his last mission, Richard says to Aga, "He won't make it in the program. He has no real appreciation of the opportunity he has here, under Dr. Brown and Dr. MacIntosh." Aga laughs as he looks back at Roger, who has now redirected his efforts in pursuit of a long-haired and -legged, short-skirted coed. "He doesn't even understand his own comment on the motivating influence of events, of convincing people to believe in and support a cause. He has no concept of how to understand a voting group's decision making, what would best influence people to change their voting decision, and how to best communicate to them to effect this change."

Richard and Aga pick up their pace, moving quickly away, leaving Roger far behind, metaphorically echoing their growing resentment of his selfish, childish, pursuit of yet "another skirt." The rub, as they saw it, was his not recognizing the once-in-a-lifetime opportunity before him.

They enter the building though grandiose arches facing the main campus, where the Department of Government and its graduate student offices are housed. They enter along with scores of undergrads heading for relief from the heat, most failing to consider the additional discomfort they will face from the man-made hot air they will soon have to endure.

Chapter Two

From his corner office Dr. Sam Brown observes his department's three Political Science graduate students entering the building. They are the last three he will ride herd over.

As chairman of the Department of Government, Sam had selected his uniquely large and open third-floor office to provide him a view including Texas Memorial Stadium, the LBJ Museum and Presidential Library, and the Clock Tower, all locations to which he feels a strong personal connection.

He had been unable to play football in college himself due to a knee injury suffered during his four-year service in the Marine Corps prior to attending college, but Sam is an avid fan and enjoys hosting pregame parties, which have, over the years, become legendary on campus. Their fame stems primarily from Sam's sinister drink servings, which lead to great conversations with his friends and associates as they monitor the festivities and crowds that gather for home games.

Many attendees of his pregame functions have been known to master Portuguese in a single afternoon while attending what he affectionately terms the Training Room. All too frequently, participants in this UT tradition have decided to forgo the game itself, preferring to simply relax at Sam's Training Room. Given this was going to be Sam's last year of teaching before his scheduled retirement in June, he decided to make this final go-round special, including a bartender and a hostess to serve catered barbecue brisket sandwiches—the cost of these added amenities, of course, coming from the departmental budget.

Sam's Training Room was notorious not just for his generous bar but also for the many bar stories told at his parties, especially prior to UT football games, when the male testosterone in the infamous room was at its highest, with Sam often lamenting his inability to play college football but filled in with stories of his days in the Marine Corps. Rufus was Sam's greatest supporter, finding gratification of a type, as he had never experienced, in Sam's prowess in fisticuffs. Sam's boxing prowess was legendary, both when he was in the service and afterward in Golden Gloves tournaments.

Rufus had, in fact, a lifetime of Sam stories he could call up and share with any willing listeners. And the more inebriated he became, which was simply a matter of time, the more colorful and detailed Sam's experiences were described.

In fact, even as a senior citizen, Sam took no guff from anyone and, on more than one occasion, found himself in front of the university's governing board for his "minor" altercations. Most potential board "incident reviews" he could easily evade, but a few over the years at UT took him to the brink of being disciplined. However, being LBJ's lifelong pal went a long way to having the board look the other way.

"Oh!" Rufus would begin with his favorite Sam story prior to almost every game, standing in the Training Room, bellowing out the "rickshaw" story of Sam once he had enough bourbon in him to provide him the confidence necessary to tell it in the boisterous style he believed necessary to carry the impact he desired.

"Oh, my God. It was great! Sam and I left for the pregame festivities at the Training Room just before ten after parking at the LBJ library. You know how hot it can be. And many of the fraternity members built rickshaws so they could transport the fans up to a mile and half from the furthest parking lot to the tailgates and to the stadium. I mean, it's a great business for them: with 100-degree heat people are more than willing to jump in their rickshaws and be delivered to their tailgate activities rather than walk. And the kids make great money."

Rufus would always take a breath at this stage of his story, along with a long pull on his glass of bourbon.

"But that day, it was so hot, as a student went by peddling his rickshaw, we flagged him down. The driver told us it would be five bucks to take us the three blocks."

Rufus would take another drink and Sam would habitually, at this point in the story, either ask Rufus to move it along or beg him to stop.

"Anyway, the kid—who was clearly an undergrad, though he looked like he could have played football himself— and Sam at that time was just, maybe just pushin' sixty-some himself. But the kid tells Sam to hurry up, because he was costing him money, and pushes Sam into his seat causing him to spill his drink. Sam looks at him, and the dumb bastard says, 'Fuck you old man, you can get a refill in a few minutes. Let's go.'"

Rufus would always laugh out loud at this stage of the story.

"So Sam, instinctively, pops him one in the chin with his left and follows up with a straight right and the kid is out. So Sam puts the kid in the rickshaw with me and pulls us both to our building, sticks five bucks in the kid's pocket, and we leave him sitting there, as he is beginning to come to."

"But the kid was fine," Sam would always add, putting Rufus's listening audience at ease. "He was just a cocky little shit. So he learned a lesson that day, that there are consequences, right there across from the old man's library next to the stadium."

Of course, both Sam and Rufus were intimately involved with the design and construction of LBJ's Presidential Memorial at UT, having to be on site daily for several years immediately after their arrival on campus, until it opened May 22, 1971, just sixteen months after LBJ left the presidency. Sam had always harbored suspicion that LBJ had organized their positions at UT to ensure his library was done the way he wanted it to be done.

The relevance of the Clock Tower to Sam was a different story. Having qualified as an expert with rifle, pistol, and machine gun while in the service, Sam outwardly loathed but secretly appreciated the shots fired from the Tower Clock on August 1, 1966, by former Marine and UT student Charles Joseph Whitman. The shots Whitman fired that day killed 14 students and citizens and wounded 32. Sam was always careful to point out that

Whitman's longest deadly shot, to the stomach of a 29-year-old electrician Roy Schmidt, was from over 500 yards away. And, he would explain for those who showed interest, just how difficult the shots had been for Whitman, from his vantage point, shooting down from the 300-foot tower that daily rang music from its carillon of 56 bells.

Sam would occasionally share over a beverage how he had helped found the Marine Corps sniper school and would point out the critical and necessary importance of a one-shot mentality. During these instructional tutorials, there was no doubt that Sam was still a Marine at heart.

Walking into Sam's office, which was the home of the Training Room on game days, gave the general observer not only a great view of campus landmarks but a view into the personal history of Sam Brown. On the wall of his office, nearest the large picture window offering a view of the campus and, further south, the downtown area, was a beautifully framed and famous picture taken at the signing of the Civil Rights Act in 1964. It showed President Lyndon Baines Johnson turning to hand a signing pen to Dr. Martin Luther King Jr. and, standing behind and to the right of Dr. King, were Sam and Rufus. Always in the background, but also always in the know about their mentor's true motives and intentions, both Sam and Rufus were showing off their absolute biggest smiles. Sam, his hair still Marine Corps cropped, his eyes weathered but clear and determined, still looked like he could kick anybody's ass. While Rufus, always ruffled, already balding, his red suspenders clearly on display, looked on, with his shirttail semiexposed, his sport coat open and unbuttoned, exposing his prematurely expanding stomach. Rufus's signature look, including his string tie, was not surprising, given he was from Fink, Texas, population comprising his own and one other family when he left for college. Fink was a once-thriving cowpoke town between Dallas and the Red River bordering Oklahoma, later known solely as a place to water horses.

Thomas J. Reynolds, Ph.D.

Rufus had come a long way from Fink. He studiously took in the events evolving around him, often smiling bizarrely, as if he were the evil cat in a comic cartoon that had just gotten away with eating the poor yellow bird. But those who actually knew Dr. Rufus MacIntosh, a University of Chicago–educated PhD in sociology, were pretty well convinced that he was the smartest guy in the room. He certainly believed that himself. "Ol' Texas smart," he would often reflect, which "was 49 times smarter than all of the rest." This personal assessment tended to be a little more likely when he was addressing his "being parched" problem with some medicinal bourbon.

The furniture in Sam's office, his colleagues often teased, resembled how they imagined a mad, rich, gunny sergeant's office might look in a tented combat zone, plain, stark, weathered, and scarred. There were six chairs circling a large conference table in Sam's office, and a large executive desk, with an encased three-foot-high, four-foot-wide, and one-foot-deep glass front that showcased a perfectly designed nature setting, exhibiting six taxidermied red-necked pheasants, forcing anyone attempting to look down or away to avoid Sam's harsh gaze to stare instead straight into a flock of dead but beautifully stuffed carefully preserved birds.

Only 15 feet to the left of Sam's desk, was his equally audacious, stand-up wooden bar, with brass spittoons on each side on the floor and an enclosed picture-box front, with several Texas quail, two black-tailed prairie dogs, and, in both corners, western diamondback rattlesnakes, perfectly posed to strike, in a beautiful and natural setting, prairie flowers all around.

Proudly perched atop Sam's campus-famous bar, there could always be viewed, standing side by side, bottles of Texas bourbon, Austin's Red-Handed Bourbon, Garrison Brothers Texas Straight Bourbon, and Red Line Texas Bourbon. The ever-present odor in the office was directly attributable to the liquids in the bottles, which were often left open. The only utensil atop the bar was a single glass eye dropper, used to add Austin branch water to

23

Sam's favorite beverage, with a two-drop maximum allowed. "One drop or two?" Sam would famously ask his guests when assuming his traditional role as bartender, serving bourbon and branch water.

Directly behind the bar, in the place of honor, was Sam's most prized possession, an elaborately framed personal note on presidential stationery: "Thanks, Sam. Without you and Rufus, none of this would have come about," and signed, "LBJ."

As Sam stood at his window, waiting for his scheduled meeting, he watched the students walk across campus, as he reflected on his life. It had been a good one, he thought, overall. He served his country, in the military and in government. He was proud of being part of a team that really made the Democratic Party. What motivated him to teach was the sharing of his political experience and vision with the next generations and the enjoyment of spending his days with his lifelong friend, Rufus MacIntosh.

Rufus entered Sam's office, as usual, without being announced or even knocking, breaking Sam's train of thought. Following behind him was Dr. Debbie Bowman, the only female of the department, and the third member of the political science PhD faculty.

Though she was 40 years of age and her two colleagues were more than three decades her seniors, Dr. Debbie Bowman enjoyed the verbal innuendo and flirtations Dr. Rufus MacIntosh, 72, often directed her way. She could not remember a time when crossing her legs had not immediately, instinctively, and obsessively drawn or commanded Dr. Mac's full attention—although she would have much preferred that such attention should come from Dr. Sam, because he could better further her career, which was her primary motivating force. But this was not the case.

She stood five foot nine with long hair and longer legs and full lips. She was fit, attractive, and, like her cohorts, of a strongly political and liberal persuasion.

While her colleagues clearly had the finish line of their careers in sight, Dr. Bowman believed she was at the starting line of her own high-profile career, not just in academia, as likely the next department chair when Sam retired after this school year, but also in state and ultimately national politics. She was acutely aware how her physical assets combined with intelligence could be used to propel her to success. Having never married, she had made the choices and sacrifices necessary to concentrate on her ambitions, making connections through countless dinners, parties, and social and political events of all kinds.

The three members of the Political Science Program's PhD selection committee sat comfortably in Sam's office, or at least so it seemed. Every time Debbie entered Sam's office, her skin tingled from the feeling of power.

Sam was traditionally clad in a sport coat, Rufus in a white shirt and his traditional red suspenders that did nothing to hide his extended belly. Debbie wore high heels and a tight skirt and blouse, always open at the collar. While Sam and Debbie were always well dressed, Rufus's clothes, like his face, were wrinkled and always looking as though he had picked them off the floor, though his loving wife Mary made every effort to see that he dressed well. "Maybe it's his posture," she had once commented to Sam.

Sam moves immediately to his bar and pours bourbon into three glasses. He smiles as he pours for his colleagues, hoping to go unnoticed as he adds several drops of water to the drinks, using the ever-present eye dropper atop the bar.

Debbie, to no avail, attempts to abstain with a wave of her hand and a polite smile.

"Last go around," Sam announces. "I'm ready to ride off into the sunset."

Sam looks at Rufus. "And how about you?"

Rufus nods affirmatively. "Let's make it a good one," Rufus says. "And let's start with a toast . . . to good friends, good whiskey, and good times. But," he pauses for dramatic effect, "you branch water this bourbon down any more and you'll have a mutiny before you have a test ready for Friday."

Reluctantly, but smiling at Rufus's aversion to water in his bourbon, Debbie accepts a glass. Sam growls, "How long have we been selecting these piss-ant PhD candidates, Rufus?"

Shaking his head, Rufus responds, "Since you almost had a full head of hair, I was almost skinny and we were lucky enough that Lyndon found me and you jobs when we left Washington, graciously providing us an honorable exit strategy."

Rufus takes a long drink, glaring solemnly at his glass. "You remember, Sam? He made us part of the UT scholarly brain trust." Rufus offers another toast, looking toward the five-white-star diagram on the wall, "To the White Stars." As they toast, both men think about this team, three of the six previously having offices in the White House.

Sam turns to the graphic on the wall as they stand and toast, while Debbie remains seated at the conference table. She studies the two men, unsure of the meaning of the reference to the framed print but realizing that any questioning of their Ol' Boys' Club formalities at this point could be viewed as inappropriate, and thus not in her best interest.

Changing the subject, Sam asks, "How about that dumb shit Carter? Iran hostages, economy running on one cylinder, and no economic plan in sight. He sure likes to get folks thinking he cares about their problems. But, truth is, he has no bloody clue what the hell to do. Great heart, maybe, but no strategy."

Intent on being part of the conversation, Debbie adds, with the sole purpose of ingratiating herself, "Reagan vs. Carter could change everything that you two gentlemen helped to build. We could be headed for a conservative course, with five Supreme Court seats at stake, and all your old programs in jeopardy. Good thing your old boss isn't around to see that."

Rufus holds out his glass and shakes it when Sam feigns to stop pouring. Reluctantly, Sam fills his friend's glass to the level satisfying him. "Fuckin' Carter!" Rufus reacts, "He ignored us all. He certainly didn't have anything like the brain trust Lyndon had. He tried to intellectualize things too damn much— and he didn't have a team with a long-term game plan." He pauses, taking a long swig of bourbon and continues, "Enough about politics! Speaking of game plans, the ass-kicking we gave Holtz and the Razorbacks was sweet revenge for last year's debacle."

Sam counters, "Yeah, I ran into Coach Akers outside the stadium yesterday. He said the Arkansas opening game was going the set the tone for the season. He was right, we are on the way."

"How do you think we'll stack up against the shit-head Aggies this season?" Rufus inquires, then taking a sip of bourbon as he waits for a response.

"We're much better this year, I think," Sam positively responds to Rufus. "The Aggies lost a lot of their starters from last year. They shouldn't prove much of a problem for our boys. There is a good chance we could run the table this year."

Rufus interjects with a smile, "Yeah, and I heard we raised minimum wage for the backfield."
Sam agrees with a smile and says, "I did hear our recruiting has also definitely improved, what a coincidence."

"I did see quite a few new Camaros outside the dorm where most or the athletes live" Sam shares, validating Rufus's recruiting observation, then adding "I did also hear that the stakes are up in Dallas with SMU. They're getting the star recruits: they got a pretty good deal on Pontiac Trans Ams."

Sam holds the bottle out to Debbie but she refuses with a gentle, almost flirtatious shake of her head.

"You sure?" Sam asks, and when she confirms it, he turns to Rufus, who warns him. "You never would have watered down Lyndon's bourbon like you do mine," his abruptness surprising both Debbie and Sam with his obvious and genuine frustration.

"Oh, hell no," Sam quickly responds, "he'd of dragged my ass into the john and forced me to watch him take another dump, talkin' all the way through it, as though he were just sitting in a local saloon."

Rufus laughs and asks, "You remember the day he was on the pot and he sent me out to get him prunes?" Sam laughs while sipping his drink. "Those stunts were his way of making everybody around him intellectualize, in a very relaxed environment. I remember the first time he did that. We were strategizing at San Marcos about how to overthrow the Black Stars. It just blew my mind that he would hold a big strategy meeting while sitting on the shitter."

"Yup," Rufus responds. "You know I always wanted to put a rubber snake, or a live one, in the john for him to discover. But I never had the nerve."

Debbie has been sitting at the conference table, listening intently, her curiosity growing. Suddenly, she can no longer keep it in check. "Are you serious?" she asks. "Did he really hold meetings like that, in the bathroom?"

Pretending to ignore her question, Sam responds, "Enough of our dirty laundry. Back to Carter. That dumb bastard doesn't even have a short-term plan. As you would say, Rufe, to quote you yet again, he's a pencil dick, chicken shit . . ." Sam pauses, searching suddenly for a word that might be less offensive to Debbie. "Son of a bitch," he suddenly blurts out. "All we built, he's just pissing away!"

Surprised at Sam's language and tone, Debbie crosses her legs, trying to break up the old-boy dialogue and move the meeting along, confident her exercise would draw their attention, and pleased when it does. "I have several test ideas in mind," she says to them, "but tell me yours, so we don't overlap. We only have today and tomorrow to prepare for Friday."

Sam engages again, "Okay, we have three candidates we all know well from our classes. We pretty much know how each will do, so let's just construct questions that will discriminate them in terms of their knowledge and insight."

Rufus confidently comments, "Yeah, I know how they'll do."

Obviously uncomfortable, Debbie crosses her legs the opposite way and asks, "Our goal is to build a fair test that measures their abilities. We cannot enter into it with any prior bias, can we?"

And, with that, Rufus takes a long drink and comments, "Right!"

Sam begins to respond, but Rufus beats him to it. "Okay, I see, maybe, three areas: First, the implications of the Vietnam War, both internationally and with respect to our societal value system and how our society will likely view the war in the future; second, our country's international affairs problems created by the Cuba fiasco, leading to the Cold War, due to our so-called foreign policy guru, JFK, which extends, unfortunately, into the current Iran hostage cluster fuck; and third," Rufus looks very intent as he continues, "of particular interest to me, in order to get the kids focused on the political unrest which is likely to continue into the future, is all the damn assassinations, which conveniently ended when our boy left office. I'm talking about starting with JFK, to Malcolm X, Bobby, and MLK. Finally, closer to home, how to characterize the motives underlying the assassinations of Lyndon's henchmen, Malcolm Wallace, and Billie Sol. I think this history is worth thinking through, for all of us, before we are on the defensive. It is a matter of time before someone will dig it all up and connect the dots. We need to prepare for this eventuality or all of our Great Society programs could be called into question." Looking at Sam, Rufus continues, "and we don't want that to happen, do we?"

Debbie was unsure how to react to the assassinations issue, so she opted to focus her question on the second, foreign policy failures due to JFK. She could not help but question the negative tone, Sam's obvious distaste for JFK, but after a moment of thought, she decided it was not in her best interest to argue with the current power elite.

"Look," she said, after several awkward moments of silence, "I break it down to questions that focus on the fundamental distinction regarding government strategies, the best path to give the disadvantaged a better life. More specifically, is the Gipper's crazy notion of supply-side economics, the belief that we could eliminate poverty and racial injustice by enabling people to lift themselves out of the cycle of poverty, the direction our government should take? Or, is our government's helping-hand strategy, which you two led the fight for," she looked back and forth between Sam and Rufus, "that is grounded in truly caring for the disadvantaged in our society, giving them a safety net to ensure their quality of life, the better option?" Debbie had prepared this question for the meeting, knowing she would strike pay dirt with her senior colleagues. And it worked. They nodded agreement, indicating it would definitely be on the exam.

Trying to gain further brownie points, Debbie continues in firmly establishing her commitment to the party line, scoffing, "Reagan is a naive, insensitive asshole. He can read a script, but he has no intellectual understanding of anything. You know the teleprompter is his best friend. He doesn't understand that folks need our guidance. They cannot exist without our type of government programs."

Rufus quickly and supportively responds, "Another version of the 'trust me' government strategy to solve inequalities in our society. Perfect. Spin the hope card, and keep 'em in the dark as long as you can with the 'great future ahead for all of us' bullshit. That's what you're describing, after all, isn't it? 'Trust me, I know best.' It plays the same on both sides, though, doesn't it? It just depends on where your ideology lies, how well you frame what you represent as truth and the vision of the future you paint."

Sam stands, walks to the window, turns, looks at Rufus, and says, "Framing the truth so folks can't see your game plan is your area, Rufus. It's what you and the old man conceived of and accomplished. But let's get back to why we're here now. We need a question or two about how political philosophy drives the development of programs, which can be sold as solutions to societal problems. Specifically, the creation of entitlement programs that directly deal with societal problems as opposed to a simple-minded practice of preaching equalizing opportunity for, or at some time in, the future."

Debbie also stands, adjusting her skirt, as if in response to Sam, and speaks confidently, "The political reality is really quite simple. It's about convincing folks that you are a leader and can deliver what they want. We know better than the uneducated masses. Without us they would never have a chance to experience the American Dream. They wouldn't even have a chance to dream. That's what our party stands for."

Inspired, Rufus, thinking about his past for a moment, proudly adds, "The old man really was the greatest politician ever, and thus he was also the greatest creator of agenda-making, leadership-believing rhetoric. He lived in reality the way a magician does. His true gift was distraction."

Debbie is instantly and obviously offended and frustrated by Rufus's remark, and now a little too bourbon-influenced to hide her feelings. "Surely you mean that the president was a political magician, in the positive sense, but not a liar, or a deceiver, right? That's what you're saying, right?" Debbie, almost pleadingly, questions.

Sam once again attempts to redirect the conversation. "Look, nobody played the political magic game better than the old man, Debbie. Nobody. He always had a game plan, but he never let on as to what it was. He was a true magician of political rhetoric and he never, ever, passed up a political opportunity for accomplishing his goals."

Rufus jumps on Sam's bandwagon adding, "Hell, he even thought every crisis presented an opportunity, didn't he, Sam? Even the war!" Still confused and totally unconvinced, Debbie responds. "Are you serious? Vietnam as an opportunity? An opportunity for what?"

Rufus, realizing his bourbon may have been speaking out of school, jumps to his feet. "And that's a damn good exam question," he comments, following Sam's lead in attempting to draw the conversation back to test questions. "It's a damn good question to come up with, even for an old jarhead like you, Sam!"

Rufus points to a picture on the wall of a very young Sam, perfectly outfitted in his Marine uniform. As Rufus looks at the picture, his mind drifts back to the first time he and Sam met, so many years before. Sam had been standing in front of him in the dining hall line at San Marcos. Rufus remembered himself, admiring but curious in regard to the new-on-campus and very young Marine, still in uniform, standing tall, his hair short and shaved on the sides.

"You a student here?" Rufus remembered asking.

Sam had smiled. "Yeah, I guess. Starting today I am, anyway."

"So," Rufus had added, "you won't be a Marine anymore?"

Sam had quickly turned then to face Rufus, speaking bluntly, crisply, putting Rufus in his place while making his situation clear, the smile disappearing from his face, "I'll always be a Marine!" Sam had snapped. This recollection brought a bit of sobriety to Rufus.

Standing in his office, Sam pours another round of drinks for himself and Rufus but purposely avoids Debbie, who still looked perplexed by Rufus's last comment regarding the political upside of the Vietnam War. She realized that Rufus was just jerking her around, which he tended to do to everyone, except Sam of course, when he was at stage one of being over served.

Just before reseating himself, and very desirous of redirecting the conversation, giving a wink and nod to Rufus as Debbie looked away, Sam says, "I, well, you know, there was a time when I actually did believe the old man's crap about his great-great-grandfather being at the Alamo."

Rufus, realizing that Sam is saving him, says, "Oh, did you, now? Really?"

Debbie, taking the bait, admits, "I thought LBJ's great-great-grandfather was at the Alamo."

Rufus all-knowingly winks at Sam but then speaks to Debbie. "Oh, come on."

Sam and Rufus laugh. Rufus says, 'Just another story, honey. I'll fill you in another time."

Sam pauses, takes another long drink, emptying his glass. He looks, longingly, as if for a friend, to the bottle of bourbon on his bar. Judging the distance to the bar as too great for the moment, he raises his empty glass and toasts, "Well, hell, I will drink to . . . to the intellectual cloud covering up political reality in this day and age, to truth, and to the old man's great-great-grandfather." His toasting with an empty glass gives Debbie a clue that he, too, had imbibed a bit too much bourbon.

Confused but still terribly interested, Debbie looks from Sam to Rufus, and then at her glass, now wishing it was full, as Sam adds, "We learned from the master."

Walking to Sam's desk, unsure how to respond to this revelation, Debbie randomly picks up one of the bottles of bourbon and pours herself a drink, almost filling the glass. "Yes, of course," she admits, wisely realizing the great-great-grandfather trap her two colleagues had set, "Politics is about winning, but it must be for the long-term benefit of society, for those we serve."

Sam and Rufus share a glance as Sam finishes his drink; both thinking how simple minded her idealism is. Sam continues with his train of thought: "Back to business. The program. The questions. Not so much why exactly they were developed, but rather what they were, and if they were effective. Design and effect should be the crux of the questions we present. How are things different because of the programs we initiated? And are we, or is the country, better or worse as a result? If yes, explain. If not, tell us why, explain why not?"

"Yes," Rufus adds, "the real question to be reflected upon is whether we are we better off as a society? To hell with truth! That's the only real question that needs to be answered, isn't it? It's all about the end result of the programs. And, speaking of being better off, wouldn't we be better off in a place like the Driskill? Where we can be served in style? Rather than here, where the drinks are watered down, where it is becoming annoyingly and increasingly difficult to be 'properly' served?"

Debbie drains the drink in her hand and says, "Perhaps I shall meet you gentlemen there?"

"A quick question to ponder on our trip," Sam adds as Debbie rises to leave. "After the exams, assuming all three of our candidates pass . . ." This causes Rufus to interrupt and say, "Fat chance." Ignoring this comment, Sam continues with "We need to also think who will chair the dissertations for each candidate." Allowing his observation to sink in, Sam continues, "Richard is clearly the brightest of the trio, and most likely to become a successful academic."

"That's true," Rufus acknowledges, cutting Sam off. "Richard attended Northern Illinois, which isn't much of a place, academically speaking, but his grades were outstanding, as were his test scores. What is curious is why he worked a blue-collar, manual-labor job for four years before even applying to grad school. He likely could have gotten a scholarship with some funding like we did?"

Debbie jumps into the fray, saying, "Perhaps he just needed to sort out his life. He has certainly been a star here at UT."

"Then there is Aga," Sam continues. "He is bright, but not a great writer or thinker. He is inquisitive, thorough, aggressive, and confident. I'm not sure why the hell he is here, but my guess is he is likely to become some sort of politico, but not a scholar, nor even an academic. He's about understanding ideas and issues, but not about the implementation of them, nor about developing any of his own."

"Agreed," Debbie responds as she wobbles slightly, then quickly sits backs down to regain her composure and balance before crossing her legs. As she sits she adds, "I would have thought a person with Aga's undergraduate pedigree would have been more inclined, more scholarly inclined," she mumbles, embarrassed by her sudden lack of coherence.

There is a long silence, broken finally by the sound of Sam pouring himself another drink.

"And then there is Roger," Sam loudly announces. "Roger dodger. Not dedicated but street smart, which is surprising given his previous surfing lifestyle at USC. Certainly not a scholar, no chance, really, of becoming an academic, but he skims by, gets by. He seems to find a way to stay on board, to keep his head above the water, hanging on by his toenails, pun intended. Not drowning."

Rufus extends his glass but Sam ignores it, as he says somewhat jokingly, "I've always thought of USC as the University of Spoiled Children. Have you seen that Corvette he drives? He's big on style and looks, short on understanding, and totally absent original ideas and inspiration."

Debbie comes to Roger's defense. "He could become a credit to us, to this university. To our program. Yes, admittedly, he struggles, but he also succeeds. He does require special support, but isn't that our purpose here? To provide the support required, needed? Roger does have potential!"

Exasperated but curious, Rufus adds. "Potential? Perhaps at being a subversive political operative. He would be a perfect, good-looking talking head, repeating political rhetoric, talking political jargon, making points someone else has developed! His rhetoric should not be legitimized by us simply putting doctor in front of his name."

After a long pause, Rufus directly confronts Debbie. "I sense you like this young man, this Roger? How is this possible? He isn't even a true believer in our political orientation."

Caught off guard by the comment, she responds quickly but carefully, avoiding any appearance of defensiveness. "I like that he finds a way to succeed," she finally responds, having struggled several moments for the words. "He finds a way to navigate through the ivy-laden academic maze, with the bullshit challenges we create."

Sam finishes his drink and attempts to laugh, but it turns into a snort and he is embarrassed by the resulting sound.

"Okay," he says, struggling for a response. "Roger will be a pragmatic practitioner without ideological baggage. And, after all, isn't that really what political science should be about?"

Rufus looks to Debbie and laughingly questions, "Are you shitting me?" He then looks to Sam and adds, "You know it's only about ideology. The biggest joke of all is giving our field credibility by labeling it Political Science. Science means searching for truth, something not often found in politics."

"Sure," Debbie confidently responds, having regained her composure. "We all perpetuate our own core ideologies. After all, isn't that why we're here? To talk about the things we want to sell, to work with the people we wish to influence? I do believe Roger shares many of our values; we'll see how he does on the upcoming exam."

Sam rises, placing his arm on Rufus's shoulder. "We are heading to the Driskill, Dr. Bowman. You are free to join us or escape. The choice is yours. But we do have to finalize the test questions by tomorrow. Be sure to have yours in my office by ten so I can review them."

As Sam and Rufus exit Sam's office, Debbie purposely turns the opposite direction.

"See you tomorrow, Dr. Bowman," Sam says, his voice following her down the hallway.

Debbie smiles and waves backward over her shoulder without turning to look at them, knowing both men were watching her, understanding they would not look away until she had disappeared.

Chapter Three

Considered by many as the one true honky-tonk beer joint in Austin, the Broken Spoke is where Roger liked to meet Amy in the daytime, as it was just far enough out of Austin that they did not run into any of his other campus female friends. He had also made it a point not to flirt with any of the waitresses and so felt safe, comfortable, there. While at night the old red rustic barn-like building had hosted such country singers as Willie Nelson and George Strait, it was always pretty much empty during the day. It smelled of stale beer and smoke and had a sticky concrete dance floor, but Amy liked it because she was always able to cajole Roger into two-stepping with her at the Spoke, which he agreed to only because they always had the dance floor to themselves on their afternoon visits. He did not like to be evaluated with respect to his dancing prowess.

Usually the first to arrive at their rendezvous, Amy Johnson, 25, was a girl so naturally beautiful she normally avoided wearing makeup and always looked fresh without it. Her hair was long, blonde, and straight and she had a model's figure, though she liked to drink beer and spent more time with her books and studies than ever worrying about her looks.

Dr. Sam Brown's granddaughter, his deceased daughter's daughter, was Sam's reason for living. He was fiercely protective of her. He knew she had taken up with the ever-philandering Roger, but until Amy could see the light, he had promised her that he would not get involved, and would give Roger the benefit of the doubt. Amy, like Roger, was also a doctoral candidate, but her field was economics. She was a genuine academic star.

Amy had been immediately attracted to Roger. His good looks, the fact that he drove a Corvette, and his being on the fast track for the doctoral program in Political Science, as he very convincingly boasted, made his story even more appealing for most of his target market.

Amy knew Roger's dream of being accepted into the final stage of doctoral program was fifty-fifty, at best, having spoken with Sam about it, but she had still been attracted to Roger, primarily by what she saw underneath the surface, and by a depth of spirit that she alone seemed to recognize. While Roger's true self was often in question, Amy, like many young girls in love, believed she could bring out the best in Roger. And she was determined to do so.

As he was only one of three candidates for the prestigious program Amy's grandfather oversaw, Amy had allowed herself to believe her support could help Roger qualify for the final step, the dissertation. But she also understood that she had been taken in by Roger's boyish charm.

As Amy enters the bar, she sees Roger sitting in a booth against the bar's left-side wall, on the other side of the tired and worn, no longer green felt, coin-operated pool table. Sitting at the bar were the usual handful of locals who strongly endorsed the credo that "you can't drink all day unless you start in the morning."

Roger smiles as she approaches. "You do realize," he asks, "that there are two old men up in their ivory tower deciding my future right now, at this very moment?"

Amy laughs. "Sam and Rufus? They're not the only ones deciding your future, or, at least, determining the questions for your qualifying exam this Friday."

Roger scowls, nods to the bartender for two beers, takes a long look, without Amy noticing, at a girl seated at the bar, quickly thinks better of it and looks away.

"You are talking about our future, aren't you?" Amy asks.

"Of course, our future." Roger, ever-correcting, notes. "But you've got a lock on finishing the economics PhD program. And not because you're Dr. Sam Brown's granddaughter, but because you're truly deserving. But I'm not sure where I'm going or what I want to do, though I do know I want to be involved at the highest level of politics."

The bartender delivers two bottles of Lone Star beer, and both Roger and Amy take long drinks, half emptying the bottles before setting them back on the table. "I thought," Amy reflects, "I thought we could just be professors together, at the same university, hopefully here at UT."

Roger responds, "Yes, that would be the best of all worlds. I think being a professor is a necessary step toward getting to where I want to be. We could do this together. You are my only friend, you know. I have never made any real friends at this school. Richard and Aga don't take me seriously."

Amy smiles. "So, you're at least referring to us as friends now?"

Amy finishes her bottle of beer and signals the bartender with two fingers in the air for another round. The bartender smiles back a friendly acknowledgment of her order, a smile which confuses Roger.

"I'm not nervous about the exam," Roger says defensively. "I know I will do well, and yes, of course we're friends. The very best kind of friends," he says, flashing his perfect smile.

Amy looks across the table at Roger, which confuses him, making him suddenly unsure of her true feelings. His patented smile apparently had not worked as planned.

"Only God in heaven knows what you mean by that, Roger," she says.

As he often does when confronted with a question he doesn't want to answer, Roger attempts to escape the situation. He gets up and puts a coin in the juke box. As he makes his way back to the table, he asks, "Let's dance," with a big smile and extending his hand to Amy.

But Amy remains seated in the booth. "No. Sit down. I want to talk." Roger slides back into the booth, grabbing and holding onto his bottle of beer for support. "I've been working on a paper I wanted to share with you," Amy informs Roger. "It's information you really need to understand. It's about supply-side

39

economics. It is at the heart of the upcoming presidential election, and meshes our two academic areas. Basically, it's about economics serving as a foundation of political strategy. It could be the basis of our partnership, the one you so unceremoniously just mentioned."

Roger laughs. "What?"

"Supply-side economics. It's a simplified view of the theory that tax revenues would be zero if tax rates were either 0 percent or 100 percent. And that somewhere between 0 percent and 100 percent is a tax rate that could maximize total revenue. It's a postulate by a guy named Laffer that the tax rate that maximizes revenue was at a much lower level than previously believed, so the current tax rates are well above the level where revenue is maximized. The econometric-based model is termed the Laffer Curve."

Roger questions, "Simplified, my ass." He looks away, certain that Amy can read the look on his face, exposing that he is lost, unable to decipher what she has just explained to him. Amy continues, "It just means that cutting taxes could lead to more revenue. That by reducing the tax rate the government will actually create more revenue, sort of an economic boom!" Amy laughs, hoping her mood and enthusiasm can influence Roger into listening to her, understanding her explanation.

"That just doesn't make sense," Roger responds. "How can that work? It's impossible."

The bartender delivers two more beers to their table unnoticed by Amy as she continues with her explanation. "Laffer thinks the problem in raising income for government isn't demand but the constraint of heavy taxes and regulatory burden."

Roger, knowing he has no escape, begins to question Amy with "What is the top tax rate now?"

She answers, "It's 70 percent."

"No! No shit?" Roger responds in shocked surprise.

"Yeah, no shit." Amy says, smiling at Roger, encouraging him while realizing he is caught off guard by the actual tax rate.

"It's not so crazy, I guess, to believe that wealthy people would invest their profits, which could help grow the economy."

Roger considers Amy's explanation, then says, "Yeah, well, I've never been on the money-making side. I'm more politically oriented, which is," he smiles and continues "on the money-spending side of economics."

Amy sips her beer after smiling and shaking her head. "You better not let Grandpa hear you say something like that."

"Your granddad," Roger responds, "helped create the Great Society. And spending money is what his Great Society is all about." Growing increasingly frustrated with Roger's responses, Amy blurts out, "The Great Society was about helping folks and leveling the playing field, Roger. It was about fairness!"

Roger finally responds in a manner that actually and surprisingly impresses Amy, because of the profoundness of his realization. "Yeah, yeah. Economics is the fuel that drives political power. It decides who pays to get what."

Amy laughs at Roger's description, aware that it is not too far from reality, and frames the issue at hand by saying, "So you think it's power versus fairness? That's the trade-off?"

Roger takes a long drink of beer, then responds, "Nope. Power provides the foundation to provide fairness. That's what being a Democrat is all about."

Amy leans back in the booth after taking a long, curious look at Roger. "Let's dance," Roger proposes, and Amy quickly accepts.

As Roger sporadically makes his dance moves completely independent of the rhythm, he is thinking and hoping that, maybe with two more rounds of drinks, they can go home and communicate on a level he understands.

Chapter Four

Roger and Amy finish making love at his apartment. Amy makes allowances for the disorganized and dirty bachelor pad, which looks more like a team of undergraduates camp there, rather than a sole PhD candidate's place to drink, entertain, and flop. Amy has often offered to help him redecorate, though she really meant to make it habitable. She has dropped discussing the topic because Roger is endowed with two not enviable traits, being both lazy and stubborn, that make reasoning with him a virtual impossibility. This is perhaps best exemplified by his strong belief that his pride and joy artwork, his masterpiece beer can collection, will someday become more valuable than she can imagine.

Roger rolls unceremoniously off Amy onto his back, pushing back his hair and looking into her deep blue eyes.

After a brief pause, he says in a serious tone, "You could help, you know. If my grandfather was one of your judges with the ability to determine your fate, I would help you. I'd do whatever I could."

Amy is not amused, wanting to relax and glow following her sexual release. This is a topic she is tired of discussing, but gives in, saying, "Of course I will help you, because I think you deserve it."

Roger remains unconvinced. "Truthfully, I'm scared. Nervous. I've never felt really accepted here, by any of them, teachers or students. Guess I have never really felt accepted anywhere."

He glances over, curious what impression his comment has made.

Amy looks at him for a long moment and responds in a serious tone, "I know it was hard for you, that your mom left when you were just a baby, and your dad's been an absent prick. I know these have been big issues in your life. But now that part of your life is over. You've worked hard. You're ready for this last test. And ready for our lives together."

Nervous, Roger presses Amy further. "I need an edge . . . something, anything."

She smiles, gives Roger a kiss on his chest, and says, "Nonsense. Besides, they continue to drop hints all the time."

Interested in the opportunity to gain any advantage, Roger rubs against Amy, as she pulls the covers over her exposed breasts. "Like, for example?" he asks.

"Like the make of LBJ's car on the ranch. Like his first college nickname. Like his favorite candy, or like LBJ's favorite alcoholic beverage?" she responds with more than a bit of sarcasm.

Roger answers resentfully. He believes that his career could rest on being as prepared as he can for his upcoming qualifying exam. "I know LBJ's ranch car was a white Lincoln Continental convertible with suicide doors. His first college nickname was Bullshit Johnson, but come on, sweetie, tell me about his favorite candy and his favorite booze, please."

"Well, I've heard from powers that be that their favorite 'bonus' question has to do with LBJ's favorite 'brittle' snack," Amy adds, with a girlish smile, and Roger smiles back.

Roger, continuing to dig for as much insight as possible, asks, "Any more possibilities?"

Amy continues, saying, "Well, LBJ's favorite alcoholic beverage is not so well known." Roger looks at her quizzically, as Amy goes on, "Think Sean Connery. Where is he from?"

Roger contemplates a moment before responding, "Got it. Peanut brittle and scotch whiskey. Thanks, sweetie."

She pushes him over and begins giving him a back rub.

"Relax, silly. You're just nervous. Everyone is at this stage. I know I will be when I take my qualifying exam. Believe me, you know everything you need to know for this exam."

Roger looks over, focusing on the three empty beer bottles on the dresser, and grunts in response to her motivational pep talk.

"What you mean is that you already know everything I need to know," he blurts out, frustrated, then continues, "and you know the mind-set of the judges."

"No," Amy forcefully responds, "I mean you know. We've been over every lecture they've given, reviewed every note you have taken from your classes with Sam, Rufus, and Dr. Bowman. We've even studied other related issues, subissues, to provide you background and a more in-depth understanding. Like I mentioned earlier, playing back the economic perspective or, more importantly, the political implications could well be worth the effort. This could help you frame your answers to appreciate why these are important questions, and which undoubtedly will be a major part of your exam."

Roger lies still, anticipating how to get additional informational insight from her, while at the same time wanting Amy to continue his back rub, and hoping she will end her after-sex motivational lecture. Noticing his frustration, she asks, "What? What is it?" Roger rolls over, looking her in the eye, responding with a sigh, "You know, Amy. It's like every time we make love, as soon as it's over you begin some scholarly lecture, some curve shit or other."

Amy laughs, unable to hide her frustration and amusement, and explains, "Come on. I know you understand the importance of the exam you are about to take. I am just trying to help."

Roger, ignoring her rationale, sits up and pulls the sheet down to her waist, "Do you ever just think about making love while we are making love? Or are you always jumping ahead, thinking of some economic theory?" Roger questions, trying to set up his next step, wanting to get back to personal issues, as he has already worked out what he thinks is a foolproof plan for the upcoming exam.

Amy's frustration turns to anger. "Jesus, Roger. I'm trying to help you. I am desperate for you to pass this exam, maybe even more desperate than you."

Finally, appreciating her frustration, Roger lies back down, pulling Amy to him. "Look, Amy. I just want you to love me. You are my anchor. I understand how important this exam is, and I am going to pass it. I promise you, I will pass it!"

Comforted by the confidence and determination in his voice, Amy interlocks her fingers with Roger's and smiles seductively, saying, "Let's see if we cured your nervousness." Roger laughs, rolls over and kisses Amy on the neck.

"Sounds like a plan, sweetie," he says. "Sounds like a plan."

Chapter Five

Two students walk down the hallway in the Government Department. Both are young and wearing shorts, his to the knee, hers barely covering her well-rounded posterior. Along with his dirty shorts, he wears an untucked UT burnt-orange T-shirt, and carries a book under his well-muscled arm. She carries a book in her hand and a purse over her shoulder. Her top is tailored, creating the appealing shape of an inverted three-dimensional pyramid, and her hair is tied in a ponytail. She sports what appears to be a more than incredible body, and her hair is long, shoulder length. He is unshaven, several days' growth evidencing an almost, but not quite, manly set of stubble.

Trying to establish his academic prowess, the male student comments, "I hate this nonsense. Grad students teaching is bullshit. What insight has he ever offered different than the text book? I came to college to learn from real faculty, professors, not some . . ."

"Some what?" she interrupts.

He goes on and counters, "Somebody who knows what they're talking about!"

She cuts him off again, "I like him. I think he asks great questions, challenging questions, penetrating, deep."

"Oh God!" the male student responds. "You're nuts over him, too! What the fuck is it with this guy?"

She tries to answer, "He's . . ."

Cutting her off, he answers for her, "Good looking?" He continues, "And he asks questions only because he doesn't know the answers, I think. He's using us to help him learn, to answer questions he is too lazy to research for himself. That's what desperate graduate students do."

The male student pauses, stops walking and she also stops, just before they enter the classroom, giving him the opportunity to highlight his point of view. "Has he ever definitively expressed a political perspective," he asks her, "that you learned something from? Has he ever offered any real insight, challenged you in a way, other than fantasy, other than turning you on?"

As she gets ready to enter the class, she opens her purse, removes a pair of reading glasses, and puts them on, instantly making her face more attractive, appealing.

"Those glasses look great on you!" he says flippantly, knowing full well why she put them on.

"Yes, I know," she responds.

As she stands directly in front of the classroom door, she turns and says to her male companion, primarily to rebut his criticisms of Roger, "Do you know anything about the Socratic method? Do you understand that asking questions is the best way to challenge students, teach them, and make them think instead of just looking up and regurgitating textbook answers?"

He opens the door wide for her to step into the classroom. And as she walks in front of him, he counters with, "Please, remind me, does the Socratic method involve looking up the skirts or down the tops of young, attractive coeds? Because that's the only kind of scientific method he seems to have in this class."

Both enter the classroom and take their seats. Roger watches them enter, but his attention is obviously much more on her, as she takes her seat.

Roger looks down and smiles at the top heavy, bespectacled coed, and begins, "Let's discuss a new political science topic today, one not in the text book. I will divide the class into five groups."

Roger waves his arms indicating who will be part of which group, and goes on to say, "Take a few minutes to outline your group's collective response to the following question in regard to our current tax system. The question is: Consider the effect of both raising or lowering taxes and the impact you believe it would have on our country's tax revenue stream. This is not a trick question; it just requires a bit of clear thinking. Basically, think about whether there is any way that cutting taxes on the rich could raise, create more, revenue for the government? If you feel comfortable with your answer, then consider the implications. Should there be one rate for all? Or should we keep our current system where many with lower incomes pay 20 percent while the highest-income people pay 70 percent? You've got 20 minutes for your group to come up with your best answer. I will circulate from group to group to discuss your thinking. Okay, get at it." The students, looking clearly bewildered by both the group discussion method and the question, move into their assigned groups, which he is indicating by pointing hand gestures.

Roger, pleased by what he believes a clever teaching idea, pauses while he scans the class to determine the students' reaction to his questions. Satisfied that they are actually involved and thinking and discussing answer options, he goes in sequence to the groups, always approaching the best-looking coeds, asking, "So, where is your group coming out on this question, young lady?"

Twenty minutes later, clearing his throat with the goal of getting the attention of the class, Roger asks, "So, what do you collectively think? Could lowering the tax rate on high-incomers actually create more money to go into government tax coffers?"

The spokespersons for each of four groups all respond the same; confirming that more revenue outcome is impossible. When their turn arrives, the fifth group spokesperson, Ms. Pyramid, stands up and takes the opposite point of view, explaining her answer. "There are three principles that in combination lead us to this conclusion. First, it is very likely that this lost tax revenue from the wealthy will be invested back into the economy, which will cause the overall economy to grow." She looks down at her notes, and continues, "Second, if the wealthy do not invest this new found money, they will spend it, with the result of creating jobs, another win for the economy. And third, and maybe most convincing, is that in terms of spending efficiency, having a private, vested interest in financial success is far more productive than the government bureaucracy alternative. Basically, if it's your money, we have determined that you will try to spend it wisely."

The class is silent, indicative that these comments challenge the general thinking. Then within the groups, discussion begins. A few groups raise their hands, asking questions of the shapely spokesperson. After clearly and convincingly fielding them all, she sits down.

When it is apparent to him that the class has endorsed her argument, Roger asks, "By a show of hands, who now believes that lowering taxes on the rich is actually a good idea?" All but 3 students of the 30 in his class agree. Roger remarks, "Okay. Very well done."

Changing topics, Roger addresses his major issue, saying, "Okay, let's get to the status of the seven groups that I assigned one question to last week. Remember, your detailed outlines are due this evening. And remember, this grade will count as your first test. So I suggest you give this exercise your complete focus. Given your significant progress today, I will give you a grading bonus. I will count this take-home, group exercise, as if it were two test grades. You should all do well if you put in the time and effort."

With this clearly advantageous pronouncement, there is a clear positive attitude in the classroom, something that hadn't happened before. Roger, believing it possible that he may have begun to turn the corner with these students, confidently raises his hand, indicating class is dismissed.

As the students file out, Roger overhears positive comments, which bring a smile to his face. He cannot help but think that he has discovered how to understand and tap into the motivating forces of people, students, and that this gift could make him special, could provide the insight to develop and be successful in the political domain. He believes he has finally experienced a positive breakthrough as a teacher.

Roger confidently puts his note papers into his briefcase while thinking about how he will execute his fail-safe game plan for his upcoming exam.

Chapter Six

The two students from the hallway who participated in Roger's class are impressed by his lecture. She gives her partner a smiling glance signifying that Roger deserves credit for his Socratic method and spot-on lecture. He notices her look but avoids acknowledging that Roger deserves more credit and respect than he had previously thought. One class, he thinks, does not make a good teacher or would-be professor. As the lecture hall empties, the pair assemble in front of Roger hoping to pick up any additional information in regard to upcoming insights as to their team projects.

Roger, sitting on the desk at the front of the room, smiles at the attractive Ms. Pyramid as she stands to his side, while he is chatting with a handful of students taking this opportunity to kiss his ass. As their turn arrives to talk to Roger, she greets him with a big smile while the young man standing four feet in from of him frowns, understanding Roger's true motivation in regard to his companion.

"Okay," Roger begins, finally throwing a welcoming look to the male student. "I assume you are here to talk about your group paper. So, tell me how it is coming."

Both students appear calm, confident, which vexes Roger, irritates him as it brings him down from the high he has just experienced, the smattering of applause and recognition he has just enjoyed for the first time as a lecturer.

"As you know, my group chose the War on Poverty and assessing its effectiveness," the young man volunteers, stepping forward, forcing Roger to acknowledge him and his question.

"My group chose the Vietnam War and its political implications, specifically with respect to the Domino Theory," the young coed submits, playing with her glasses but refusing to remove them, knowing how much they improve her appearance.

Realizing why they are there, Roger reaches into his satchel and pulls out his notebook.

They outline their ideas for Roger, each reading short, scripted summaries of 100 or fewer words, as he has always demanded of his students in such meetings, his obvious thinking being that this format was much easier for him to summarize in outline form. Roger pens bullet points as they detail their key ideas, trying to make his interest seem casual, calm, but concentrating to get every specific point of their thoughts into his note, while the students both sit down immediately in front of the podium.

"Good job," he responds, after taking a deep breath, "but, as you know, details are really the key. They key to academic success is effecting a comprehensive outline before one begins writing. So an outline should be your immediate and first priority. This is the framework that leads to clear thinking," he exults, feeling good as a result of his breakthrough teaching success.

The young man catches himself halfway through a moan, having heard this outline description more times than he wants to remember.

Already defensive, he quickly continues, "Well, the War on Poverty, again, is primarily a war on segregation, prejudice, inequality, and the spreading, sharing of wealth. It involves and employs the tax system, which was an integral part of your lecture today, as you astutely pointed out." While watching Roger take notes, the student can't believe he actually said that, but, hell, he thinks, getting grades is only a game. So why not play to win. He continues, adding, "It is also a key part in the development of many government programs, to change and hopefully extinguish, once and for all, the societal power-based legacies including control of the rich over the poor, the oppressors over the oppressed, the haves over the have-nots."

Roger has been writing frantically in his notebook but is anxious to conceal his true motives and note taking.

"I'm sorry," Roger offers, "I just had to write down some details from my lecture today, follow-up thoughts I want to make sure to cover in my next lecture. I do think your key points exactly extend and address the questions we were discussing. I do think you should be sure to bring your summaries out at the beginning of next class." With that defensive cover in place, Roger looks at the young man, suggesting he continue.

"Welfare," the young man says confidently, not buying Roger's note-taking cover, "levels the playing field for those who fail to make it on their own. It's about fairness, ultimately."

Without looking directly at the young man, Roger responds, "The issues you raise regarding inequality in our society are on the right track. But, I repeat, the fundamental to keep in mind is to organize all of your diverse thoughts in a detailed outline."

Unable to conceal his frustration at another mentioning of Roger's "detailed outline" speech, the young man groans again and almost laughs, but, knowing that laughing in Roger's face would be over the line, catches it short and pretends to cough.

Angered, but unwilling to acknowledge the young man's dig, Roger smiles and continues looking directly into the eyes of the female student, trying to engage her. He thus directs the conversation, "So, back to you."

She anxiously jumps at the opportunity for one-on-one communication and eye contact with Roger, and also the opportunity to present her views uninterruptedly, with perhaps a window to her personal interest.

"In my group's view, the Vietnam War says it all about our nation, our true goals and ambitions. We know Vietnam was about controlling the economic breadbasket of the Far East, not about fighting communism, as we were led to believe. It was about controlling what actually fuels political economies, oil and food, which represent the historical basis underlying world order."

Roger's interest in the young girl grows as she speaks, her intelligence overcoming her insecure need to cover her face with glasses and makeup. He is obviously taken with her in several ways, but he is even more interested, if possible for him, in her topic under discussion.

"Yes," Roger responds, "very big, very good ideas. Good subjects for your group paper and well-chosen topics presented in classic order. I think these topics can have the most potential of the seven options. So, think like a squid, an octopus, tackle your subject by coming at it from a variety of directions."

The young man groans again, thinking, *What bullshit.* This time he made a very minimal attempt to hide his frustration with Roger's obvious ploy for information, for insight that apparently he does not have.

Roger smiles, ignoring the young man, confident he has made a positive impression on the coed, and continues. "Spread your ideas around, look at all connections involving other political issues, think about all direct and indirect dimensions of your subject, and make sure you don't miss important implications."

Roger hesitates, unsure if he should attempt to continue, still glowing in the aftermath of the positive, reinforcing applause following his lecture and realizing the potential value of the student's insights that he had never even thought of.

But, with the hint of newfound confidence overshadowing his realization that the undergrads could connect the dots better than he could, he adds, trying to elicit more of their intellectual insights, "Also, perhaps, consider how government can best help the poorest among us in regard to taxes. Perhaps all wealth should be passed to the government, for care of the needy, when rich people pass on? Basically, consider a wealth tax, so that, instead of simply keeping the money in a family, who did nothing themselves to create that wealth, perhaps all of one's wealth upon death should simply be given to the government?"

Both young students look at one another and are obviously, simultaneously both surprised and impressed by Roger's seemingly innovative and totally new idea, not understanding it to be the basis of Marxism 100 years earlier. The young man appears impressed and surprised, and the young girl, looking over the rim of her glasses, feels inspiration, with a strong dose of true admiration. They both nod, believing his idea makes sense and truly would serve to level the playing field in society.

The male student organizes his thoughts and stands to forcefully make his contribution to developing this radical idea, but he is cut off as Roger, before one word can be spoken, sticks his open hand out to the male student to silence him, "Yes, this is just food for thought. Hopefully you can chew this a bit by our next meeting. Now back to your group business. Again, as I said, outline your subjects. Develop your ideas further and bring them to my office by the deadline, no later than 10:00 p.m. tonight. You've got about nine hours to wrap up your topics, but this deadline is absolute. Pull your teams together, finish your outlines and think as best you can about what the underlying assumptions are that the strategies of these programs are based upon."

Roger pauses, and then continues, "I will be working late. I'll be in my office."

Roger leaves with the students and walks down the hall to his office, thinking this could really be what he is cut out to do. As they separate, Roger winks at the coed before heading to his office. As he walks away, he remembers what his dad told him when he was about to enter high school: "If you pass one up, you're one behind." He smiles, thinking, *Words to live by.*

Roger arrives in the grad student offices and is greeted by Richard and Aga, who appear in serious conversation. He enthusiastically interrupts, and begins discussing the students' ideas with Richard and Aga as though they were his own. There is no reaction from either. Roger becomes disturbed by their nonreaction and their calm confidence in their own game plan, and struggles to control his emotions. These arrogant sons of bitches, he thinks, are sure he will fail the qualifying exam.

Aga, his clothes, as always, neatly pressed, sits down after pouring a fresh cup of coffee, ignoring Roger. "I'm sure that one of the questions on our exam," he begins, "will be about a woman's right to choose."

Richard says, "Maybe, but I don't think there is much of a question there, unless you are checking our political union card." Richard continues, "But there should be a question on what a cowardly president Carter has been, letting Iran walk all over him, allowing them to hold our people in captivity." Richard continues, "The future implication of this lack of reaction to the hostage situation of our citizens, long term, is really the essence of the question, and thus the answer.

Aga responds, "Yes, and this is only the first implication step. Once other countries figure out the US will not respond, they will continue to bite off bigger and bigger chunks. It is only a matter of time. They're hostage strategy involves reinterpreting being a Muslim, an Iranian Muslim, to be aggressive, and defining the US as their archenemy, for the political purpose of unifying their power base. It is perfectly predictable, and unless the US steps up, they are going to lose the support of other nations, in particular the Muslim ones in the Middle East."

Richard honestly reflects, "Well, it could be interesting to see what Reagan will do, if elected."

Aga looks at Richard and says, "Look, he never served in the military. He doesn't understand the military. He talks big, but all he knows is how to play a soldier in a movie. It looks like he will inherit this mess, but I doubt if he will do anything about it. Unless someone writes his strategy on a teleprompter, he won't know what to say, or think, or do." This pointed critique evokes a chuckle from Roger, with a corresponding nod.

Richard shakes his head and says, "I think you two may be surprised by what happens if Reagan is calling the shots."

Having addressed the world situation with nothing more to add, and hoping to gain additional insight about the upcoming exam, Roger refocuses the conversation, saying, "You know, Dr. Sam has shown a strong, positive bias for welfare policies, and I think developing ideas in this area will definitely be questioned."

"I know," Richard comments, while getting up to pour himself a cup of coffee. "There will certainly be a question or two on the political economics of Great Society programs, as Dr. Sam and Dr. Mac were both so heavily involved in their creation. And I think there will also, certainly, be another on the political implications of our current tax policy, and the pay-your-fair-share strategic positioning idea as outlined by Dr. Mac in his seminar last spring. And I also anticipate a question in regard to overall Democratic strategies of the past, their success and failure. This will likely follow the theme of Dr. Bowman's seminar last spring. And another on potential future Democratic policies—what is viable and what is not? This is the bread and butter we have learned from Dr. Sam. But," looking up from his cup of coffee, directly at Roger, he continues, "of course I'm confident you are well prepared for all the various avenues of questioning they could choose?"

Aga, picking up on Richard's attempt to pile on Roger's obvious lack of confidence, adds, "Yes, I agree. I think we all know the most important eight or nine questions that must be asked. If only Carter had folks working on his staff with the insight we've experienced from Dr. Sam and Dr. Mac. I don't see any possibility whatsoever for Carter to win a second term, which also could be worked into a question. But, I mean, how embarrassing, losing to some Hollywood B actor. It could be a new low for the Democratic Party."

Richard laughs out loud, relaxing into his seat and continues in the undermining of Roger's confidence. "You have both previously expressed doubt in regard to Carter's reelection, and I respect both of your opinions. His lack of leadership, compounded by economic problems and the Iran crisis. Well, I also can't believe he decided our country should not participate in the Olympics. Yeah," he laughs expressively, "Carter is dog meat! The American people care more about winning gold medals at the Olympics than they do about foreign policy. Shit! Remember what Dr. Mac taught us about formulating political strategy:

'Remember, two-thirds of the voters in the US have a below-average IQ."

Roger and Aga both laugh in agreement, but Roger's laughter is tinged with a hint of anxiety, anticipation. He has never understood how that particular statistical fact could possibly be true and has always been afraid to ask anyone to explain it to him. He assumed it was just a reference to how dumb the American population really is when assessing issues and political candidates.

Following up Richard's statistical reference, Aga said, "Most people vote for the candidate they believe has the best vision for the future, for their own future, not issues, because they simply either do not know them and or don't care to learn. So, even a person like Carter would have a chance given the general stupidity of voters, but his lack of taking any sort of positions and his lack of action, makes folks believe he is a crappy leader. Thus, any dumb shit that paints any type of vision, which is the linchpin of being perceived as a leader, has a clear advantage. So, get ready for some more of what we have now, not so much in terms of having any well-thought-out strategy to deal with economics or the world situation. Bottom line is that you're fucked. Get used to it."

Roger, not knowing exactly how to react to Aga's rant, says, "Oh, enough political mumbo-jumbo predicting what will happen come November, maybe we should just sit down and outline what we all think will be the key questions on the exam."

Both Richard and Aga laugh, clearly indicating to Roger that they have no time nor interest in last-minute tutorials, as though such cramming were unnecessary, beneath them. They both realize his collaborative idea is no more than a desperate plea for help from an ill-prepared cohort who hasn't taken his classwork very seriously for the last three years.

Recognizing this discussion isn't getting him anywhere, Roger leaves, but isn't even gone for ten seconds before Aga turns to Richard and says, "Actually, it probably would be a good idea to have one last review. Let's both write down the seven or eight questions we think will be on the exam, and compare them. We can share our questions and answers when we meet tonight for our search for a needle in the presidential haystack. I was planning to stop by and help for a while tonight, anyway."

As they begin independently summarizing, Aga smiles, laughs. "Poor, dumb-shit Roger. He just has no fucking idea, does he? No idea at all."

Chapter Seven

Roger and Dr. Debbie Bowman sit at a table in a small bar just outside Austin. They choose a table in the back of the room to avoid any chance of someone from the university seeing them together.

While Roger is dressed in wrinkled slacks, open-collar shirt and a well-worn sport coat, Debbie wears a red designer dress with thin silver shoulder straps. It is the type of dress that is low cut when worn well with appropriate posture at the beginning of the evening, but that drops severely as the evening wears on, the posture slopes, and appropriate libations make its low-cut design all the more revealing.

They have been drinking for several hours, both slurring their words a bit as they discuss possible questions for the doctoral program exam. While their chairs had been facing one another from opposite sides of the table at the beginning of the evening, their chairs now are nearly touching at one corner of the table. Rogers legs are spread, allowing Debbie's chair and her legs to fit tightly between his. Debbie uses this arrangement to sporadically and suggestively exercise her groin muscles.

"Do It to Me One More Time" by the Captain and Tennille plays softy in the background.

"After tomorrow," Debbie says, looking Roger in the eye while performing isometrics with her thighs, "you and I will be one step closer, almost as close as we are now."

Roger rubs his hands along the sides of Debbie's legs, pulling her dress up slightly, assessing the results of her barroom exercise regime.

"We're getting closer all the time," Roger says, moving his gaze upward toward her face.

Debbie puts her hand on his, causing Roger to look her in the eye, and in a devoted tone, she says, "It'll be interesting to see just how close we become, once you pass that exam."

"Come on, Deb, I know you know the questions on tomorrow's exam. Why don't you just share them with me, give me a heads up. Fuckin' Richard and Aga are such cocky bastards; they are so confident and make it so obvious they anticipate doing better than me. Just share a few of the questions, give me a head start, it's all I ask."

Roger's request frustrates Debbie.

"Jesus, Roger. Leave me some dignity. I have already shared far more with you than is appropriate. Honestly," her earlier mood changed, her frustration now clearly visible, "if you can't pass the damn exam with all I have already shared, you probably shouldn't even be in the program."

Her comments obviously strike a nerve with Roger. He looks away in anger and frustration. Her exercise program ceases, and she slides back into her chair.

She tries to soften her comments: "Oh, look. I'm sorry, Roger. Really, I'm sorry, honey. Just trust me. You know enough of what's on the exam already to do very well without knowing any more. If you do too well tomorrow, it would be a dead give-away."

Stunned by her comment, and realizing he is not getting anywhere, Roger decides to play the anger card, blurting out, "Really? A dead giveaway? Of what? Of that I'm not really smart enough to pass this exam without your help?"

Realizing she has struck a sensitive nerve, but a little too inebriated to cover for her remarks, she makes an attempt anyway. "No, no. That's not true and no one knows I have helped, worked with you as much as I have, or at all, really. No one is even aware that we have been seeing one another . . . that we have drinks . . . that we enjoy a few laughs and . . . one another's company."

Knowing the next gambit is bitterness, Roger says ironically, "Look! I'm sorry, but I have to go. I need to get home, spend the rest of the night prepping for this exam. It's the biggest exam of my life, sweetie. Thanks for all your help."

Roger rises to leave and reaches for his wallet hoping she will acquiesce and give him more clues. But she doesn't.

"No, no. This is my treat tonight. I got it," Debbie insists.

Roger reflects a moment on Debbie's condition. They have been drinking for several hours, but executing his game plan demands his priority. He looks her in the eye and in a serious voice asks, "You gonna be okay? You gonna be able to get home all right?" fully realizing the necessity of mending fences, as she will soon be grading his exam.

She laughs. "Sure. Don't worry. I'm a big girl. I can take care of myself. You go home. Study hard. Go bone up, my little surfer boy!"

Debbie pats Roger on the ass as he departs, motions to the bartender for the bill, and then smiles widely when she notices the bartender smiling at her, his expression exposing his curiosity as to why a middle-aged chick as hot as her needs to suffer an insecure young man just to satisfy her, some sort of . . . instinct. Definitely worth an expository smile to see where this could go, Debbie thinks, knowing herself inebriated to the point of making a mistake, but anxious to change the expression on the bartender's face.

Once outside, Roger climbs into his Corvette and scribbles the test question topics he just learned from Debbie into his notebook. He looks at his watch. It's 10:15. Right on schedule, he thinks.

Chapter Eight

Instead of going home, Roger drives back to campus, parking his car in his usual spot next to the LBJ library, next to Aga's Mercedes and Richard's piece-of-shit 1970 AMC Gremlin. He first thinks, those sons of bitches are studying together without me. Arrogant shitheads. The realization that his game plan for tomorrow's exam is in jeopardy undercuts the effect of the alcohol. "Fuck," he says aloud, thinking if they are in their offices, in the building, he is screwed. Wondering what his options are if they are there, he begins walking to his office.

He passes two male undergrads, passed out on the lawn in from of the government building, beer cans and an empty brown paper bag lying next to them. This sight for a moment takes his mind off the dire predicament he will be confronted with if Aga and Richard are in the vicinity of his office by reminding him of his college days at USC.

Roger walks down the corridor to the windowless grad student offices, checking the classrooms as he goes. They are all dark. He goes by his office and checks the classrooms on the other side, and they are dark as well. He realizes his plan can now be executed. He is greatly relieved but cannot help but worry.

Unlocking the door, Roger enters and views the students' group papers, containing their outlines to the questions he assigned, on the floor, having been slipped under his door. He smiles while counting them. All seven are there and he gathers them up, giving each a brief scan as he unceremoniously seats himself behind his desk.

Roger puts on a pot of coffee. As it brews, he begins summarizing the papers, copying key points from the students' papers to small pieces of paper he has cut to fit, without folding, in small envelope. After he finishes transcribing the first group's outline, he pours himself a cup of coffee, sits down and continues, drinking a celebratory cup of coffee with the completion of each outline.

When his crib sheets are finalized, Roger folds them neatly, opens his desk drawer for an envelope, then exits his office and walks down the hall to a small men's restroom next to the room where the doctoral exams will be conducted the following day. He places the crib notes in the envelope and puts the envelope behind the towel dispenser. Having completed his mission, Roger reflects on the critical importance of the next day. He reflects a moment to store the picture and the scene of the crime in his memory. The room is stark in its coldness, a gray-streaked travertine on the walls and floors, cracked around the toilets and sinks, making the room look old and somewhat dirty, like an ancient Roman bathhouse.

Roger considers the action he soon would be taking, but not questioning either his strategy or his motives. He does recall another one of his father's catch phrases used when describing how to approach life, "If you ain't cheatin,' you ain't really tryin.'" Hell, he contemplates, maybe the old man would finally be proud of his son's disreputable ingenuity.

Roger's mind wanders and, as if in a dream, he leans back against the cold wall, envisioning himself, years before, as a fourteen-year-old boy seated on the floor of his bedroom, leaning against his bed, just as his father enters the room in a drunken stupor and stands over him, both his hands tightened into fists.

"You ain't nothin,'" his father bellows at the boy crouched on the floor, attempting to hide, make himself smaller, to somehow escape his father's coming diatribe. "You ain't nothin' but an ungrateful little shit. And you got some big test at school tomorrow, ain't you? Some test for honors classes or somethin'? Ain't that what you said? But I bet you ain't done nothin' about it. I bet you ain't been studyin' or nothin'. You just wanna coast, don't ya? Like always, you just wanna coast, take the easy way. Hell, you ain't never gonna be nothin', nobody! You're no better 'n yur stinkin' mother."

63

Roger remembers his father stumbling from the room and sitting alone, wishing, somehow, that he could live with his mother and her new husband, who, he knew, were the financial support in his life anyway.

He longed to be with her, away from his father, even if, as she had explained, she had no time for him. And he knew that his father kept most of the money she sent, spending it on gambling, drinking, and other self-indulgences.

Roger's entire life, in those early days, was spent daydreaming about escape, growing ever more desperate to find a way out of the grip of his father, away from the house and control he knew only centered on the monthly stipend his mother and her new husband provided.

Roger locks his office and goes home, in a state of equilibrium, the seven cups of coffee balancing out the alcohol. He goes to bed, but is unable to sleep until he finally dozes off at 6:30 a.m. His alarm awakens him two hours later and he prepares for the day ahead.

Roger arrives in the designated testing room at 9:25 a.m., just before the exam is to begin. Sam and his secretary are preparing for the test, and exam booklets are on the desk in front of the room.

Roger looks around. He has been in the exam room many times, but today it seems different to him, stark, colder in appearance than ever before, the atmosphere heavy with fear, anticipation, and excitement. This was to be the most important exam of Roger's life.

Richard and Aga arrive in an obvious good mood, making their arrival apparent by the laughter and noise they create in the hallway just before entering. Both seat themselves, smiling at Roger, as if both appreciating some private, inside joke. Their mood stems from the fact that Richard struck pay dirt earlier in the week, following a trail of correspondence between LBJ and Rufus two nights before that definitely had the potential to facilitate his retirement. Aga was motivating Richard with retirement lifestyle images from his own personal experience.

Sam passes out the doctoral qualifying exam notebook to Roger, Aga, and Richard who are seated 10 feet apart from one another, smiling as he drops six blue booklets, all with 16 pages, on each desk for each of the three men.

"You will have four hours to take this exam," Sam explains, "which describes six key problems faced by recent presidential administrations. Describe these programs as completely and precisely as you can, and be sure to focus upon what you think were the underlying political strategies and long-term implications. I suggest you outline your thoughts first, then write your detailed answers in the blue exam booklet, one for each question. Your tests will be graded by myself, Professor MacIntosh, and Professor Bowman."

Sam points to his secretary, an attractive young woman in her early thirties. "Miss Jones, my assistant, will monitor the test." Sam starts walking toward the door but turns and stops and, with a grin, explains, "There is a bonus question, making total number of possible exam questions seven. That bonus question is: 'What was LBJ's favorite White House snack? Write this answer at the end of booklet six." Sam pauses, looking at each of the three grad students, then adds, somberly, but sincerely, "Good luck, gentlemen. And remember it's not the quantity of words here that counts, it's the quality of thoughts."

Sam departs. Roger briefly looks over the six political exam questions and confidently writes in the answer to number seven on the last page of blue booklet six, mentally thanking Amy.

After waiting for 25 minutes, Roger smiles charmingly at Miss Jones. "Miss Jones, I'm very sorry but I need to use the restroom. Nerves, I guess? Just nerves." His smile wins the day, and he knows he has won her confidence, as she smiles back.

"Of course, but hurry, please," she answers. "You know I'm not supposed to let anyone leave the room during the exam, I . . ."

Roger stands, shoots her another winning smile and departs for the restroom. The clock on the wall shows 10:02 a.m. Ten minutes later Roger returns.

An hour and half into the exam he signals Miss Jones again. "I am so sorry. A few too many Lone Stars last night at the Branch Saloon. You know it? You been there?"

With a smile, she confirms she knows and has been to the Branch Saloon.

"I'll be headed there later, after the exam. I'd love to buy you a drink," he offers.

She smiles, her eyes widen. "Okay. Go, but this must be the last time, so please, hurry. I don't want Dr. Brown to know I let you leave the room."

Roger leaves with a pencil behind his ear and blank bits of paper hidden in his hand.

Richard and Aga exchange looks; Richard shakes his head in frustration.

Roger returns with a new burst of energy, writing furiously, for the first time.

"Un-fucking-believable!" Aga mutters in Arabic, just under his breath, expressing both his and Richard's disgust. Aga shakes his head but quickly returns his concentration to his exam.

Exactly at 1:30 p.m., Miss Jones announces that the exam if over, walks to each desk to collect the booklets.

The three men rise, acknowledge Miss Jones and depart.

In the hallway, Roger is the first to speak. "Hey, beer is on me. I'll meet you guys at the Longhorn to celebrate if you like." Both Richard and Aga appear flabbergasted at Roger's invitation.

"Sure," Richard responds, as Roger disappears down the hallway. Aga is surprised at Richard's acceptance. "What the hell did you do that for? We just watched that son-of-a-bitch cheat his ass off, and now we're going to celebrate with him?"

"Sure," Richard responds. "It'll be fun to watch him squirm when we question his two bathroom breaks during the exam. What the hell would he have done if Dr. Brown hadn't left Miss Dumbfuck Jones in charge?"

Aga doesn't answer, but seems equally perplexed.

"I mean," Richard continues, "he will probably pass the damn exam now and we'll be stuck with him for another year. But who wouldn't be able to pass it if able to run from the room and look up the answers to any questions he's stuck on?"

Aga, wondering aloud, jokingly says, "Gee, who do you think he can get to write his dissertation for him?"

"You know that isn't going to work," Richard says taking a serious tone. "Having to work on a regular basis with his advisor, Roger will never be able to hide his true ability."

Aga laughs, "Yeah, and even if he does get his dissertation done, what's he going to do when he has to face the oral exams, sitting in front of a table of scholars anxious to cut his balls off? What the hell. If we do well enough, maybe one or both of us could be asked to monitor his final orals—if and when he actually gets that far."

Both men laugh. "Let's go ahead and meet the cheating fucker at the Longhorn. It could be interesting," Aga adds.

Chapter Nine

Richard and Aga arrive at the Longhorn Saloon in downtown Austin in Aga's Mercedes. Roger arrives moments later in his Corvette, parks next to them, and the three men begin walking the 40 yards or so to the saloon.

As they approach, Roger, smiling, asks, "Can you believe it? Can you believe it's over?

Anxious to get out of the Austin heat but believing an immediate response was necessary, and anxious to challenge Roger on his test-taking tactics earlier, Richard stands his ground just outside the entrance. "So, Roger? You feel good about the exam?"

Roger smiles, laughs, his exuberance showing. "Relieved!" Roger responds, moving past the two men, anxious to avoid the Austin heat as well as questioning about his feelings.

The saloon is an eclectic place, deserving of the label saloon rather than bar. It is a saloon because at least 90 percent of the patrons are men, and Austin eclectic because roughly half are wearing boot-cut Wranglers and cowboy hats and the other half are UT students in shorts.

They sit at a large round table near the rear of the bar, and Roger waves one hand in an imaginary circle signaling for a round of drinks, with the order having been acknowledged by the barkeep when he points to the Lone Star sign behind the bar, with Roger nodding yes. With his nod, Roger also points to himself indicating he will buy and to start a tab, which surprises both Richard and Aga. Roger's generosity is but a strategy, they both believe, to get Richard and Aga in his debt, in the hope they will drop their perceived investigation into his exam behavior.

Their corner table is surrounded by UT memorabilia, mostly football related. To clean the table for the celebration, Roger deposits the remaining popcorn onto the floor with a swipe of his hand.

"Really?" Aga asks, realizing he didn't even ask him what he wanted, and incredulous that Roger has offered to buy the first round. "You know I really wanted a Crown Royal, today."

Roger hesitates, not knowing quite what to say, and Aga lets him off the hook, volunteering, "Very well, I will lower myself to drink the blue-collar Lone Star swill you always order." With that, the Lone Stars are delivered.

"Good!" Roger replies, relieved. He lifts his Lone Star for a toast and adds, "We all made it. I'm sure we all passed. Time to celebrate!" Roger raises his bottle in a toast, and the three click their bottles together in unison. For a short moment following the toast, the three men sit in silence, enjoying the drink and reveling in having finished their exams.

Again, wanting to avoid questioning, Roger smiles at Aga, asking, "You have to explain to me how a good Muslim can indulge himself in Crown Royal, or any alcohol for that matter?"

Aga, sensing Roger's well-earned uneasiness and attempt to avoid questioning, responds in a somber tone, "My religion is geographically restricted to public areas in my country. Which is one of the reasons I came to this heathen country."

"I don't think this place even stocks the high-price stuff you prefer," Richard comments to Aga, as he glances at Roger, unable to control his curiosity. "Tell me, Roger, you were a wreck before the exam, and now you're riding on a cloud of confidence. Did you really find it that easy?"

Ignoring the tension and the intent of Richard's question, Roger deflects, "I thought they were great test questions, well framed, well thought out . . . and totally predictable, don't you agree?"

Richard pauses, reflecting, then continues his attack, "Does that include the one regarding the long-term implications of stopping the draft under Nixon? You anticipated that one?"

Roger ponders a reasonable answer, knowing Richard's attack involved the one question he had no clue about. "Well," Roger answers, "I thought there were several possible questions regarding the implications of the Vietnam War, and that definitely was one of the possibilities."

Both Richard and Aga are cognizant that Roger's answer is total, unmitigated bullshit. Aga rolls his eyes in disbelief, while Richard decides to have some fun at Roger's expense and sets Roger up with a question: "Yeah, it was unclear to me, though, what they were after with that question."

Aga, not understanding Richard's comment, adds, "I thought the question had to do with what long-term impact the cessation of the draft will have on our country and your country's value systems."

With his new confidence, Roger attempts to bring some humor into the conversation: "Wouldn't have had to sacrifice so many young hard-dicks if they had been able to avoid the draft, and maybe more of them would have ended up on welfare, right?"

Frustrated and annoyed, not understanding this was Roger's lame attempt at humor, Richard cannot hold himself back. "Jesus, Roger. That is such a dumb comment, even from you."

Aga jumps on Richard's bandwagon, "So not sacrificing the poor bastards would be your answer, Roger? Really? That's your brilliant assessment of long-term societal impact? That's the reason you are so confident after the exam, with comments like that?"

Roger ignores their criticism. "Look, I was kidding. Just a joke." Deciding it best to change the focus, Roger continues, "But you're both old enough to have been in the draft. Did either of you go?"

Aga shakes his head and laughs. "Not a citizen!"

Richard looks away but responds. "I was 4F due to a high school football injury. Knee. I was relieved to have escaped that responsibility, however."

The bottles of beer arrive. Richard and Aga glance at one another. "You really thought the test questions were predictable, Roger?" Richard asks, his frustration obvious in his voice.

"Yes," Roger responds, "Democratic dominance? Educational programs? Redistribution of wealth? Social programs and the coming importance of a potential free trade agreement with Mexico? All things we discussed in class. All very predictable, I believe."

Aga smiles, suppressing a laugh. "It's almost as if you had insight into the process, my friend. Unless you're into thaumaturgy'?"

"Thaumaturgy?" Roger questions.

"Sure," Richard responds as he winks at Aga. "It's the science of crystal-ball gazing."

Aga smiles, his point made, delighted to have embarrassed Roger and to have had Richard slamming down the intellectual hammer on the cheating dumb shit.

Electing to ignore Aga's taunt, gulping down his beer, Roger finally responds, "Oh, well, Aga, it was all there. In their lectures and, if you listened carefully to their informal conversations, there were no questions that we had not discussed at one time or another."

Not buying Roger's dodge, Richard puts the question to him while looking directly at him, first saying, "Including the societal implications of a free-trade agreement with Mexico?" Richard continues his inquisition, "Perhaps you were somehow just more attuned to the private conversations of our good professors or had a spy within the academic confines?" Looking at Roger, Richard asks, "Miss Jones, perhaps? Amy? Or hell, knowing you, Dr. Bowman?

"Yeah," Aga follows, "perhaps more directly, in tune, in touch?" Now getting to the immediate issue, Aga continues, "And that was so convenient, well timed, so opportunistic of you to charm dear, sweet Miss Jones. I could see that your step, your confidence increased magically following each of your trips to the john, especially the second trip. Don't you think, Richard? Don't you believe he returned from relieving himself with a demeanor and attitude that were, well, inspiring?"

Richard almost gleefully adds, "Oh yes. And will the dear, sweet, so easily inspired and manipulated Miss Jones be joining us here for drinks? Or will that be later?"

Unable to control his reaction, Aga laughs out loud. And Richard, enjoying Aga's inability to hide his reaction, also laughs, loudly, boisterously, sure of having split Aga's arrow, upping Aga's derision of Roger's too obvious manipulation and apparent game plan.

Surprising them both, Roger confidently smiles, no longer feeling like the third rail in their push for acceptance to the doctoral program, believing, perhaps for the first time, that he did as well on the test as they did. And certainly not giving one iota of a damn as to what he had to do to achieve the results, feeling justified, somehow, to have equaled or bettered his comrades, by whatever means necessary. He gulps down the bottle of beer in his hand and signals, with his free hand, for the bartender to bring another round. *Fuck them*, Roger thinks, following up with one very clear additional thought, *I'm going to get drunk and celebrate.*

Knowing that the exam results would bear out his joy, Roger responds with all emotion carefully removed from his professorial voice, "It was all there, in their lectures, boys. You just had to separate the wheat from the chaff."

Several moments of silence follow. Richard and Aga are frustrated, especially Richard, but, without evidence to support their claim, without any ability to prove that something was wrong with what occurred during the exam, they are forced to accept the day's events, knowing Roger's time will come, that Roger will eventually face a true and legitimate reckoning with the writing of his dissertation.

"Look," Aga finally says, breaking the ice, ending their game of gotcha on Roger. "If we all pass, I have a surprise. I will take you both flying. Anywhere you want to go, within a reasonable range of the Cessna 182 I just soloed in."

"Flying?" Richard asks.

"Flying," Aga follows. "You both knew I was taking flying lessons this past year. Well, I soloed in July. I got my pilot's license last month."

"No shit?" Richard comments. "Well, congratulations, Aga. A grad student getting his pilot's license? That must be a first, but nice. Guess it fits with your new Mercedes."

"Well," Richard adds, "that sounds good to me. How about flying to a football game in Chicago at my alma mater, Northern Illinois University. I'd love to see a few of my old buddies. So how about it, Aga, you willing to fly us to the Windy City?"

Aga, at first a bit taken aback by Richard's choice of Chicago, slaps Richard on the shoulder. "Yes, of course. Let's plan on it! If we all pass? Right, Roger? We'll go to Chicago if we all pass?"

Roger, happy to end the third degree, focuses the conversation on the fact he has never been to Chicago, and agrees the Windy City would be a great destination for the three of them.

As Richard finishes his beer, he turns to Aga, asking if he can take him back to his apartment so he can get dressed for dinner.

Roger, never having seen Richard dressed up or on a date, asks "Do you have a date?" Richard nods in the affirmative, and smiles. Surprised, Roger comments, "No shit. Congrats, big guy. I was beginning to think you hit from the wrong side of the plate."

Following another poor attempt at humor at Richard's expense, Roger does not realize how close he came to taking a well-deserved nap, from a short, hard right Richard had imagined as an appropriate payback for Roger's violating the academic honor code. Instead, Richard abruptly gets up and departs, followed by Aga, leaving Roger the chore and responsibility of settling the bill.

Chapter Ten

Roger and Amy once again lie in Roger's bed following love making. It is the day after the exam. Both are happy, playful. Amy cannot resist challenging Roger.

"You can begin to see it now, can't you?"

"See what?" Roger asks.

Frustrated but unwilling to allow the mood to be broken, Amy counters, "The future, Roger! Our future!"

"Well, no. I mean, I don't know," Roger finally blurts out.

"Sure you can. You will complete your dissertation, earn your doctoral degree, and begin teaching, probably here, given there will be two openings with the retirement of grandpa and Dr. Mac."

Roger rolls over following Amy's challenge and sits on the edge of the bed. "Well sure, that would be wonderful, sweetie."

Amy smiles, ear to ear. "We could both be here. Both teach here, live here, and raise our family here."

Roger reaches for his pants, pulls them on and begins buttoning his shirt as he says, "It would be great. Yeah. It would be," suddenly anxious to depart.

Amy gets up, suggestively allowing the covers to fall from her shoulders. "Do you really have to go?" she says with a mischievous and highly suggestive tone in her voice.

"Yes," Roger responds, looking at his watch. "Sorry. Got to grade the final paper outlines so my students can pick them up tomorrow. I'll call you later at your place, sweetie. We can meet for a drink or dinner."

Roger smiles as he rises and walks out of the bedroom, causing Amy to question what is going on with them. She begins to get dressed.

Roger exits his apartment, quick-walks to his Corvette, opens the door, and sits behind the wheel. He exhales for a long second, looks at himself in the rearview mirror with raised eyebrows, and smiles. He starts the car and quickly exits the parking lot. Minutes later he parks in an alley across the street from a popular downtown Austin bar, climbs out of his car, and trots across the street.

Entering the bar, Roger sees the female student, Ms. Pyramid, seated alone in a booth at the back of the bar. He walks up to the young girl, smiles, and seats himself next to her, close enough so that their legs touch as he slides into the booth.

"Been here long, sweetie?" he asks.

She smiles shyly, demurely, sliding even closer to him as she places her hand next to his leg, slightly touching it and leaving it resting there.

"I would have been here earlier," Roger smiles, thinking the best way to get into her pants is to play the academic card, "but I was thinking about your ideas regarding the tax-revenue discussion. You were really on top of that." Nice line, Roger compliments himself as he goes on, "You convinced almost everyone in the class, changing the way they thought, by your clear, detailed rationale. Ever think about becoming a professor? You definitely have the right mind-set."

She smiles back, more conscious of his flirtatious manner than he realizes, more aware of his intentions than he knows, and responds, "Yes, in fact I am thinking about going to grad school. You do know that my major is sociology?"

Roger waves for the bartender while the girl nervously fiddles with a bottle of beer already in her hand.

She looks at him, continues to smile and squeezes her hand on his leg. "So, I will be getting an A in your class, right, professor? Because I need the grade. I need an A to help me qualify for grad school."

Roger loves the salutation of professor, and smiles confidently at the girl. "I will help you any way I can. Seriously, any way I can. You are far and away my best student."

"And you are someone I can trust?" she asks, a seriousness, genuineness, in her voice that troubles him in its forthrightness and sincerity. "Can I trust you? Can I trust that you will keep your promise?"

"I always keep my promises," Roger tells her, as the bartender arrives with two bottles of beer. "Always." Roger takes a drink and says, "I can also keep a secret, can you?"

Ms. Pyramid smiles, knowing exactly where this going, where she really wants this to go.

Chapter Eleven

At two o'clock in the afternoon on a blazingly hot, hell-like Austin day, Amy enters Sam's office, sweating profusely. She runs to the air-conditioner and stands in front of it, unselfconsciously holding up her bare arms, exposing her powdered armpits to the cool air blowing on high from the window unit.

She wears very short shorts, a red sports bra covered by a white half T-shirt, battered and worn running shoes, and no socks. Relaxed, sitting with his feet resting atop his desk, Sam is dressed casually in a gray UT T-shirt, a tan pair of pants, white gym socks and white, red-striped and pristine Adidas running shoes, which had been a gift from Amy and look new, though they are almost a year old. His ever-present sport coat and tie rest on the back of his chair as he struggles to ignore his granddaughter's scant and revealing outfit.

"This testing program is making me sick to my stomach, grandpa. And watching what you have put Roger and the others through, really, it's enough to make me heave. Really, I mean actually heave!"

"It's supposed to be tough, Amy. Gotta weed out unwanted intruders, you know that."

Amy isn't buying Sam's explanation. "Grandpa, really, I just think . . ."

Sam cuts her off. "It's a necessary rung on the educational ladder. And I don't know why you would worry. You and I both know you'll ace it."

Amy looks away. "I, I worry about . . ."

Sam cuts her off again. "You worry about your boyfriend. Well, don't worry. Let him be a man; at least let him act like a man, maybe act like a boy learning to be a man. Shit, I don't know. But he'll make it or he won't, and your worrying isn't going to make any difference."

Sam peers over the top of his granny glasses as Amy continues her diatribe.

"I mean, I'll be taking my exam later this semester and I hope I don't have to go through anything like you're putting Roger through."

Sam again looks up, removing his feet from the desk and swiveling in his chair to face Amy. "You'll do fine," he says, smiling. "You're the smartest candidate in your department. Your professors told me that back when you were an undergrad. So, just relax into it, honey. Enjoy it! There won't be anything in it that you don't know inside out. I promise."

She turns from the fan, allowing cool air to filter back into the room.

"Did you have to go through this, back in your day?"

Sam laughs. "Sure, of course, but it was more difficult back them, with ink wells and all."

Amy laughs uncomfortably, and Sam realizes she has taken his joke seriously.

Avoiding Sam's question, Amy moves to a chair across from Sam's desk and unceremoniously seats herself. She is always relaxed when in Sam's presence, more like a young school girl than the beautiful young woman she has become, who is often uncomfortable with the way men look at her, but always comfortable and girlish, at ease and happy in the company of her grandfather. She senses that he still sees her as a 10-year-old and thus often tends to behave in such a manner when with him, knowing he enjoys it, is more comfortable with it, and happy herself to feel so genuinely and sincerely loved.

"Grandpa, I'm very worried about Roger."

At that moment, Rufus and Debbie Bowman enter Sam's office. Amy, happy for the reprieve, departs, kissing Rufus on his cheek as she passes. She looks back at Sam and he nods, acknowledging what she hopes, that he will give Roger a fair shake, perhaps even an edge in the process.

Rufus and Debbie, both dressed comfortably for the extreme heat, Debbie in a patterned sun dress and Rufus in thin running pants and a Hawaiian shirt, with outrageous large red and yellow flowers on a white background, seat themselves at Sam's conference table. And Rufus bellows out what he came to say, looking directly at Sam, "I assume we have all scored the three candidates. Debbie and I have compared notes, using our usual, traditional formula."

Rufus, with a touch of bravado, sets the papers on the table and continues without looking up, "Two points for excellent, one for pass, zero for fail."

"And?" Sam asks, looking to Debbie, "Where did you two score them?"

"Richard received two points from Rufus and two from me," Debbie explains, "Aga we graded two and one, two by me and one by Rufus."

"Okay," Sam acknowledges, "so both pass. And what of Roger?"

Rufus looks across the table at Debbie and then to Sam.

"Debbie gave him a two and I gave him a zero!"

Sam positions himself in his chair, obviously uncomfortable and unsure how to continue.

"So," he finally responds, "you're putting it on me?"

Rufus smiles. "It does take a total of four points to pass, so, yeah. It's on you."

Sam starts for the bottle of bourbon on his bar but hesitates, catching himself and thinking that it may be a bit early to indulge, especially with the negotiation he anticipates with both Rufus and Debbie. He does, however, look longingly at the unopened bottle before returning to the subject at hand.

"So how do you two explain the discrepancy over Roger?"

Appearing uncomfortable with the question, Debbie adjusts her skirt. "Well," she submits, "I scored him on his test results. He impressively dealt with the subjects, framed his ideas succinctly and noted key implications. I believe he did a very good job."

Rufus, apparently not happy with Debbie's assessment and obviously having a big itch, scratches his chest and adjusts his suspenders. "Yes, yes. Roger outlined it," Rufus responds, "much like it would have been done in Cliff Notes. There was no depth of critical thinking, none. His answers were right out of an elementary poli sci text book. Hell, an undergraduate could have done just as well on the exam."

Surrendering to his desire and delaying his reaction, Sam moves to his bar, opens the bottle of bourbon and begins pouring, almost filling three glasses. No ice will dilute the bourbon.

Carefully watching Sam pour, Rufus responds. "Oh, so that's how it's going to be."

Wanting to avoid a long, drawn-out meeting over the issue of Roger, Debbie attempts to take some command of the situation. "Are we going to be here long?" she asks. "I mean, if we are, I need to make arrangements."

Sam distributes the drinks. "As long as it takes," he says calmly, confidently.

Debbie nods her understanding and sits back in her chair, confident she has made a good argument.

"Look here," Rufus offers, "Roger can spit it back okay, the importance and evolution of civil rights, federal aid to education and funding for cities, medical care for the aged, poverty programs. He knows them but he doesn't really understand them with respect to their political implications. He has no feel for the political reality. He cannot comprehend why we fought so hard for them, why they were so important at that time. And, most importantly, what the long-term implications are."

Seemingly taken aback, Sam responds emotionally, "Important? They were important because they built the party's base, for the future, appealing to large constituencies, creating assistance for those in need. It was Lyndon's key political principle: fuel voter loyalty, creating dependence for and on assistance! Hell, that's the political reality. That's the long-term implication, putting the party into position to address the issues facing America that they think are in the best interests of the people."

Rufus suppresses the hint of a sarcastic smirk escaping his mouth as best he can, while reaching out to accept the glass of bourbon from Sam. He looks up once the glass has been successfully transferred to his hand and, attempting to corner Sam, asks, "Does fuel mean buy?"

Sam ignores Rufus's implication and responds, "Well, Roger can certainly be bought. He's clearly just a surface-level sycophant. But I read his answers. As Debbie said, he does clearly understand the background of key issues, and he did note many of the key implications."

Rufus interjects, "Bullshit. Are you kidding? Implications, my ass."

Debbie attempts to negate Rufus's comments by referring back to Sam's commentary. "Sycophants, no shortage of those in our profession. It's a critical function in the political arena, after all," she says, then questions, "and I'm sure you boys are just funnin' when you talk about buying loyalty. I know you mean earning, deserving, right?"

Rufus responds, ignoring Debbie's question, while looking at the picture on the wall of him and Sam standing next to LBJ for effect, "It is true that the old man liked smooth-talking sycophants, and that he always said it was necessary to keep them close, even closer, frequently, than your most trusted advisors."

Sam hesitates for a moment, looks at the amount of bourbon he has poured for himself and, without looking up, continues pouring until the glass is completely full. "That kind of behavior," Sam reflects, "wasn't one of the old man's better traits."

Rufus appears insulted. "Oh?" he asks, and looks at Debbie. "He hid more than he ever showed. He was a sly old fox and he could charm the pants off a woman a block away. And he could con a friend while looking him square in the eye." Clearly the bourbon had increased Rufus's honesty factor.

Sam challenges Rufus with the question, "You got something you want to say, Rufus?"

"No, no," Rufus responds, "I'm just an old man, with not too good recall at times, talking, maybe, when I should just shut up."

Sam senses the importance and necessity of coming to Roger's defense. "Roger accomplished what we put before him, Rufus. We challenged him and he's the only one of the three that took an interest in digging deeper, answering question number seven about the brittle. So I would like to give him the nod."

Rufus drinks his glass of bourbon in a large gulp and holds out the glass for a refill. Sam fills it.

"So," Rufus summarizes, "based on Roger's ability to replay the party line, or on his insights into digging deeper into preferred White House snacks, on that impressive basis, you believe we should pass him?"

Frustrated, Sam exhales deeply and seats himself behind his desk. "I think," he says, "that, well, that, he has done what we asked him to . . . and," at this point believing it necessary to surrender to truth, Sam admits, "and Amy really likes him."

Debbie looks away uneasily as Sam continues. "So there has to be something there, beneath the surface, perhaps, but there, for her to care so much about him. And I think he does have potential."

Flippantly, Rufus waves his hand in the air. "So, the bottom line is that this process is really all about Amy?" Then, sensing a need to soften his stance, he goes on, "Maybe it's just Amy's motherly instincts." With that, Rufus rises from his chair, obviously headed for the door.

"Okay," Rufus adds, without turning to look back, "This is our last go-around, for you and me anyway, Sam. If you want to go out helping a, well, providing Roger with an automatic pass . . . well, he's going to need a lot of help. I hope you folks have the time. Is it going to be you, Sam? Or," finally turning to look at Debbie, "or you?"

For Rufus the meeting has ended and he gets up, grabs his drink, and begins walking. Just before Rufus makes his exit out the door, he turns and, just before disappearing down the hallway he says, with a smile and grand gesture of his free hand, which still holds the half-full glass of bourbon, "Thanks for the drink! I'll see you later."

Sam rises to stop Rufus from leaving, believing it bad form for a tenured senior professor to be caught in the hallway of the school's government building with a glass of bourbon in his hand, but stops, laughs and shakes his head.

"Oh, what the hell! It's his last year."

Debbie hangs back as Rufus makes his exit, seeming to want a final word with Sam. "Thanks, Sam. Don't worry. I'll personally see to it that Roger makes you proud. Makes all of us proud."

Sam pours himself another bourbon, though concerned that he has already allowed himself more than his daytime allotment. He sits at his desk, glass in hand, and peers over his granny glasses. "Sure," he says. "But make sure you go lightly on trying to prove anything with him. I'll let you know what I decide about who will be assigned to whom."

Debbie acceptingly nods, smiles at Sam as she departs, saying, "Fine."

Frustrated, feeling like he has betrayed his academic credibility while more importantly supporting his granddaughter's wishes, Sam sits once again behind his desk, drinks the remaining bourbon in his glass, looks at the half-full bottle on his bar, and laughs.

"Oh what the hell. It's not like I betrayed the entire world."

Chapter Twelve

The sun was setting, but waves of heat still rose from the asphalt in front of the Driskill Hotel, Austin's most upscale gathering spot, as a wedding reception crowd mingled out front and in the lobby.

Most Austin residents take advantage of the landmark for their important events. It is where a young Lyndon Johnson had his first date with a Texas socialite named Claudia Taylor, who would later become Lady Bird Johnson, in 1934.

Founded in 1886 by Cattle Baron Jesse Driskill, the hotel was a favorite of Johnson's all his life. He once awaited news there from Sam and Rufus, who had teamed up to deliver the "necessary tasks" that led to his successful 1948 Senate bid. And it was also at the Driskill where LBJ waited for the results of the 1960 election promoting him to the office of vice president, and it was where, four years later, that he watched the results of his presidential election, from the Presidential Suite.

Lyndon liked to say that every room at the Driskill had a story, and that Sam and Rufus had something to do with every one of them. He even credited his two loyal associates with getting air-conditioning installed after Lyndon spent a sultry and uncomfortable evening there back in 1950.

Sam and Rufus had lovingly carried on the tradition of the Driskill, while serving on the UT faculty, making it the location of choice whenever an event was deemed worthy. And thus they had selected it for dinner, as always, following the PhD exam review.

Upon arriving, Sam worked his way through the crowd gathered at the hotel's entry into the famous bar, where he was pretty assured that Rufus was already there holding court. And he was right.

Upon joining Rufus in the bar, Sam intoned, "I love this old place. Hell, it's older than we are." Rufus waves at George, their favorite bartender, indicating that they would be heading to their usual table.

The two sit down, Sam after he customarily takes off his sport coat, hanging it behind the chair. "How many dinners have we had here, through the years?" Rufus rhetorically questioned. "In this very room, most at this same table."

Their table in the bar was nearest to the hotel's entry, with a view of the front of the hotel and the street out front, and it had been their favorite table for over 40 years. And Rufus often bragged that he could see the comings and goings of all of Texas from this vantage point.

Without fanfare, having recognized Sam and Rufus when they entered, a waitress brings the two men their favorite non-watered-down drinks, sets their drinks in front of them and, without comment or fanfare, hurries to another table.

Rufus, in an attempt to put behind them the earlier meeting, raises his glass to Sam, saying, "I have witnessed you downing a few of these over the years here, Sam."

"Yeah, true," Sam quips to Rufus, pointing at his bulging suspenders, "but you've obviously had more dinners here than me." They share a smile and laugh, allowing the day's earlier frustrations to dissipate.

The two men drink in silence for a few minutes, as the crowd out front finally makes its way into the lobby and then into the banquet room.

As Sam finishes his first drink, he reflects, "It's obvious now that Carter has no chance in the upcoming election. Imagine if you can, Reagan, a B-movie actor, a teleprompter politician intent on undoing all we have done, accomplished . . . all of the old man's programs. I'm glad we are retiring, that this really is our last go around, our last group of political disciples to train to our way of thinking, and to then unleash upon the world."

As Sam completes his thought, the ever attentive waitress arrives with a second round of drinks.

Rufus shakes his head, disagreeing with Sam's statement, then responding, "Our programs are ingrained in Our Great Society. They will live through the next four years and be born again with the election of a clear-thinking Democrat president four years from now. With his strategic insight presented, Rufus stands to deliver a toast, "To the old man."

"To the good we did," Sam counters simply raising his glass, "to what we were able to accomplish."

Sam smiles as Rufus sits back in his chair, looks outside, and then comments, "You know, Rufus, you were the real genius and author of most of LBJ's programs. Your vision launched 435 grant-in-aid programs, five federal agencies, including Housing and Urban Development, and Health, Education and Welfare. You, a cowpoke sociologist, did all that for the president, for our country."

Sam raises a toast to Rufus, and Rufus raises his glass in response and says, "Sam, I didn't know you were counting. Where did you come up with all those numbers?" Sam smiles. Both men then sit silently, starring into their ice-filled but now empty bourbon glasses.

"Actually," Rufus adds, "you wrote his speeches, including the Great Society speech, only four weeks after he became president. And you were his liaison to Congress, the guy who, when he spoke well, was credited with making even ol' Landslide sound like a smooth talker."

The waitress walks by, drops off menus for them as a courtesy, along with fresh drinks, but does it in a manner in which she appears to keep walking, having served them almost without hesitation. Over her shoulder, as she departs, she explains, "Steaks rare, potatoes loaded, and salads Italian dressing with blue cheese sprinkles? And another round of drinks, in seven minutes?"

Both men chuckle, ignoring their menus, and both wave in unison.

Right on time, seven minutes later, she returns, drops off their next round of drinks and removes the menus without either of them ever having been opened.

"Looking ahead," Sam says, while glancing out the window, "it seems so hard now to predict the future. But we were once so hopeful. It's hard to know where all this will go, but I hope it never goes backward, that's for sure. I thought we were all about giving equal opportunity to all."

Rufus laughs. "Intent, our intent was good. We had the long-term best interest of our country in mind. We changed America by giving a more equal chance to the underprivileged. And built a political party on their loyalty."

"Best interest?" Sam questions his friend. "A more equal opportunity, Rufus? We? No, my friend, it was your strategic plan. I just drafted legislation. I wrote speeches based on your plans and performed a little sales magic on Capitol Hill."

"Don't kid yourself," Rufus counters, "we both had the country's best interests in mind, didn't we?"

Sam smiles, waving his napkin in surrender, "Best interests, Rufus? Well, intent can be a slippery slope. The blacks for example."

Obviously troubled by Sam's comments, Rufus starts to speak, "Let's not . . ." but he doesn't finish.

"No," Sam comes back, "let's! For once, Rufus, you be straight with me."

Rufus nods in agreement, making it seem like surrender. "Okay. We wanted those colored folks as a voting bloc and decided to do what it took to get them . . . and most importantly to keep them voting our way. And we got 'em!"

Obviously in disagreement with Rufus, Sam comments, "We gave them welfare, laid the foundation for food stamps, a number of other programs designed to give the needy opportunities, a better life."

Rufus appears to glow as Sam lists the accomplishments, until Sam reflects on the ever-escalating outcomes of those programs that "squelched their work ethic" and ultimately "broke up their families."

"Not only did we break up the families," Sam continues, "but we created single-parent homes, then increased their benefits if they remained broken. And then we allowed drugs to be introduced into their culture, society, compliments to a great degree of Vietnam, and the drugs eventually put a shamefully and increasingly high number of black men in prison. We destroyed their neighborhoods, their family structure, pride, their dignity. We took away their jobs, so that the only avenue available to them was one of crime . . . and all by creating dependence."

Sam's reflection has put Rufus in a foul mood by the time the waitress arrives with their food. Both men sit in silence as she sets their steaks and salads, always served at the same time, on the table. "Rather negative view, don't you think?" Rufus comments after the waitress leaves.

"A true view, Rufus," Sam says, "and you know it. We did that. And we knew that we were doing it. I was conscious, even then, that our legislative means were justified by our political end goals. But I never fully understood what path our programs would lead the country on a downward spiral."

"We did what we had to do to get in power! And to stay in power," Rufus comments, ignoring the food in front of him, his appetite suddenly diminished. "We got things turned around, didn't we? Lyndon got civil rights passed, voting laws passed. None of which would have happened without us taking the path we took!"

Sam begins cutting his steak. "Nice to think so, anyway. But we're beginning to go down the same road now with those from south of the border who are coming for the opportunities our country offers, aren't we?"

Rufus begins eating his salad, knowing full well what Sam means by his use of the plural of opportunity. He is desperate to change the conversation, uncomfortable, breathing heavy and obviously on the verge of physical distress. Sam is so angry at his realization, brought out by his life reflections as retirement time approaches that he is generally unaware of Rufus's condition, until he sees that Rufus is sweating profusely.

Sam then decides to change the subject, smiles and waves for another round of drinks. "Look, Rufus, I know you have serious doubts about Roger, but it won't be the first time we helped a candidate, while ignoring a few rules. And I want you to be his chairman. One last request from your lifelong friend."

Rufus smiles, a curious, but appreciative, suddenly relaxed smile, appreciative that Sam has elected to change the subject, even if it was to discuss Roger. "She loves him, doesn't she?" Rufus asks. "And they want a life together, don't they?"

"Yes," Sam admits, "she loves him. They want a life together. And I owe my daughter. I promised her, on her deathbed, after the car crash, that I would take care of Amy. I'm all she has, and she's all I have."

Rufus breathes easier as the waitress serves their drinks and removes their empty plates. "Let's quit playing," Rufus tells the waitress. "Just make 'em doubles from here on in, okay, sweetheart, that means only every 14 minutes before refills."

She smiles. "Yes, of course, Dr. MacIntosh."

Rufus laughs. "So you remember me by name, you don't just recognize me by my drinks and dinner favorites?"

"Of course. I took your class several years ago."

"And how'd I do, my dear? Please tell me."

"Well," she said, "I really did learn a lot. I'm in law school now. I just work here when I need extra money."

Rufus attempts to stand, but remains in his seat. "Well then," he says, "Congratulations, Miss . . . ?"

The waitress smiles widely, happily, and strikes a pose, "Why I'm Miss South Dakota. Least that's what you used to always call me, Miss South Dakota, because that's where I'm from, originally."

Rufus smiles and nods in remembrance. "And I certainly do remember you now, my dear. I certainly do."

The waitress smiles and moves away.

"She is a nice girl," Rufus tells Sam. "I do remember her."

"She is beautiful," Sam shares. "Miss South Dakota?"

"Yes. Yes, and bright too."

"And is there a story there?" Sam asks, with some humor in his voice.

"Has the bourbon dimmed your senses?" Rufus responds, then electing to return the subject to Roger. "Look, Sam, Roger is shallow, an intellectual lightweight. He will contribute nothing of significance in the long run. But, okay, yes. Because of our history together, I will do this for you. But, if he doesn't perform to my standards, he won't make it. Agreed?"

Sam smiles. "Deal. I think I will assign Richard to me, and that leaves Aga for Debbie. I think Richard is a great candidate. He will be a wonderful addition to academe. Aga is above average. I'm unsure of his true intentions, direction, not even sure if he is a true progressive or just courting favor. But who are we to say?"

Rufus smiles widely, genuinely, once again at ease with his friend.

"I will give Amy's man the chance for the life she wants. I'll go along and give him a simple topic that doesn't require too much intellectual work. My last effort for my pal. But this dinner is on you, Sam!"

Rufus looks out the window to the street, but his mind travels into the past. He sees himself in LBJ's congressional office, with LBJ's arm on his shoulder. It is 1948, just days following the "landslide" victory for the Senate primary, which guaranteed the position to any Democrat with a pulse.

LBJ speaks almost in a whisper into Rufus's ear. "Come on, Rufus. Stay with me in Washington, and you can bring Sam with you. I'll triple both of your university salaries. The three of us together again, we'll have fun and get things done, just like our San Marcos days, a reuniting of the White Stars!"

Rufus fumbles for an answer to the invitation. "Sam isn't like us, Lyndon. He's a pure heart, a good soul. Hell, he still thinks he's a Marine." He pauses again, grows serious, almost somber. "It's not like the old days, Lyndon. Sam is all about the future of our country. He won't look the other way when the really dark, political work must be done. But he's a great writer, as bright as me. He's just not as grounded as you and I are, Lyndon . . . or as understanding of how things work, how things really get done. He doesn't have the stomach to make sausage but he enjoys eating it, and sharing it with others, if he believes in the desired outcome."

Lyndon Johnson lets go of Rufus's shoulder but continues to speak into Rufus's ear. "So, let me be clear, Rufus. I will always be able to count on you for what needs to be done? I can count on you also to keep an eye on Sam, so I don't have to worry?"

LBJ steps back, then forward once again, pressing against Rufus. "I'm so glad you see it my way," LBJ whispers into Rufus's ear, "I knew you would."

Without looking at LBJ, Rufus responds, "Yes, yes sir."

Rufus is brought back to the present by Sam's comment, "Let's finish up and go home. I'm full," referring to his daily bourbon quota.

Chapter Thirteen

Richard and Aga stand in the hallway outside Sam's office waiting for Roger. Both are frustrated, as he is always late. Both Richard and Aga compulsively look at the sign above Sam's door, which reads, "Dr. Samuel Brown, Chairman, Department of Government." Roger walks casually, confidently down the hallway and smiles as he reaches his friends.

"Late, you're always late!" Richard barks at Roger as he arrives.

"Really," Aga adds. "And don't act so confident. Miss Jones may have turned you in."

Roger smiles as he reaches them. "Never let 'em see you sweat, boys. Never!"

The trio enters Sam's office and is greeted by Sam's secretary, Miss Jones, who is paying close attention to Roger and smiling. She departs and enters Sam's private office. The three men stand silently looking at the photos on Sam's outer office wall, of Sam as a young Marine; of Sam with LBJ; of Sam and Rufus, both young men looking ambitious and confident in the Oval Office; and of Sam at LBJ's ranch, sitting alongside the president, who is behind the wheel of his long, white Lincoln Continental convertible, top down, though a very rare winter snow is falling all around.

Miss Jones continues to smile broadly as she passes Roger. "Good morning," she says to all three of them. "Dr. Brown will see you now."

Seated at his desk, Sam looks up over his antique, '60s reading glasses and motions for them to be seated at the conference table. "Don't believe in drama, boys," Sam begins. "You all passed your PhD qualifying exam and can officially begin work on your dissertations."

Unable to control their excitement and relief, all three candidates smile, sit up in their chairs, and congratulate one another as they also thank Sam.

"Don't look so happy," Sam admonishes them. "At this stage you boys are all hat and no cattle. So each of you needs to put together the rest of your five-person committees to support your dissertation work. I have already selected your chairs."

For a long moment, Sam looks over each candidate. "Aga," he mentions first, "you will work with Dr. Bowman. Roger, you will be under the supervision of Dr. MacIntosh, and Richard, that leaves you with me as your chairman."

Richard is obviously pleased, Aga a bit uneasy, but Roger looks frustrated, confused, and upset.

Sam continues with his instructions, "Each of you will meet with your assigned chair as soon as possible to begin work. Make us believe we have chosen wisely."

Sam shakes hands with each of them warmly and sincerely as they begin to exit his office, and the three young men continue shaking hands and congratulating one another.

"Later, Richard, Aga," Roger says. "I have to find a phone and call Amy."

Roger rushes down the hallway to the grad student offices at the end of the hall to call Amy, anxious to share his good news, genuinely excited to share his information, knowing she will see this news as confirmation of a future for the two of them, side by side, beginning their life together.

"Amy," he says, reaching her at her apartment. I did it, honey. I did. We did. We made it! Now on to my dissertation. One last step!"

As Amy listens to Roger, her mind wanders to 1965 when she was 10. Sam had taken her on a special trip to Washington, D.C., to celebrate the passage of the Medicare Bill, which she had not clearly understood at the time but sensed it was a great moment, a time of real significance, and she was proud that he had chosen to share it with her.

She remembered standing next to Sam and Rufus in the Oval Office, watching President Johnson sign the bill and how, immediately after picking up the first pen and making a very small mark on the page, he had turned, smiled at her and handed her it to her. And, while she had no understanding of the importance or significance of his gesture at that time, the pen had grown more and more important to her over the years and was framed now and hanging in her apartment.

"Here honey," the president had said, "this pen is for you. Your Grandpa Sam worked hard to make this bill a reality."

President Johnson had smiled widely, allowing the cameras to capture the moment.

"I know you just turned 10 years of age," the president had continued, "and I know you just recently lost your mommy and daddy in a horrible car accident. But I hope this pen, in some small way, can give you a new beginning, and provide you with a moment of happiness that you can treasure."

Amy had attempted to smile at the president but was confused and afraid. Sam moved to her side and placed his hand on her shoulder, reassuring her, comforting her.

The president had continued, "Do you know anything about . . . understand anything about this bill, honey?" he asked as the cameras flashed all around them.

LBJ had turned to Sam. "Does she know anything about this bill, Sam?"

Confused how to best answer the president's question, Sam responded as best he could under the circumstance. "No, Mr. President. I don't think she understands, but I will explain it to her and, in time, she will appreciate your kind act in presenting her with a pen to commemorate this wonderful and important day."

Even though she hadn't understood much of anything that was going on that day, the emotional thickness was too much for a 10-year-old, and tears had rolled down Amy's cheeks, thinking about her parents. The truth was, she knew nothing of the accident that had killed her parents, only remembering Sam arriving at her school to pick her up, comforting her, later explaining that her parents were in heaven.

Reflecting on her childhood with her grandfather, she did learn not to believe the stories she often heard him and his friend Rufus concoct. Even as a child she could tell they spent more energy trying to make their stories believable than they ever spent trying to explain the truth. She very much enjoyed this entertainment, which she thought then was only for her.

Sam carefully moved Amy away from the activity around the president and, as they reached a safe corner of the room, away from the photographers and supporters anxious to get a pen or be in a photo capturing the moment for history and posterity. Amy, holding her pen tightly in both hands, had turned to her grandpa.

"I was okay until the President talked to me, Grandpa. I wish I knew what to say."

Sam answered, with a rare tear, "Honey your look said it all. I'm so glad you are here today. I love you."

Chapter Fourteen

Two days after the meeting in Sam's office, Richard and Aga sit at a conference table in the graduate student offices. The conversation moves from Richard's progress on his presidential library research to discussing potential ideas for their dissertations, gleeful that they had actually made it to the final stage of the program.

Roger walks in and begins listening to their ideas. Moments later, Amy joins them. Roger stands as she enters the room, surprising her, and, in a seemingly gentlemanly gesture, he pulls a chair out for her in which to be seated.

"Hey, sweetie," he says, smiling, winking at her as a surprised but appreciative smile spreads across her face, lighting up the entire room.

Turning to Richard and Aga, Amy asks, "Mind if I sit in with you, boys?"

Both men graciously welcome her. "Happy to have you here, Amy," says Richard, as Aga smiles and signals with a hand gesture for her to be seated.

"We are working on outlining ideas for our dissertations, Amy," Roger explains.

This comment causes Aga to look at Richard and roll his eyes back into his head. Richard then asks Amy, "But I'm sure you are pretty much already settled for your topic, your dissertation topic. Right?"

"Oh, hell no!" Amy responds, explaining, "I'm torn! This coming election has thrown me a big curve. It's such a big deal. It could ultimately determine government as a force for good or evil for generations . . . at least the foreseeable future. I'm not sure how to attack this idea of supply-side economics and some crap theory appropriately labeled as a trickle-down effect."

Aga injects, "It's not so crazy, hell, and trickle-down is how Kuwait functions."

Richard laughs, "But, Aga, your country is fundamentally a dictatorship!"

"Oh no," Aga responds to Richard, "not quite that. We are really more like a family-owned business."

"One with allegiance to Russia," Richard retorts.

Aga explains, "Yes, playing both sides makes the most financial sense, you know."

Amy jumps back into the argument, stating, "The question is, where there is a democracy with equal opportunity, then, is the trickle-down theory really best for the people, and of course in our case, the American people?"

Richard wastes no time asserting his political idea. "Reagan's end to 'trust me' government and his focus on personal opportunity and responsibility versus Carter's despair and pessimism campaign has us all in a fuss, confused, anxious. If Reagan convinces folks of his philosophy, our entire party is at risk," Richard goes on. "Carter has caused this; he has screwed it all up. He has no credibility at this point, absent any semblance of political vision, leading us to 21 percent interest rates, a 14 percent rate of inflation and double digit, 12 percent, unemployment. And his hands-off approach to economics and the central bank adds up to an absolutely perfect failure."

Richard pauses, then continues, "I do admit, however, that I am struggling with Keynesian issues supporting government intervention to improve the overall economy with respect to balanced budget issues, which seems totally at odds with Reagan's unrealistic commitment to a lower tax pledge."

Surprised by the abject fierceness of Richard's tirade, Amy responds immediately.

"Oh, blasphemer!"

"Yes," contributes Aga, "somebody get a bar of soap! But, Amy, Carter does bring to life a perfect, though unfortunate, example of a 'malaise' strategy. He's a follower, unlike President Johnson, and not a leader. He is a man without vision, I'm afraid."

Unhappy with Aga's assessment, Amy contributes her own opinion. "We all have to pull together, fight the good fight, bring critical issues to the attention of the country. I do admit, however, that I'm struggling some with the Keynesian approach, supporting government intervention to improve the economy. But, as compared to Reagan's insensitive, truly unfathomable economic rants, I think governmental control of the economy is clearly the better path. Good Lord, if we let this ignorant bastard become president, it could well be catastrophic."

Anxious to contribute his own ideas, Roger jumps in. "I'm leaning toward Vietnam as a dissertation topic, the impact of the end of conscription, which was the most interesting exam question, I believe. My guess is that it was Dr. Mac's sociological implication to put it on the exam. But I'm also considering the tumultuous period of assassinations over the past 20 years which, I have learned from Dr. Mac, coincidentally ended in conjunction with LBJ's leaving office."

Aga looks at Richard, and smiles, thinking that is the discovery that Richard has recently found in the library documents, specific references with reverse-coded initials of the recently and, as indicated by the dates, the soon-to-be departed.

Amy, obviously offended by Roger's comment, jumps into the fray. "Please, Roger. Tell me you are not going to attempt to indirectly link President Johnson to any of the assassination theories. You're not doing to do that, are you?"

Roger doesn't take Amy seriously. "Assassinations are a subject Dr. Mac brought up, not me. I think he wants it researched for the DNC to be ready, prepared, should any such accusations arise."

Amy sits back, accepting Roger's explanation, not able to understand why Dr. Mac would suggest such a topic. But Aga continues the debate, "Interesting, isn't it? Dr. Brown and Dr. Mac were true believers, insiders into all the issues we are considering for our dissertations. They set the stage, in many ways, for Reagan's rise to the presidency."

Amy is aghast at Aga's suggestion. "Oh, Aga! Shame on you! Say it isn't so!"

Aga is defensive. "Look, Amy. You know it is. Reagan will win this election. He will be the next president."

With this comment, Richard jumps in. "Which has to be just killing Dr. Sam and Dr. Mac. You know it's about tapping into folk's value systems, just like Dr. Mac taught us, that's what drives the voting decision."

Amy eyes Aga. "So, Aga, what is at the top of your list?"

"Power," Aga responds. "How to create it and how to govern with it—how to keep it. This is the centerpiece of what I came here to learn, from the masters. This is the core of political strategy, even though you seem to refer to it very inappropriately, I think, as political science."

Richard laughs and points at Aga. "We all know where your power comes from in the Middle East, Aga. It is oil! It is your and your sisters' countries' economic currency. But the question," Richard remarks with a philosophical tone, "seems to be how to optimize the use of this natural resource in order to gain even more power, through controlling an ever-increasing share of world economies. Isn't that really our view for future control, or in your terminology, power, upon which you ground your strategic thinking?"

Sternly, directly, Aga responds to Richard, taken aback by his friend's directness. "It's no different a view than what guides the political parties in the US. It's about maintaining power for the long term. You kid yourself if you think it is about doing any type of social good. Remember, everything in politics is personal, according to Dr. Sam and Dr. Mac, which they both attribute to their Oval Office pal, LBJ."

Feeling somewhat ill at ease and somehow threatened by Aga's response, Amy attempts to lighten the mood. "No lack of interesting topics here. Though I do believe smart economics is the driving force underlying good political strategy. It determines the long-term success of the ruling party, because it builds loyalty. And gaining loyalty is the linchpin of political strategy."

"But following this line of thinking," Aga interjects, "doesn't this just mean if you build a linchpin system that pays folks off, you will build loyalty?"

Roger comes to Amy's aid, feeling uncomfortable with the direction the conversation is going. "Absolutely, no better time possible to study and unearth the strategic underpinnings of LBJ's social programs, having one-on-one contact with two of his most trusted insiders, his brain trust."

Aga laughs. "Unearth? Is that really a word? Get serious, do you not think they won't direct the choice of our topics and then edit our findings down to suit their own personal ends, making those findings more supportive of the issues and programs they spent their lives creating? If you don't agree with this, you don't understand the academic process here, or any place else."

Amy, feeling Aga's comment directly impugns her grandfather's motives, starts with, "Yes, unearth is a word, but my granddad would never . . ."

Seeing where this is going and wanting to cut it off, Richard stands and interrupts. "Enough." This very uncharacteristic move by him results in silence.

Amy understands what Richard is doing, and asks, "Okay, what's your dissertation idea, Richard?"

Richard begins with, "Look, I am trying to contribute something to the national discourse. I've worked hard here, and am ready to dig in. I believe I would like to study the long-term strategic viability of race-based preferences."

"As a minority yourself," Roger says, "I assume you are going to look through a lens that will result in you scientifically concluding they are good for all."

"No," Richard surprisingly responds. "The issue I believe worth focusing on is the long-term societal outcomes, the direct and indirect, long-term consequences of race issues."

Roger surprises everyone as he barks out, "Are you nuts? Race-based preferences are about achieving equality of opportunity for all. That was one of the main points of Dr. Bowman's governmental affairs seminar."

Richard smiles at Roger's response. "So," Richard asks, "you think race-based preferences should be applied to all hiring practices?"

"Yes!" Roger responds, without thinking through his answer. 'By all means. It will level the playing field for those that our society has abused in the past."

Roger seems pleased with himself, knowing he has exactly repeated the party line.

"So, how about airline pilots—should these hires include race-based preferences?" Richard asks Roger. "So, do you think equal opportunity should apply to evaluating and hiring them, lowering the qualification standards? What do you think the average American would say to hiring the less or not qualified when lives are at stake?"

Richard's quicksand example is followed by silence. "Well," Roger finally responds, "maybe not in the case of pilots." Realizing he was cornered, Roger goes on, timidly, "I see your point, but that is a unique case. I do think a racial preference to balance the opportunity equation makes sense."

Amy gets up and announces, "Got to go do some work. Enjoyed our chat." She looks at Roger and asks, "See you later tonight for our celebration?" Roger nods in the affirmative and smiles. With that, Amy gets up and walks out.

For several moments after Amy leaves, nothing is said, apparently all three exhausted by the arguments. Finally Richard says, "We've all got a lot to do. I'm heading over the library to begin researching the background for preferences." And Aga follows with, "I need to go over there too."

Aga and Richard depart. Roger sits alone, wondering for the first time if he will be able to argue successfully for his dissertation when the time comes, if he will be able to defend his work adequately. He answers his own question. He will find a way— he always does.

Chapter Fifteen

"Sailing" by Christopher Cross plays in the background of the Sixth Street Bar in Austin. Roger and Amy are celebrating in a booth near the back, hoping to escape the large number of undergraduate students and locals near the front.

"I'm so proud of you," Amy says to Roger. "I knew you could do it."

Roger embraces Amy's congratulations and basks in the glory of his moment.

"Yeah. But you still need to help me, Amy. Dr. Mac is my chairman and he is not going to cut me any slack. Really, I'm scared. He's a hard man, harder than you know, and he can see right through me."

Amy is unwilling to allow any negative change to their celebratory mood. "Nonsense. Sam picked him for you because he believes in you. I've never heard Rufus say a bad thing about you. Sam paired you with Rufus because he believes he will bring out the best in you."

Unconvinced by Amy's defense of Rufus, Roger empties his bottle of Lone Star and waves to the female bartender for another. He smiles widely, remembering how dedicated she is to servicing her customers, unaware that Amy has monitored his obvious familiarity with the bartender.

"I hope you're right about Dr. Mac, sweetie. But I know I will continue to need your help. To do well, to really do well and get Rufus's approval, I will need you to keep asking Sam how he thinks I'm doing, so you can tell me if Rufus has said anything about how I'm doing."

Amy looks at the pretty bartender, who looks away under Amy's gaze as Roger continues.

"Rufus's support will make all the difference in my attaining a good academic position, Amy. To be able to remain here, with you, it's critical I always know where I stand with him."

Disturbed by Roger's flirtation, Amy's voice cannot hide her discomfort. "You worry too much, Roger. I feel like dancing tonight." Amy stands, grabs Roger's hand, and pulls him to the dance floor. Later, when Roger and Amy return to the table, a bucket of Lone Star beer sits in the middle of their table.

"'Hungry Heart' is a cool song," Amy submits to Roger, ignoring the sudden appearance of beer no one ordered, "but pretty hard to dance to."

Roger nods in agreement, ill at ease as he also notices the ice bucket and several bottles of beer he had not ordered. "I think great when I dance," he suggests, anxious to avoid the subject of the newfound beers.

Upon returning to their table, Amy elects to ignore the ice bucket of beer and decides a bit of humor is in order, offering, "I'm surprised you can think about anything when you dance, or is it surfing?"

Roger notes her election to ignore the mysterious free beer and responds, "You know, Amy. You are so confident with your work in economics. Maybe I should follow your lead. We could work together, draw strength from one another, go in different directions, of course, but discover different truths. It would be so great to work with you, alongside you."

Amy smiles, understanding why the conversation has changed, "Your focus needs to be on your dissertation, which makes it impossible for you to concentrate fully on your moves, your dance moves—that's it, isn't it? That's why you can't dance?" She laughs at her own humor.

"Okay, so I dance like a white boy. Is that what you're saying?" Roger responds, happy to have the conversation about his dancing.

Amy decides to have some fun with him, as part of her celebration. She thinks for a moment and says, "Okay, surfer boy, what do you think of this academic stuff, that I think we could partner on? I've been reading Schlesinger and John Kenneth Galbraith. They scoff at Reagan's supply-side tax-cut ideas. They scoff at the Laffer Curve and suggest Reagan's ideas will bankrupt the government. I think this could be the foundation for my dissertation. Does this fit in any way with what you are thinking about?"

Roger fidgets for a moment, happy to be clear of the bartender issue but out of his league in discussing economics with Amy. "Yeah, the Laughing Curve," he chuckles. "Isn't that an economic-effect measure of a TV laugh track?"

Amy shakes her head almost in disbelief of his perpetual idiocy. But she thinks, he is funny and so cute. This thought brings a smile to her face.

Springsteen's voice launches into "Sherry Darling" and Amy grabs Roger's hand, pulling him back to the dance floor, purposely parading him by the pretty young bartender. She's become used to the problems Roger's flirtatious habits create, and once again elects to ignore it, determined to enjoy the great celebration they have planned for later.

Chapter Sixteen

Early the following morning Roger's Corvette crests over a small Austin hill, the early morning sun at its back. It descends into a well-kept neighborhood, and Roger parks in front of a stylish ranch home. Roger gets out of his car, walks up to the front door, and knocks loudly.

Debbie answers, dressed only in a T-shirt, her long legs immediately commanding Roger's eye.

"Are you the milk man?" she asks.

"No," Roger responds, "but I am here for a morner."

She allows him entry but turns and walks away. Her home looks like it is out of a fashion magazine, more stylish and accessorized than any home Roger has ever been in, more perfectly coordinated than he could ever imagine. "A morner? What's a morner?" she asks, over her shoulder, without looking back.

He smiles as he enters her home, the exact opposite of his apartment. "A morner," he answers, smiling, "is like a nooner, but sooner."

He can hear her reacting moan to his attempt at humor as he follows her into the bedroom.

Hours later Roger and Debbie are still lying in bed. Debbie reaches for and lights a half-smoked doobie, pulling the sheets up around her. She inhales deeply and asks Roger if he wants a drag. He declines with a head shake.

Debbie exhales, realizing she needs to address his situation and says, "I couldn't convince Sam to let me chair your committee. I tried. I teased him that I would refuse to wear a headscarf in sessions with Aga, but it made no difference to him."

Pulling a pillow off his face, Roger responds. "Any chance that Dr. Sam is suspicious about us?"

Debbie smiles confidently. "No. God no. You and I have been so very careful."

Roger rolls over, and Debbie begins rubbing his back. "It would have been great to have worked with you," he says to Debbie.

She smiles, laughing to herself, knowing that what he truly meant was that the process for his dissertation would have been easier if she had been his chair. "Don't worry," she tells him. "For your final committee review I know what both Sam and Rufus look for. I'll make sure your work makes a positive impression. I do have a vote, you know. After all, you know I want you right here, with me. After you complete your dissertation we can move in together. Sam and Rufus will both be gone, I should be the next chair, you will be my first hire, and we can run things. We'll share careers. It couldn't be any better than that."

Roger smiles but turns away, wondering how he would ever explain such a thing to Amy, but grateful at the thought that Sam would be gone, unable to punish him for his infidelity toward his granddaughter.

"Yeah. That will be great. Both of us on staff. We won't need to hide our relationship. We'll be able to do what we want."

Debbie, with a big, seductive smile asks, "Are you up for sharing our 'careers' again?"

As she asks Roger the question in a lighthearted manner, she also mentally challenges herself on the issue. She has wondered many times why she has allowed herself to be so easily seduced by this young man, when she has evaded so many previous such advances, from men so much more successful than Roger, men not only more successful academically in their chosen field, but also more mature and clearly much more sophisticated. Why this guy, she had often asked herself? But she always avoided thinking it out, truly challenging herself for any answer. Truthfully, she knew, she liked controlling him. And while it was fun and even exciting for her to discuss a life together with him, in reality, she didn't believe it would ever really come to that, that she would ever allow it to come to that.

So, when Roger would become uncomfortable when she broached the subject of them someday becoming more serious, it also provided her a sense of relief that she was still in control, that he hadn't become too attached to her—that she could still exit in a comfortable, respectable and simple manner whenever she wanted, or whenever it became necessary.

Her conclusion: I seduced him for my own personal ends. Hell, life is just a political game. Control is the strategic driving force. Feeling comfortable with her Freudian self-analysis, she begins to play out her political positioning of sharing their "careers."

Chapter Seventeen

Following her celebratory night with Roger, Amy arrives to take part in the weekly ritual of sharing family time with her grandfather at Pete's, a small coffee shop just off campus. Sam is always the first to arrive.

The place is frequented by an early morning crowd of men in boots and hats, blue jeans and belt buckles, men on their way to work, or just getting off work. And there are always a few students trying to sober up before beginning their school day. There are also always several trucks parked nearby, as it is considered one of the best breakfast restaurants in Austin.

It is a gem of a find, which Sam and his wife originally discovered many years earlier, but which has become his and Amy's favorite meeting place. Recognizing his long tenure at Pete's, which entitles Sam to the same booth every day, most regular patrons tip their hat in a good morning welcome to him. Most of the regulars have appreciatively watched Amy grow from a young girl to an attractive woman.

Amy enters and sees her grandfather, as usual, reading the morning paper, already firmly ensconced in his semireserved booth, waving at the waitress for his second cup of coffee. She smiles, shakes her head at his rituals, such as always arriving before her, and joins him. "No matter how early I come, you are always the first to arrive," she scolds him, knowing he will pay her no attention.

"Well," he responds with his standard morning wit, always enjoying her frustration with his habits, "I don't sleep. After work each day, I just come here and sit, drinking coffee, hoping you'll show up."

Amy takes off her backpack and slides into the booth across from Sam. Sam asks "So how are your scholarly pursuits coming, young lady?"

Amy answers, "Pretty well. I'm really having fun. The faculty has really accepted me as one of their own. They stop by my office to discuss ideas, which is their way of giving me direction as to what I should be thinking about."

Sam finishes a sip of coffee and nods, then says, "Yes, scholarly stuff can really be fun. What other profession pays you to think about and learn about whatever you want to?" He pauses and continues "so, what's piquing your interest now?"

Amy responds, "Well, believe it or not, I've been thinking most about the economic implications of political policy, or maybe better said as the reverse of that, the respective validities of competing economic rationales leading to the political policies of President Carter and Reagan."

Sam, smiling, says, "So, what do you think about this supply-side crap?"

Amy shakes her head. "Actually, I'm not sure." Wanting to get to what is really on her mind this morning, Amy bridges to saying, "I am really worried about Roger. Please tell me you guys will go easy on him."

"No chance of that, honey," Sam informs her. "You know that. He has to perform. He has to pass muster. Rufus will make short work of him if he doesn't perform. But it will make him a man, maybe even a scholar, if he has it in him."

Amy seems in anguish as the waitress pours her coffee.

"Same as always?" the waitress asks.

Both Sam and Amy nod in unison, each unaware that the other has physically acknowledged their order to the waitress.

With a nod to Sam the waitress says, "Steak and eggs, steak rare, hold the toast and the potatoes, and for you," she says from memory and looking at Amy, "a cup of fruit and cottage cheese." And, with that, the waitress walks away from their table.

"Oh God," Amy laments," any time you employ those old Marine Corps slogans like 'pass muster' I get nervous."

Sam smiles proudly. "Well, it did make a man out of me. Those years were some of the best of my life, all for the good.

Why, hell, I met your grandmother, God bless her soul, when I was in the service. And, you know, you are the spittin' image of her. I swear."

Amy isn't buying Sam's purposeful diversion from the discussion of Roger. "Grandpa, I think Roger was hoping to work with you or even Dr. Bowman. He aced all of her classes and she showed genuine interest in his work and his future. She really believes in him. I'm just not happy with your decision to have Rufus chair Roger's committee. I think you or Dr. Bowman would be a better choice."

After a brief interlude of silence, the waitress delivers their breakfast and Sam fiddles with his food, dropping his fork on the plate in frustration.

"Amy, Roger is . . ."

But Amy cuts him off. "Look, Grandpa, Roger is my future. I love him. We want a life together, and you can help me realize that dream. Please think about it. Please."

Sam shakes his head and smiles.

"You really do remind me of your grandma. She was always smarter than me, better at figuring out people, understanding them."

Sam picks up his fork and knife and cuts his morning steak. Before he puts it into his mouth, he looks lovingly at his granddaughter and says, "You know, Amy. More than anything in the world I want you to be happy."

"I know, grandpa. I remember you and grandma together. And I want what the two of you had. You two taught me what true love is, Grandpa, and I want it with Roger. We want a future together."

Sam smiles, cutting happily into his steak and nodding a "good-morning" greeting to a just arrived patron.

Amy realizes what is done is done in regard to Roger, that there is no changing Sam's mind. And she engages the culinary challenge of locating her fruit cup somewhere behind the blocking side cup of morning gravy for Sam's steak, and partially hidden by the morning paper and Sam's hat.

Chapter Eighteen

Roger drives on campus, parks half in and half out of a handicapped parking space close to the Economics Department offices, and changes into a clean shirt that he pulls from behind the driver's seat of his Corvette. As he walks, he habitually checks out each attractive coed he passes.

He enters Amy's office in the Economics Department and exclaims, 'I'm exhausted! All that dancing! I had to take a nap when I got home this morning."

Amy slides up next to him and hugs him.

"I called you early this morning to tell you that I love you . . . but there was no answer."

Unsure where the conversation is going, in fear of what the next words coming out of her mouth will be, Roger stiffens himself for whatever is coming next.

"I guess all that dancing really wore you out?" Amy suggests, and Roger almost slides to the floor in relief, catching himself, understanding such a reaction would give him away. She continues, "Relax, you need some quality time after your exam. Things will be fine. Just another hill to climb, but you'll be fine, you'll do fine."

Amy continues, "Have you talked to Dr. Mac any more about a topic?"

Relieved, Roger does relax. "Yes, I ran into him again in the hallway yesterday. He elaborated in detail ideas for the assassination idea."

"I don't know about that," Amy admits. "What did he say, exactly?"

Roger sits in a chair next to Amy's desk. "Assassination! He suggested that I write my dissertation on the supposed involvement of LBJ in the Kennedy assassination and offer multiple alternative scenarios, which will become the options to be considered, none of which, of course, will involve LBJ one iota."

Amy is still confused. "Why? Why would he . . ."

Roger interrupts, "Because he's sure the far right is going to eventually make it an issue, try to undermine Great Society programs by damaging LBJ's reputation, after Reagan gets in, which sadly looks like is going to happen."

Amy's expression changes from shock to confidence, as she understands the logic. She smiles widely while announcing, "Of course! He wants you to be ready for the coming attack. To head it off, set the groundwork for an argument immediately depriving it of any credibility." She laughs out loud, a wonderful, gleeful, girlish laugh. "It is so smart! Ingenious! And he's giving you the opportunity of a lifetime," she gushes.

"Don't you see," Amy explains, "you would be the expert witness against it. You will have thought out every argument. You'll be prepared, experienced in argument to thwart their attack."

Roger still seems confused. "Yeah? Well, okay. I hadn't thought of that. I thought he was trying to, well, maybe you're right."

Amy moves into action mode.

"You need to talk with Rufus and get all of his insights. He can lay out the entire game plan for your dissertation. All that you have to do is execute it. I'm sure he has already thought it through, in great detail, knowing him. He knows more than anyone about some of that stuff, about where the bodies are buried—and not buried. I've heard him and Sam share stories. And I'm sure Dr. Bowman and the other committee members will be highly supportive of this proactive strategy. It's so exciting! Why, you'll be on all the Sunday talk shows, a hero of the left."

Roger smiles, and a genuine sigh of relief escapes his body. "This could be my ticket to a great professorship, and career, I guess?"

"Yes," Amy responds with sincere relief and happiness expressed in her voice as she tells Roger, "Given the potential impact of this topic, it will be a cinch for you to receive an offer from UT. The powers that be will all want the publicity that this will provide. It will go a long way to erase the negatives of the JFK assassination on Texas soil."

At that moment, as Roger looks into Amy's eyes, she appears as happy as he has ever seen her. "And I'm pretty confident I will also get an offer as well, right here at UT," she says to him, her eyes never leaving his. "It is our professional pathway to happiness."

Suddenly, once having feared even gaining access to the program, Roger now finds himself involved with two women, both of whom have mapped out successful paths for him to follow, not only to be with them, but to gain professor status at UT. He appears rattled, confused, which Amy takes for excitement, happiness.

Roger is suddenly overcome with emotion, shocked by his reaction, unsure of what it means or how he will actually respond in the days and weeks ahead. He wants to kiss Amy but holds her tight, not wanting her to see the concern in his eyes, the confusion apparent in his voice and demeanor, the fear noticeable in each breath he takes.

What the fuck, he thinks. What should I do, which way should I go? Then he recalls, *if you pass one up,* which brings an anticipatory smile to his face.

Chapter Nineteen

Rufus and Sam sit comfortably in easy chairs in Rufus's office. Both are relaxed, happy, and comfortable in one another's company, until Rufus raises his hand in the air and waves it around, as if defining and describing everything around them.

While Sam's office shouts and expresses his personality with each item, each piece of furniture, art piece, memorabilia item, all the books and papers, Rufus's office expresses only disorganization, sloppiness, and confusion, and, while his office looks no different than it had ever looked, Sam felt something was, indeed, very different. It made him uneasy, though he knew not what it was or why it was affecting him so. Either something of great significance was missing, or something so obvious and profound, that he should certainly recognize in an instant, that was looking him right in the eye, but that he was unable to see—that was readily and obviously apparent—threatening.

His office looked as if he was moving, or as if he had never moved in, given well more than a dozen, two-foot-high piles of papers. It was, to say the least, one very unique filing system.

"I'm struggling with a good idea for Roger," Rufus explains to Sam. "One he can accomplish without too much challenge, hopefully. Debbie even asked for my guidance in terms of a topic for him. So my thought is, with all of the committee's help, of course, I wanted to give him a topic he can handle. Something that is pretty limited in scope, not much research involved and that cannot be very easily counterargued."

Sam is already tired of hearing about Roger. "Oh hell," he says to Rufus, "this sounds like you are thinking about having him write a short story, not a dissertation."

Rufus shoots Sam a perfunctory smile and says, "Something a bit more challenging, perhaps?" Rufus looks away, out the window, suddenly lost in thought and goes on, "I threw him the assassination idea, you know?" Rufus explains. "I assured you I would give him an easy subject and I did. Disproving conspiracy without any knowledge of the facts is about as easy as I could think of, actually."

"Yeah, so how'd he respond?" Sam asks.

"Confused," Rufus explains, "frightened, ready to crap his pants."

Sam laughs, "Yeah, okay. Got the picture."

Rufus points to Sam, "You did ask. I thought this solves your problem."

Sam replies, "Well, if you would have asked me, Rufus, I would have suggested the societal outcomes of welfare economics. I know sociology and societal effects are your academic strong suits. It's Amy's idea, actually, but they could have worked on it together, looked at it from different perspectives, possibly even teamed up down the road for a book."

Rufus thinks very carefully before responding to Sam's suggestion. "Indeed, that would make for a great collaboration for you and me, Sam. Such a wonderful topic, illustrating how we created wonderful opportunities for people with little previous chance or opportunity in our society," he equates with an almost serious delivery.

Sam starts to speak. "You and I both know, Rufus . . ." but Rufus cuts him off.

"Now, Sam!" Rufus interjects, "I do believe Amy would do a wonderful job with such a topic, and I would be happy to recommend it to her, even serve as the outside member of her committee, if you want me to."

"Well," responds Sam, "thank you, Dr. Mac."

"And you are so welcome, Dr. Sam!"

Sam takes a serious tone. "Look, Roger could be very good with your guidance, your helping hand. Perhaps as your classmate at the University of Chicago did, Saul Alinsky. He helped you with your understanding and appreciation for organizing, organization. You always said he was the organizational genius that provided you the theoretical foundation for your dissertation."

Rufus laughs. "Good old Saul. He died in '72, you know. And he was one smart son of a bitch. I mean really smart. Too damn smart for his own good, I think. But he was my guiding light, for a time. Ol' Saul taught me to analyze things by focusing on the difference between what we know, what we think we know, and what we really don't know. I've been able to frame problems with this approach ever since."

"Actually," Sam explains in a serious tone, "the critical difference is between what we think we know and what we think we don't know, and the accuracy of our perceptions to reality. Which requires the specification of the precise, testable assumptions that underlie the relevant perceptions."

Rufus nods in agreement, with the comment, "Your philosophy background continues to be a pain in the ass. You don't need to complicate things!"

Sam rises slowly out of his chair and points to the door.

Rufus understands from the look in his friend's eye that he is headed for the restroom, but Sam turns and asks, "What's wrong with your office? Something is different, strange."

Rufus laughs, "I'm just beginning to pack and organize my stuff for retirement, to get the hell out of here. I'm throwing one box of crap out every week."

As Sam departs Rufus's office, Roger enters and they exchange a perfunctory greeting, Sam thinking he is placing Roger in good hands, Roger believing his ass is about to be grilled over an open fire.

Rufus is seated at his desk. Roger seats himself across from Rufus, "Thanks for agreeing to meet with me, Dr. MacIntosh."

"Sure. Happy to. What's on your mind, Roger?"

"I've come about your idea of studying assassinations during Johnson's tenure as vice president and then as president. It's an interesting concept, though one I'm not fully prepared to undertake. That is, without some strong support with lots of background insight. I'm hoping you would be willing to provide me the guidance I will need, with possibly the added support of Dr. Bowman. Maybe joint chairs is worth considering?"

Rufus carefully studies Roger.

"Oh, well, bullshit, Roger!" he finally blurts out. "She couldn't carry my jock strap. She's your standard poli sci liberal academic, shallow, value-driven, which is based upon some vague notion of creating a societal greater good, which drives liberals like her to a borderline semirational view of issues."

Rufus stops his speech only to give himself a rest, to draw some breath. He continues, "Let's understand one another. First, I will help you. Second, I'm not so sure you are truly capable of finishing this program. I don't know if you are really up to it. Compre-fucking-hende? Do you understand?"

Roger nods uncomfortably, quietly saying, "Yes, sir. I do. I most assuredly do."

Rufus smiles. "Then I suggest two things. One, you best keep Amy on a pedestal and worship the ground she walks on or Sam will have your ass, if there is anything left of you after I get done. Second, you best get to work. Now!"

Chapter Twenty

Roger and Amy, dressed formally for dinner, pull in front of the Driskill Hotel. Roger's version of formal is a Hawaiian shirt under a blue blazer with khaki pants and a pair of just-that-afternoon polished cordovan loafers.

Roger stops close to the curb, handing the keys to the valet, and rushes to open Amy's door, offering her his hand and smiling warmly as she delicately extricates herself from the small passenger seat of his Corvette, in a manner and with the comfort, ease, balance, and dignity of a prima ballerina.

Amy is dressed in a simple, flower-patterned summer dress, medium heels, her hair pulled back and resting atop her head, showing her ears, highlighting her face and forehead and eyes, showcasing a beauty natural in its own right. Her outward appearance is elegant. Her presence draws the attention of every person within eyesight, which Roger relishes, capturing the moment in his memory, hoping he will draw upon it many times in the lifetime of their relationship, however long that may be.

She carries a small bag and wears a thin, almost transparent shawl that is gently wrapped over and around her shoulders, in a manner and with the confidence that only women of an extremely delicate and sophisticated nature are capable, and which few are courageous enough to attempt. Yes, he thinks, she is a real show dog.

They are seated at a table by the maître d', and Amy smiles proudly as they are given one of the best tables. She casually glances around the room, recognizes no one, but is thrilled that two young men sitting at the bar, who had watched her entry, were still looking at her, in a courteous and respectful but envious manner that she knew would make Roger happy.

Roger also visually searches the room, well aware of the attention Amy's entry has caused. He orders champagne, and as soon as it is opened and served he raises a toast. "To us," he says, suddenly and mysteriously overcome with emotion.

They touch glasses, and he watches as her delicate lips accept the rim of the glass, which warms his heart and touches his soul as she smiles and giggles, in a sophisticated yet girlish and elegant manner that makes him flush with pride.

"I love this old place," Amy says.

"Best cocktails in Texas," Roger counters.

For a moment they sit in silence. Amy breaks the quiet with "Oh my God!"

"What? What?" Roger asks.

In a very solemn voice Amy announces, "We're making some kind of transition here, from beer in loud bars and horrible dancing, to cocktails with dignity at the Driskill."

Roger sits back, also now appreciating the moment. "Yes," he agrees, "from students to faculty in training."

The two laugh and agree to drink only champagne for the rest of the evening.

"Oh, and also," Amy offers, "we should learn to share our vision, as Sam and Rufus have shared their vision with one another over the years. We'll teach students how to think, how to form opinions as we've been taught, and we'll share graciously what we have learned, as our mentors shared so generously with us."

"Good God," Roger responds, "you sound like a Jesuit."

"A Jesuit?" Amy curiously questions.

Roger expounds, "Sure, give me your children and I'll give you good Catholics. Old story, I suppose. It's about the only thing I remember from my religious experience as a kid."

Amy smiles, proud to be with Roger, excited and already thankful for the future she anticipates. "You're smarter than you look," she says, "and you look good all dressed up."

Roger smiles. "You think we're ready?"

Amy smiles back. "No, but we're getting ready. And we're learning from the best."

"Okay," Roger agrees. "I accept that, and together we will make it. We will be happy."

He pauses, then continues in a soft, sincere voice that is controlled but riddled with emotion just below the surface, which Amy notices. "Rufus has agreed to my topic and said he will help me develop the idea, get it done. So we should celebrate tonight, because I'm going to have many a late night in the months ahead."

Roger downs his glass of champagne and, surprising Amy, signals for the check. "Let's forget dinner tonight," he says, smiling at Amy. "Drink up and we'll head for home."

Roger escorts Amy back to his Corvette, again opens the door for her and proceeds to drive her to his apartment, but as they near his place, which is only two minutes away, he recognizes Debbie's car parked just outside his front door.

Terrified that Debbie is waiting inside, as he often leaves a key for her under the doormat, he awkwardly attempts to create an excuse for staying at Amy's apartment instead by sheepishly saying, "You know, Amy, my place is such a mess. And you look so wonderful tonight. Would you mind if we stay at your place instead?"

Quiet for a moment, worrying Roger, Amy finally responds, "That's fine, Roger. But is there a problem? Is something wrong? Is there anything I should know?"

Roger shoots Amy his most confident model smile.

"Just embarrassed, sweetie," he explains, then watches nervously as Amy scans the parking lot as they drive away, saying nothing, but terrifying him with her silence.

Chapter Twenty-One

Early the next morning, Dr. Deborah Bowman meekly, reluctantly, and sadly, much like a condemned criminal climbing gallows stairs, steps into Sam's outer office. She is immediately, graciously, and, much to her dismay, enthusiastically greeted by Sam's secretary, Miss Jones.

Perplexed by Debbie's arrival, aware that Sam had no appointments for that morning, Miss Jones looks up and down at her calendar, searching anxiously while expending time, hoping Debbie may offer an explanation for her early-morning presence; give good reason for her unexpected, unscheduled and professionally unacceptable intrusion upon Sam's time.

When no such explanation is rendered, Miss Jones quizzically offers a greeting. "Good morning, Dr. Bowman. Do you have a meeting scheduled with Dr. Brown?"

Flustered already, chagrined, Debbie fumbles in her purse, searching frantically for her cigarettes and lighter, more in an attempt to avoid the secretary's curious gaze than for any nicotine craving she may be experiencing.

"Do you have a lighter? No, no, I don't have an appointment," Debbie stammers, "but I do need to see Sam, uhhhh . . . Dr. Brown."

Politely, respectfully, Miss Jones smiles and offers a chair for Debbie to be seated. She exits the outer office toward Sam's office thinking this arrogant bitch finally got her long overdue comeuppance. Yahoo. Miss Jones knocks and enters Sam's office, announcing "Dr. Bowman is here to see you. She doesn't have an appointment."

Sam is in the act of removing his sport coat to put it on the back of his chair, frustrated by this surprise visit, he puts his coat back on, not knowing what to expect given it is protocol that all know to make an appointment prior to coming to his office. Except, of course, Rufus.

"Okay, well then, bring her in."

Miss Jones holds open the door for Dr. Bowman and is sure not to close it completely behind her, making sure she could overhear what was going to be said.

As Debbie enters Sam's office, she is nervously searching her purse, avoiding looking Sam in the eye for as long as possible. Finally, after as along a pause as she can reasonably maintain, she looks up. "Good morning, Sam. Dr. Brown."

She seats herself unceremoniously in the chair across from his desk before Sam even has a chance to offer. "Sam," she blurts out, speaking softly, then emboldening herself, speaking in a more steady and professional tone. "There's something I need to tell you, share with you. I received a call from Amy earlier this morning."

Sam startles at the mention of his granddaughter in the context of this surprise visit and nervously begins to rise from his desk.

"No. She's fine. But, well . . . it would appear that Roger has, well, has been seeing . . . sleeping . . . with her, with Amy and, well, actually . . . with both of us. "

Flustered, aware of her inability to come up with any acceptable excuse to properly explain the situation, Debbie smiles weakly as she pulls the pack of cigarettes from her open purse and, without seeking permission, fumbles to extract one from the box and lights it, inhales the smoke deeply into her lungs, all the while purposely avoiding Sam's gaze.

Sam's face changes from friendly curiosity and surprise to instant, but controlled anger. "Have you lost your mind?" he blurts out. During the silence following his very direct and appropriate question, he sits back in his chair, giving her a moment to come up with a response to rationalize her stupidity, while also giving himself a moment to harness his anger, intent on reining in the words of his true emotional reaction.

"You knew they were seeing each other, in a relationship, Dr. Bowman! So are you telling me that you have been having an affair with a graduate student? That you were having this affair behind Amy's back, behind my back, behind everyone in this university's back?"

Unsure how to respond to his outburst and obvious anger, or if she should even make the attempt, Debbie takes a second deep puff of her Virginia Slim cigarette.

Sam continues, speaking now almost mechanically, robotically, in a controlled, emotionless manner. "This is the same grad student you, a member of our senior faculty, scored on his qualifying exam as 'excellent.' The same student you argued so convincingly and emphatically for . . . and that we have just accepted into our doctoral program."

Debbie squirms uncomfortably in her chair, but then, realizing not only her situation but her position at the school, sits up straight and looks Sam in the eye, while also looking desperately and anxiously for an ashtray. She analyzes the situation and determines it is totally political. So she decides to lie.

"I didn't know he was sincerely involved with her, with Amy, or with anyone else. I didn't know he had real feelings for her. We never talked about it. It hasn't been just a fling for me, Sam. I thought he and I had a future, that these other relationships he has, has been having, were just flings. I know he is young, impetuous, but I thought that, by the time he got his doctorate, we would be in the same place, that he would be ready for a serious relationship. Sam, I . . . I am so desperately in love with him."

By using "desperately" to describe her love, Debbie is thinking this descriptor of her commitment would soften his reaction. She knows it was a long shot, but at this point, why not try?

Sam glares across his desk at Debbie, knowing himself to be too angry to speak at this point. Finally, with the patience only time and experience can muster, realizing that the truth will bear no more significance than a good lie, he utters his reply, "So, the answer to all of my questions is 'yes'?"

Debbie does not hesitate in her reply. "Yes! Yes! But it's the real thing for me. We've been seeing one another for some time now, Sam. I know Amy is upset. I knew she would be, so I wanted to tell you. I wanted to come here first, to face you . . . with the situation."

Obviously disgusted, Sam struggles to answer, "Well, isn't that nice. If you have any interest in keeping your position at this university, I strongly suggest, Dr. Bowman, that you resolve this immediately. And by resolve I mean break it off! And I mean right now, with all concerned, or you can kiss your dog-smellin' ass goodbye as a professor at this university."

Tears now rolling down her cheeks, realizing there would be no sympathy for her or in regard to the situation, she struggles to answer. "Sam, I . . ."

Cutting her off, Sam demands as he rises from his chair, pulling on his sport coat, "Where is he? Where is that piss-ant son-of-a-bitch? I'm going to put his nuts where they won't be able to harm anyone else, anymore . . . ever!" Sam rises, drops his glasses on his desk and departs, leaving Debbie seated alone in his office.

She makes no attempt to deal with the tears rolling down her cheeks, looking instead to her one remaining friend in the room, the bourbon on Sam's bar. But she is also forced into looking into the blank, empty, dead eyes of the stuffed pheasant and quail permanently on display in Sam's desk and bar, wondering if she could end up like them, or even to become one of them.

She takes a last puff of her cigarette, allowing the cigarette to slip from her fingers and fall on to the table next to the ashtray as she departs. Miss Jones remains seated at her desk in the front office and does not look up as Debbie quickly passes. And, for a moment, she smiles to herself thinking, she made my day. But her moment of triumph quickly vanishes, as she realizes how close she came to also having an affair with Roger, how he had manipulated her during the doctoral candidate exam—how close she came to surrendering to his charm, how interested she was in his flirtation, how easily she could have succumbed to his advances. This would have cost her job.

Smelling the wood burning, she goes into Sam's office and picks up the burning cigarette and puts it out in the ashtray.

Miss Jones returns to her desk, shuffles some papers, then smiles upon further reflection, thinking that the department princess got what she deserved.

Chapter Twenty-Two

Later that same morning, the phone rings in the graduate student offices and Roger answers it. A moment later he hangs up the phone, a look of astonishment mixed with fear spread across his face. He turns to face a grinning Richard and Aga.

"What the hell, Roger?" Aga asks. "Somebody die?"

Roger spits out an answer.

"Shit! God damn it! Amy found out about me and Debbie. Somehow, she found out. So I guess it's over."

"What's over?" Aga asks, a wide smile spread across his face. "You mean you and Dr. Bowman?" he asks with a grin on his face.

Enjoying the moment, Richard joins in the fun at Roger's expense. "Or do you mean it's over with you and Amy, Roger? Which do you mean?" Roger ignores their enjoyment of his dilemma. "I think," Roger finally responds, "that it is over with both of them. Fuck."

Enjoying Roger's obvious discomfort, Richard follows with "It all finally caught up with you, your credo of 'if you ain't cheatin' you ain't tryin' bullshit, and all that screwing around, thinking you're putting one over on everybody." Richard looks to Aga.

Aga, taking his cue, piles on with "Nice timing don't you think? Our boy, Roger, just beginning his dissertation. It would have been good strategy to be involved with the department chair's granddaughter, but not such great strategy to piss that away and go after one of Dr. Brown's colleagues! Roger, my boy, you are sooooo fucked! I don't know how Dr. Brown is going to handle this, but I can only guess. But you have hurt and embarrassed his granddaughter, and you have soiled her in the eyes of the academic community. In my country . . ."

Roger cuts Aga short. "Oh fuck you and your country, Aga!"

Roger, intent on leaving this verbal abuse, starts for the door.

"Where you going?" Richard asks.

"On my way to the sacrificial altar," Roger confesses, "to throw myself on the mercy of the court. To meet with them, both of them, in Deb's, in Dr. Bowman's office. They're waiting for me."

Aga gleefully remarks to Richard as Roger passes, "This could be a great plot for an episode on *Dallas*, don't you think?"

Roger leaves the room, walks from the graduate student offices to Debbie's office and stands in front of her door, agonizing on his next move. He comes to the conclusion that his only option is to fall on his sword and say something that gives him the best chance of surviving this . . . situation. After staring at her door for several seconds, he knocks and enters. Both Debbie and Amy are seated at a small conference table, across from one another. They both look at Roger as he enters and watch silently as he seats himself at the table with them.

"Well, look," he begins. "I owe you both an apology, a big apology."

"Really?" Amy responds, obviously indignant, her voice lacking any of the sensitivity or caring he had grown to love hearing. "You think?"

Debbie quickly determines it will be her role to mediate and help Roger clean up his mess and to protect her own territory, or whatever she can salvage of it.

But Amy continues her diatribe, cutting off Debbie before she can begin. "This is just humiliating, Roger! How could you?"

Roger visually scans the room, wishing, searching for an escape while realizing there would be none, that it was time for him to do his best to deal with the situation he had created. He repeats, "I sincerely owe you both an apology. A big apology. I am sorry, really sorry. It was juvenile, stupid. I just . . ."

Debbie interrupts, smiling, her voice tinged with sarcasm. "Oh, Roger, I'd say it was all very well planned. I'd say you knew exactly what you were doing, or at the least, exactly what you wanted."

Amy angrily stares at Roger, desperately fighting back tears, intent not to let him see the pain he has caused, the suffering he has created, and she struggles as she verbally supports Debbie's assessment, spitting out her words. "You are such a self-centered prick!"

Roger is caught off guard by the venom in Amy's voice and the tears that had been welling in her eyes, now rolling down her cheeks. But Debbie speaks before Roger can. "Amy, he played us both. Me he played for personal gain, for advantage. You, he, well, actually, he also played you for advantage, for gain, for an edge in getting into the doctoral program."

Amy glares at Debbie, obviously uninterested in anything she can say. "Don't talk to me like you care about me. All you have cared about is what you wanted, and obviously, he was willing to provide it!"

"Look, Amy," Debbie starts to speak, but Amy quickly cuts her off.

"Look at what, Dr. Bowman?"

Debbie laughs, almost under her breath in response to Amy's outburst, and looks at Roger. "No one," she begins, "is going to bail you out of this one, my dear."

Debbie again turns her attention to Amy. "I am sorry, very sorry, Amy, for any embarrassment this will cause you. But you'll get over this in time, and maybe even be better off for the experience. I'm the one who has really been damaged here, my reputation, my career."

Amy is unwilling to listen to anything else Debbie has to say. "Fuck your career, Dr. Bowman! And fuck you! Stay away from me, both of you. Never approach me again. Understand?"

Both Roger and Debbie nod their heads, but Debbie also responds, "Yes." she says.

Amy turns and faces Roger. "Fuck you, and your career, and the life you almost had, the life we almost had."

Roger is trying to think about what would be best to say. Not having a solution in mind, he goes back to his standard, play the sympathy card combined with what is in their best interest.

Amy stands, but Roger stops her from leaving. "Amy, my life, all of our lives are at stake here. It is in all of our best interests to end this amicably, if possible, here and now. No one wants the scandal this will bring," he says.

Amy starts to depart but stops, turns, and looks at Roger, clearly expressing her point of view with regard to his verbal gambit, "What part of fuck you, don't you understand?"

Amy walks out the door and both Roger and Debbie sit, unable for several moments to look at one another. Finally, Debbie speaks. "That is one very angry young lady."

Roger laughs, the tension lessening in the room.

"Yeah, and I'm worried about her."

Debbie's thinking about her future, or lack thereof. To temporarily take her mind off of the professional quagmire she is facing Debbie laughs in response. "Her? Oh, she'll be fine, Roger. I'm anxious to see just what Sam has in store for you, lover boy."

At that moment, Sam bursts into the room. He starts for Roger but catches himself and holds his ground. Both Roger and Debbie step back, wishing they had a place to hide. "Sit down, you little piss-ant!" Sam commands, "Nobody hurts my little girl, my granddaughter, and gets away with it!"

Sam again steps toward Roger, catches himself once again, gathers himself, and turns his glare on Debbie. "Just what in the fuck were you two shitheads thinking? Both of you just looking for a piece of ass? So why involve my Amy, why hurt a young, inexperienced girl? You two shitheads could have easily dicked with each other without ever having to involve her."

Neither Roger nor Debbie answer, sure that no answer would be of any help in their defense.

Sam continues as calmly as he can, "Why don't we all just take a seat at your table, Dr. Bowman? Probably best for you, Roger, if you sit at the far end, as far away from me as you can.

Debbie, you can sit in the middle, between us. I figure you're probably pretty comfortable there, in the middle. Now, let us discuss how you, Roger, are never going to go near Amy again, and you, Dr. Bowman, are going to clean up the mess you have created for yourself, for our university, and for my granddaughter."

Chapter Twenty-Three

Sam storms into Rufus's office with a look and manner indicative of his mood and foretelling of his frustration and intentions. It is a happening unique in their forty-plus year relationship, an event Rufus can compare to none other.

Rufus begins to rise from behind his desk, as he realizes he has never witnessed Sam more emotional, troubled, disturbed, but stops, remaining seated, frozen, almost too afraid to rise.

Sam stops just short of the desk and wrings his hands in a very imposing, choking motion, while uttering, "That little piss-ant Roger!"

"What?" Rufus responds. "What'd he do? Can I have him killed?"

"Maybe! Maybe!" Sam responds.

Rufus smiles, trying to calm his dear friend down, and says, "Lyndon's old black ops team is still available."

Sam appears confused, frustrated by this reference, asking, "What black ops team? What the hell are you talking about, Rufus?"

Rufus waves his hand in the thinking that he succeeded in lightening the situation, with "Never mind."

Sam continues, "The son of a bitch has been two-timing Amy, with Debbie."

Rufus confused, asks, "Debbie?"

Sam clarifies, "Dr. fucking Debbie Bowman! Our Debbie!"

Rufus smiles. "I knew he didn't deserve our support, consideration. But this is the type of situation you were never very good at handling, Sam. So let me handle it."

Sam sits across from Rufus, who has remained in his seat at his desk.

Rufus stands, walks to his bar stock on the top of his filing cabinet and begins pouring bourbon from his finest bottle.

"I just want that piss-ant son of a bitch gone!" Sam blurts out.

Rufus raises his eyebrows. "Gone?" he asks.

"Yes, gone!" Sam repeats.

"Okay," Rufus says, smiling. "Just like the old days, all you have to do is look the other way."

Sam looks up at Rufus as he hands him a glass full of bourbon. "What are you talking about, Rufus?"

Rufus repeats, "Just let me handle it."

Irritated now, Sam looks at his lifelong friend. "Rufus, I don't know what in the hell you are talking about. He hurt Amy and, by God, I'm going to make him pay. You just leave him alone. Just let me handle it!"

Rufus waves both hands in the air and across his face, a sign of surrender, picks up his drink and reflects, "You know you were never very good at the necessary things. Things that had to be done. Things that you always preferred to let me, us, handle."

More frustrated, Sam responds. "Rufus, I really don't know what the hell you are talking about."

"Sure, okay," Rufus says, as he smiles in celebration of Roger's demise and downs his entire drink in one gulp.

Sam gets out of his chair and starts to leave, but turns to face Rufus, declaring, "I know I need to cool down. I'll talk to you more about this tomorrow."

Sam walks out of Rufus's office and down the hall to the stairs. He goes down to his floor and then has an idea as to how Rufus can execute Roger's upcoming dissertation failure. He turns around and returns to Rufus's office. But when he enters, Rufus is nowhere to be seen. He sees Rufus's turned-over glass on the desk. Worried, Sam looks behind the desk and finds Rufus collapsed, gasping for air. Sam pleads, "Rufus! Rufus!"

Rufus is unable to breathe on his own, and Sam immediately begins giving him mouth-to-mouth resuscitation.

"Call 911!" Sam screams out and students from the hallway look in and make the call.

Within minutes the emergency services arrive and work on Rufus, even though it is obvious Rufus is not responding. It takes four men to lift Rufus onto the cart. His suspenders hang over the edge, and Sam picks them up and tucks them under his lifelong friend's lifeless body.

Students in the hallway mill about, not wanting to leave, talking among themselves about "Dr. Mac."

"We'll take him to the hospital," a technician says to Sam, who understands that the message is simply a courtesy, that his friend is gone, and that the hospital will be a short stay on the trip to county morgue.

The man he had been sharing his frustration with only moments before, whom he had worked with for the past 50 years, has passed away, Sam thinks. He's gone, but what was it he was saying, there just before he fell, "You know you were never very good at the necessary things," Rufus had teased. For a moment Sam's problem was not important.

But what had it really been, this teasing? Sam struggled, what were these "necessary things," Rufus had remembered? What "necessary things" could Rufus have been talking about? "Those things," Rufus had said, "that you always preferred to let us handle."

It bothered Sam that he couldn't recall "the necessary things," but it bothered him even more that Rufus had added, "that you always preferred to let us handle."

What things? Handle what? Sam thought, as he followed the cart carrying his old friend to the waiting ambulance, and then helped as they loaded Rufus aboard and sped away, leaving Sam standing alone on the campus where he and Rufus had spent what was the final chapter in their professional lives.

Chapter Twenty-Four

Sam stands in front of the large wooden front door of Rufus and Mary MacIntosh's home, wishing he didn't have to be there, wishing he didn't have to bring her the news about Rufus. He tries to knock but is unable to bring himself to do it. He tries again, but fails. He sits on a small wooden bench near the front door and places his face in his hands.

Rufus's wife, Mary, opens the front door wearing her usual apron and sees Sam, sitting on the stoop wall, a sad and tragic look on his face.

"Where is Rufus, Sam?" she asks, knowing, understanding without being told what has happened. "Is he gone? Is my Rufus gone?"

Sam stands and hugs Mary, as she sobs, his mind wanders to the Oval Office in the White House, to the day he and a room full of supporters stood celebrating the election of LBJ as president.

LBJ noticed Sam as he entered his office that day and motioned to him. Sam joined the president behind his desk.

"Where's Rufus, Sam?" the president asked him.

"I don't know?" Sam responded.

The president smiled, waved, and pointed his finger at someone in the room. "Well, you see here, you find him for me, you understand? I need something done."

Sam hesitated but then offered his services to the president. "Anything I could do for you, Mr. President?" Sam asked.

LBJ patted Sam on the shoulder and smiled, responding, "No, Sam. This is a job for Rufus. Now you just go on and find him for me. You do that now." And, as Sam left the president, he added, "I'm glad you see it my way."

Sam departed to find Rufus, confused by the president's comment, unaware but strangely interested and simultaneously relieved to not know specifically why the president needed Rufus, what he wanted him to do, what task needed to be done.

Mary breaks Sam's hug, bringing him back to the present, and asks, "Did he have his pills, Sam? His nitro?" Sam can only respond by shaking his head, indicating he does not know.

Wiping a tear from her eye, Mary, her loss showing in her eyes and face, comments lovingly, "Oh he always needs them, and I always have to remind him to take them. He is so forgetful now."

Sam pulls Mary close to him. As the reality sinks in and the initial shock subsides, she begins to weep intensely, occasionally shuddering. As she calms down, she steps back and looks up at Sam, asking, "Where is he now, Sam? Where did they take him?"

"He's at . . . he's at the hospital. He didn't suffer, Mary. I was with him. He just fell to the floor, right in his office, and was gone. There was nothing I . . . not anything anyone could do." Sam can only hope that his white lie in regard to Rufus may make Mary feel better.

Mary reaches for Sam's hand and leads him into her home. She takes him into the kitchen where Sam and Rufus had enjoyed so many conversations, while imbibing with their traditional elixir. Thoughts of their mutual past bring a smile to Sam's face.

"He loved you, Mary. You were always the lady in his life," Sam tells her, comforting her.

She smiles. "Yes, of course," she says, and then adds, "but I need to go to the hospital."

Sam shakes his head and says, "Please, Mary, I think you need to sit down and relax and take some time." Sam grabs her hand and they sit down, not saying anything for a minute or so.

For an hour they discuss the early days at San Marcos, how they had all met, Rufus and Mary's wedding, with Sam and LBJ standing up for them. The days in Washington, the many long nights when Sam and Rufus were away.

Looking around the house, Sam realizes he has seen the same furniture, the same trinkets and souvenirs for all the years they have worked together in Washington and at UT.

"You know, Mary. Nothing in this house has changed much, not even from the early days. I remember Rufus and I carrying that easy chair into the house, after 'acquiring' it from the university, when they chose to remodel."

Mary laughs. "We didn't change much. We never needed to. As we didn't have kids of our own, no one ever did much damage." She laughs again, delighted to be reliving those days. "We could have had kids, you know," she tells Sam. "But Rufus just didn't want to. He said this was no world to bring children into. And he said it was going to get worse."

Her sudden, overwhelming sadness moves Sam to again take her into his arms.

"I'll be here for you, Mary. Just as you and Rufus were here for me when I lost my Janis and our daughter, my family."

"Oh that was a horrible crash," Mary reflects. "Rufus said that was never supposed to have happened. I know he felt horrible, because it was our car she was driving that day. Janis was my best friend ever since your wedding, and your Kate was the daughter we never had." With a little smile, she turns and says, "And your Amy is really like our own granddaughter, you know."

Mary's memory of the crash, which Sam had never heard before, drives him to inquire further. "Do you remember anything more he said about that, Mary, about your car?"

Still in Sam's warm embrace, Mary responds, "No. I just thought he was referring to our Lord having taken them. That he had taken them both at too young an age."

Sam does not respond, not wanting Mary to concern herself in regard to his questioning, but wondering to himself exactly what Rufus could have been referring to with regard to the crash.

Sam calls a friend of Mary's, a neighbor, who immediately comes to the house to sit with her. Sam leaves with the arrival of the neighbor, with Mary laying on the sofa, in the living room, her friend in the armchair at her side.

As Sam walks to the car, he decides on the only destination he can think of that is appropriate to the occasion, the Driskill Bar.

Once at the Driskill, Sam seats himself at his and Rufus's favorite table. A waitress approaches and starts to question if Sam will be alone but, upon seeing his face, asks only what he would like to drink. "Bourbon and water on the side" Sam responds, "and don't bother bringing the water."

Chapter Twenty-Five

Richard and Aga walk into the graduate student offices. Richard clumsily seats himself at the conference table while Aga paces unsteadily from the door to the window and back again. Both men have obviously been drinking heavily.

After watching Aga make the trip several times, Richard grows frustrated.

"Okay, Aga. You're nervous. I'm nervous. The entire campus is nervous, upset, sad! He was a very rare street-smart academic, he and Dr. Sam shared experiences we all would give our right arms for, but he's gone and, sad as that is, there will no doubt be changes in store, especially for our boy Roger, and maybe some for us too."

Aga doesn't look at Richard as he continues pacing. Finally, he stops in place, throws his hands in the air and asks, "What does this mean? I hope I can get a different advisor because of this. It is likely that Dr. Bowman will be gone very soon, so where does that leave me? It's difficult for me, having just been assigned to her."

Richard, surprised at Aga's outburst, offers, "I seriously doubt anyone is worried about who your advisor will be. Besides, you were assigned to Dr. Bowman, and I see no reason for them to want to change that. Why would they?"

Aga returns to pacing, from the door to the window.

Frustrated, Richard can only offer a recommendation, "How about going from wall to wall for a while. Just for a change?"

Aga pays no attention to Richard's suggestion, but then suddenly does change direction and begins pacing just as Richard suggested, from wall to wall.

Richard smiles. "Gee, thanks. That's so much better." He moves to the small refrigerator and looks over the contents.

Aga again stops in place, walks to the large picture window, turns and looks at Richard as he rummages through the items in the refrigerator.

"What do you think will happen now, about Dr. Mac?"

Richard pulls a Coke out and holds it up. "Coke?" he asks Aga.

Obviously irritated and nervous, Aga gets to the real reason he is nervous and blurts out, "I mean what's going to happen to all his work? To Dr. Mac's work. I'm sure he was working on something important, but that he never formally published."

Richard calmly and confidently reacts to Aga's comment, "Maybe he has memoirs of his political history, or some such? He always seemed to be working on something important."

Richard takes the bottle of pop to the counter, finds an opener and opens it.

"Did you hear me? Did you hear what I said?" Aga asks, obviously frustrated.

Richard, after taking a long drink from the bottle of Coke, responds, "No. I'm sorry. What was the question?"

At that moment, Roger walks into the office, obviously drunk.

"So? It appears you have heard the news?" Richard says, confronting and admonishing Roger with the same question.

Angry, frustrated, Roger appears in no mood for any additional bad news. He believes he has had, with Amy and Debbie, about as much trouble as he can handle, and is in desperate fear of having to face Sam.

Sam walks in and the room is suddenly, sadly silent. Roger is justifiably terrified and braces himself for what he is sure to be a physical confrontation with Sam in regard to his unforgiveable behavior with Amy.

Richard and Aga are curious to see how Sam will dismantle their more-than-deserving colleague, Roger.

But all three men are surprised when Sam suddenly explodes not at Roger, but with his feelings about Rufus, "My best friend in the world, is gone. . . . Rufus is dead!"

Richard responds without hesitation, "We all heard. We're all very sorry."

Desperately wanting to say something, but with no idea what, Roger meekly asks, "Where? How did it happen? Did he . . . ?"

Sam cuts off Roger's steam-of-consciousness questioning. "It was a heart attack. He died of a heart attack in his office!" Sam then pauses, as if it was his first opportunity, the first chance he has had to catch his breath since the attack. Having discovered a sense of calm, evidenced by his voice, Sam continues, "I just left Mary. Rufus's wife, Mary. I just left her, with a friend, at her house."

Roger, Richard, and Aga all realize that Sam is in a state of shock. They stand, frozen in place, unsure how they should behave, unable to move.

"Is there anything we can do?" Roger finally blurts out.

Sam turns, then suddenly begins to walk out. But he stops, as if remembering something he was supposed to say. "There is nothing any of you can do," he responds. "Except to be there for his service. So be there!"

Sam leaves the three men standing in the room.

A moment later, Richard and Aga sit, but Roger remains standing. "I feel like shit," Roger says. "I want to comfort Amy, but I don't know what to do . . . what I should do, what I have the right to do. I just don't know."

Richard looks with disgust at Roger. "Nice timing, Roger," he says. "But the time for compassion was before you decided to play Mr. Stud with Amy and Dr. Bowman, and God knows who else?"

"I am really sorry for all of that," Roger responds. "I wish . . ."

Aga interrupts Roger, jumping into the conversation. "In the Koran," he offers, "God accepts repentance from his servants, and if their repentance is genuine, truly genuine, it can even become a blessing."

Richard chuckles, parrying Aga. "Your citing of universal wisdom offered by the Koran will certainly bring us all relief. I am especially interested in what you don't reflect upon, in your divine Sharia law, and its teachings with regard to no women's rights, or to gay rights, or stoning as a penalty, and the mandate to kill all nonbelievers."

Aga is taken aback by Richard's statement, with his depth of knowledge regarding Sharia law, but answers directly, "Well, the political and legal system in Kuwait, which go hand in hand, do not follow Sharia law," explaining further in an emphatic voice, "Look, our masked democracy avoids being a religious body politic, which under Muslim control runs the risk of becoming extreme. Why? Because once you ground your politics in religion, it can never be questioned. The lunatics that run it can do whatever the hell they want to. Our family in Kuwait weighed this. The religious lunatics of Iran, who now hold your hostages, are a perfect example. There is no end to their craziness, and if it is not stopped, it will propagate. Look, politics is always about power; having democracy avoids total lunacy, because you have a legal system. Most Muslim countries do not."

It is apparent that neither Richard nor Roger expected such clear, definitive discourse on the peril of combining religion and politics from Aga, and the three men stand silent.

Richard finally breaks the silence, saying, "I have to go to the library," and he walks out.

Aga looks at Roger, telling him, "I've things to do," and also walks out, leaving Roger to his own thoughts, revolving selfishly around what his academic future will be. He announces it verbally, to himself, "I am so fucked!"

Chapter Twenty-Six

Rufus's express desire to be buried in the Oakwood Cemetery, on a hill just east of Austin and the I-35 freeway, with a view of downtown Austin, the UT campus, and the Capital Dome, was executed by Mary and Sam. From this vantage point, the Dome appears to be located at the end of the long road leading in and out of the cemetery.

The views from his hilltop gravesite had been of great significance to Rufus, Mary knew, but his true attraction to Oakwood was the opportunity to be buried near Susanna Dickinson. As the sole adult survivor of the Alamo, Dickinson, 1814–1883, was true Texas royalty and, since Rufus knew they wouldn't allow him to be buried alongside Lyndon at the ranch, lying close to "true Texas-style royalty" was, in his mind, the next best thing.

Everyone dressed in their finest for Rufus's funeral, which made it a grand and unique affair, as most of Rufus and Mary's UT friends and associates rarely found reason to dress formally and, in fact, avoided it with a passion whenever possible. Such dress was to be "avoided at all costs," Rufus once lectured his university associates, but on this occasion, all had desired to show their respect, dress in their finest black, ladies in long dresses and shawls, men in dark jackets, hats, boots, and silver belt buckles. Just as Rufus would have wanted, True Texas all the way.

Even Sam wore his best shit-kickers paired with Mary's offering of Rufus's prized black Stetson, which he proudly wore and, like the other men at the funeral, only removed it during the formal reading of the eulogy.

Mary stood next to the casket as the minister read the eulogy, with Sam at her side, Amy standing just behind Sam.

Richard and Aga stood a few yards behind Amy, also dressed in black, while Roger stood next to a tree about 15 yards behind the gathered friends and family. Debbie, dressed in a black summer dress with a wide black hat, stood as far away from Roger as possible, not wanting to even have to look at him during the service.

Thirty-some other friends and associates of Rufus stood respectively around his grave, including Miss Jones, Sam's secretary.

As Rufus's coffin is lowered into the ground, the preacher offers a prayer.

"Dear Lord, I send your son, Rufus Macabus MacIntosh, for your safe keeping, in your loving arms. May he rest in peace for eternity."

Following the ceremony, Sam and Amy take turns staring at Roger, who stands in line with the others to offer condolences to Mary, keeping his head bowed, not only to avoid Sam and Amy's eyes, but in genuine reverence and sadness. Rufus had scared Roger half to death, he had admitted, but he also had ignited a spark in Roger, challenging him to step up and perform and not to simply take the easy way out. Approaching Mary, Roger looks up only when he reaches the grieving widow. "Your husband was a great mentor," Roger says to Mary, "a real leader in political science and a genuine inspiration to all. He will be missed."

Mary smiles at Roger. "You must be Roger?" she asks, with a smile and sincere interest that thrilled him.

"Yes, ma'am. Yes, I am."

She reaches out and pulls Roger toward her, sincerely expressing her feelings, "My Rufus believed in the common good, Roger. He often repeated to me that the common good is what politics should only be about."

Roger is taken by her genuine tender and friendly manner and stumbles with his words. "We all greatly admired Dr. MacIntosh and his accomplishments. He truly inspired us all. He was a true visionary."

Mary smiles again at Roger, adding, "Yes, he was a true thought leader and he spoke of you, started to tell me about you on our last night, but he got a call and never had a chance to finish. I do know that you were going to be his last student, so I assume you must have been very special to him."

Mary smiles again at Roger, reaching out to him, touching his hand and reflecting, "His work, all politics, all those programs and ideas, took him away from me too much, too often. Even recently he was still obsessed with his life's work, frequently reviewing his notes at all hours of the day and night. Every time he did so, they always changed his mood. It was the only negative in our 50 plus years together."

Mary looks into Roger's eyes, making it very clear to him that she thought these notes were like a mistress to him, one that he could never completely get his mind off.

Roger, seeing maybe an opportunity suggests, "Is there anything I can do for you, Mrs. MacIntosh"?

Mary thinks for only a moment and says, "Yes, yes you can, Roger. I want my Rufus to rest in peace, and I think the only thing stopping that is those damn files he obsessed on. I think he'd want his last graduate student to have them, to carry on his tradition. Would you mind coming by so I can tell you how to pick them up. It would make me sleep easier that these notes and papers are not part of my life anymore" and she adds, "They must be important, we've been paying for storage for them ever since we left Washington."

Roger says, "Sure, I'd be happy to do whatever makes this easier on you. It's the least I can do given all that Dr. Mac has done for me. I'll give you a call to make arrangements to pick them up."

Mary leans in and kisses Roger on his cheek. Roger could only respond with, "Thank you, Mrs. MacIntosh. It would be my honor."

As Roger walks away he realizes two things. First, if the phone call had not been interrupted, Mary could have a very different view of him. And second, Rufus's papers may be his way out the mess he is in.

Sam overhears this discussion, and is shocked at Mary's incredible generosity toward Roger, but unable to say or do anything to dissuade her at that moment, even though he knew exactly what Rufus had actually believed about Roger.

Both Richard and Aga strained to hear her and noticeably flinched when they heard her offer Rufus's papers to Roger, realizing what this could mean to decrease their library time. As Richard and Aga walk away, Richard turns to Aga, "You think there could be anything in Rufus's papers?" he asks.

Aga looks away, then answers in a hurried, confused manner. "No. Maybe. Look, I'm meeting some friends tonight, so let's talk about this later, sometime later. If you need some help, let me know."

Aga walks away, leaving Richard standing alone, the last one to leave the grave site. Richard looks back as dirt is piled into Rufus's grave. And he wonders, "What secrets did you take with you, Rufus, and what did you leave behind?"

Chapter Twenty-Seven

After leaving the funeral, Roger immediately goes to the closest Austin bar and sits alone for several hours thinking about what, if any, future he would have. An empty bottle of Lone Star stands next to a half-empty bottle in front of him. The music seems loud to Roger and he covers his ears. A television set above the bar announces the death of a college professor at UT, and Roger moves his hands from his ears to his eyes.

"Can you turn that thing off?" Roger asks the bartender, pointing to the television set. The bartender shoots him a quizzical look.

"You want another beer?" the bartender asks, ignoring Roger's television request.

Roger removes his hands from his eyes, replying, "No, give me a shot. Bourbon!"

The bartender moves away, gets a shot glass, places it in front of Roger and fills it.

Just at that moment Miss Pyramid enters the bar, approaches Roger, and sits down in the adjacent bar stool.

"I saw your car," she explains.

Roger smiles at her, and politely asks, "Would you like a drink?"

"Sure," she responds. "Thought you'd never ask."

Roger waves the bartender over, orders her a Lone Star and, by pointing at his empty shot glass, orders another for himself.

"You all right?" she asks.

Ignoring her question, Roger sips on the half-full bottle of beer in front of him.

A moment later the bartender delivers their drinks.

"Roger, you're going to have to tell me what's wrong. Obviously, something is wrong."

Roger fights back tears, mainly because funerals and death made him very depressed. Roger smiles, laughs insincerely, thinking how to leverage this situation, and looks at the girl. "I buried my major professor today. A good man, I really liked him. He was my advisor in the doctoral program. We were working together, to finalize the topic for my dissertation."

Impressed by his emotion, the young girl smiles and takes a long swig from the bottle of beer the bartender just delivered. Miss Pyramid then explores, "Okay, so, you'll get a new advisor, right? I mean, they'll give you a new one?"

Roger acknowledges her question nonverbally with a nonchalant nod indicating it was of no great importance to him at this time.

"So he must have been special to you, like you are to me. You know, I really have learned a lot from you. In class, I mean," she laughs, smiling, pushing him gently. Feeling sorry for his situation, she suggests, "We should get out of here, Roger. And you certainly don't look like you can drive. Come to my place? Okay? You can stay at my place tonight."

Roger pays the tab for 9 shots and 14 beers and stumbles toward the door, with Ms. Pyramid providing a much-needed stabilizing force.

Roger wakes up the next morning in the girl's apartment, having slept on her sofa and still in the same clothes he had on the previous night. Realizing he did not sleep with the girl, he sits up, looks around the room, and then at this watch. A moment later he stands and immediately puts his hands to the side of his pounding head. "Oh my God," he remarks aloud to the pain and overwhelming sickness he feels.

Slowly, he makes his way to the door and walks outside. He has his car keys in his pocket, but his car is nowhere in sight. After a bit of painful thought trying to remember exactly how he ended up there, he finally reasons it must still be at the bar and begins walking down the street.

Two blocks later he stops at a McDonald's, walks in, orders coffee, gets it and sits alone in a far corner of the fast-food restaurant, praying no one recognizes him and that the pain in his head will subside.

He sits in the McDonald's contemplating his next move, and comes to the realization that his only real opportunity at this point, the only chance he has to create a positive future for himself, probably lies in the disclosures, ideas, and maybe even new findings he may discover in Rufus's papers that he can base his dissertation on. By some chance, some lucky, fortunate circumstance, Roger thinks this may be the way out of his dilemma. Even Dr. Sam, he thinks, would be on his side if he memorialized his best friend's life work.

Now on a mission, Roger goes to a phone booth outside of McDonald's and looks up Rufus and Mary MacIntosh. He tears out the phone book page, folds it and shoves it into his back pocket. He finds his way to the bar, which is only about a mile away, locates his car, and drives to his apartment to shower and clean up. At 8:30 a.m. he arrives unannounced at the address, knocks on the door and, moments later, Mary answers. "Oh, Roger," she says, paying no attention to the oddness of this early-morning visit. "You look terrible. Honey, you come in here right now and I'll fix you some breakfast, give you some coffee. Come on now, no argument." She thinks he has really taken Rufus's passing to heart, dear boy.

Roger enters, sure he will not be able to hold down any breakfast but thankful for the coffee Mary places in front of him.

An hour later, feeling like shit but trying to keep a smile on his face, he is relieved when Mary hands him the key with the address of the storage facility and the unit number on the chain.

"Thank you, Mrs. MacIntosh. I will put these to good use. I will make Dr. Mac proud."

Mary smiles, saying as she walks with him back to his car, "I do hope something good comes from all this, all Rufus's notes and papers and as to how they developed the programs they created, and plans for those that they never did create. There has to be a basis in there for others to learn from. I believe Rufus would want that. He always said that truth should be our first priority."

Roger waves at Mary, who walks back to her house and stands in the doorway as he pulls away.

Two hours later, with the second load of boxes in his car, having already deposited one full load at his apartment, Roger returns the key to Mary. Roger drives back to his apartment anxious to investigate what he thinks has the potential to finish his PhD that could even make him famous, that could force others to see him in as he wanted to be seen. He could outdo his two critics who make fun of him. Now, through sheer luck and bravado, he has the opportunity to rise above them all.

Roger drives with one hand on the wheel and the other resting atop the boxes in the passenger seat. His new best opportunity, he laughs, sensing that he will find information in these boxes that will help him not only to attain his goal of a doctorate from UT but make him famous in the process. He smiles at his good fortune.

Chapter Twenty-Eight

A few hours later, five miles south of downtown at Austin-Bergstrom airport Aga is parked in the pick-up area under the Southwest Airlines sign. Appearing to recognize a dark-skinned man clearly of Arab lineage, of medium build with a full beard wearing a Chicago White Sox T-shirt and carrying a small travel bag, Aga gives a quick honk of his horn. The man nods with a slight bow and approaches the Mercedes. Aga waves him in. Taking his seat, the man bows his head again and says, "Your holiness."

"No, no," Aga corrects him. "I am not Ahmad Al-Sabah here, in this country, at this time. You must not treat me as royalty. Call me Aga." With that, Aga puts the car in gear and they depart.

The man appears confused, uncomfortable. "But your highness, you are very possibly the next Emir of Kuwait; you are a crown prince. I cannot in good conscience treat you as though I am an equal. Please do not ask such behavior from me. If anyone of our country ever witnessed me behaving in such a manner, they would be obligated to execute me immediately, on the spot."

Aga smiles and places his right hand on the man's shoulder, inhaling the smell of musk, the standard fragrance of his countrymen. He stopped using it when he entered the US, coming to the realization that it likely was primarily used to cover the horrible, lingering scent of camels.

"There is little chance of that here, Jaber, my friend. Here if you wish to serve me you must not allow anyone to question my identity. We are too close now. The papers we were after are likely finally in play."

The man is unable to hide his excitement. "That is wonderful, your highness. I apologize, Aga." He immediately then bows in shame, unable to stop himself from behavior ingrained in his nature and culture.

"How can I serve you?"

"Be on alert," Aga instructs the man. "After I drop you off, remain close to your phone; don't leave your hotel room. I will let you know what our next step is after I do a little research. Our opportunity to get the papers, which we have worked years to obtain, is ripe for picking. Allah has answered our prayers." Aga continues, "For such an opportunity as this, these papers can give our country the opportunity to demand the respect from the US and others, the power that these papers will unleash, has been many years in the making. These people have been foolish to allow their history to have been recorded and documented. We would never make such foolish mistakes in our country, Jaber."

Not another word is spoken until Aga pulls up to the Austin Motel located just south of the Colorado River, five minutes from downtown Austin. As the bearded Kuwaiti opens the door, Aga commands, "The room is in your name. It has been prepaid. After you check in shave your beard, no need to stand out." As the man begins to exit the car, Aga adds, "And get rid of that shirt. Turn it inside out if you must." The man habitually bows after closing the Mercedes door, then catches himself, turns and walks into the motel.

Chapter Twenty-Nine

More than a dozen boxes and files lie open and scattered across the floor of Roger's apartment. Coffee cups, paper plates, and a pizza box lie strewn about, making the apartment an even bigger mess than usual.

Roger sits on the floor in the center of the room reading a file. He has been reading for more than 12 hours, sorting through the papers, taking notes.

Speaking out loud and to himself, he mutters, "My God!"

He sits up, shakes his head as if confused or throwing off sleepiness, unbelieving of what he has just read. He continues reading the same page, over and over again, his face displaying the horror, confusion, and excitement of his discovery, but his mind having difficulty accepting it. If true, he knows, his prayers will have been answered and he will have the material needed for his dissertation, in fact, for a book. But he knows he must be able to do more than present Rufus's notes. He must be able to prove the information. He must turn it from dramatic and seemingly important information to fact.

And for that, he needs evidence. And, growing even more exciting than his original discoveries, he keeps finding damning, in-depth Democratic Party history. Story after story points to the information in the files being true and factual. Dates, times, places and people all line up.

Roger stands, dances around the room, laughing, smiling, and goes to the phone and dials it. "Amy," he says into the phone, "Amy, it's me. Please don't hang . . . Shit!"

He dials the phone again.

"Amy, don't hang up! This is a life-and-death call. Please, believe me. I'm serious! Okay?"

He takes her pause for acceptance as confirmation that she will listen to him. "Amy, you won't believe what I found in Rufus's files. It's hard to believe, even as I read it. There are special ops, plans that were never intended to accomplish good but were, actually, truthfully, meant to do harm, all for political gain. The LBJ White House was a political machine. The Great Society they sold us, told us about, bragged about, Amy, it was just crap. It was not great, Amy, and you need to see it, read about it yourself. I've been reading Rufus's files all day, and they expose the truth about it all."

He listens for a moment to dead silence.

"This is earth-shattering stuff. Okay, not here," he says. "I'll meet you in your office in 20 minutes. I'll bring some of the key files You're not going to believe what's in them, what I have found, discovered."

Amy thinks over the situation and decides the files must in fact be very revealing, and decides to see exactly what Roger has discovered.

Twenty minutes later, Amy arrives first at her office and waits nervously for Roger to arrive. It has been more than thirty minutes since he called, ten minutes longer than he had told her.

Finally, he opens the door to her office and enters with one box of files and with a look on his face like the cat who caught the mouse, and slowly, carefully he begins placing individual files on the conference table.

"Look, Amy, I know we're done, but I couldn't talk to anyone else about this. I couldn't trust anyone else. So, please, just listen to me, let me explain to you what I've found, what's in these files."

Amy nods agreement, a seemingly perpetual frown spread across her face. Roger hands her a file.

"Take a look at this. Read it."

Amy scans the first couple pages, then, uninterrupted, reads the summary file undisturbed for almost thirty minutes. Her expression as she reads changes from one of doubt and confusion to one of anger and bitterness. Her reactions and demeanor after a few minutes no longer have anything to do with her feelings toward Roger but have turned to feelings of doubt, fear, and dread.

She is being forced, as she learns more from each page she reads, to redirect her feelings and beliefs about the Great Society, the programs her grandfather helped create. She is dumbstruck after thirty minutes of reading, unable to stop tears from rolling down her cheeks. Her bitterness toward Roger has dissipated, almost disappeared, and seems inconsequential compared to the magnitude of what she has read, discovered.

After almost an hour of reflection and note taking, her anger seems to have subsided, and Amy looks at Roger and asks, "How did you get these files, Roger? They're worse than the bubonic plague. Unbelievable! This information could cause a revolution, and I'm not kidding, Roger! If true, these files could destroy lives, and change the America we know!"

Roger explains how he came to have the files, how Mary MacIntosh shared them with him, gave them to him, trusted him with them. He explains to Amy how he picked them up at a storage locker and spent all day reading them. He speaks quickly, faster than Amy had ever before heard him, adrenaline mixed with exhaustion rushing through his veins.

"She gave me all of Rufus's stored files. They have been hidden for years. I don't think anyone even suspected anything like this existed, let alone that Dr. Mac was dumb enough to keep them. Did you ever hear any talk about these between your grandfather and Dr. Mac? Did you?"

"No. Of course not," Amy responds. "If I had known about them I would have made some noise. I assure you, I would have made some noise! I would have demanded to see them. I would have found them."

"There are boxes and boxes of them," Roger explains. "And some of them outline in detail their thinking, what they really thought, believed, in regard to the Great Society. It's what Rufus, and I assume Sam, developed for LBJ. And it outlines their real goals, which the Great Society was actually meant to accomplish. There are also handwritten notes all over these files, with corrections, suggestions. These are true strategy papers, Amy.

They even have signatures and initials. It is so sad, so unbelievable. So terribly disgusting, yet... I don't know... it's also energizing, thrilling, and exciting. I'm not sure why, maybe... because this is the first time I actually feel enlightened... have an opportunity to contribute something of importance."

For a moment, Amy tries to take it all in as she and Roger sit on the floor, staring at one another in astonishment, as if in shock.

"Most of the signatures and initials are from LBJ and Rufus, but some are Sam's," Roger tells her, as if warning her.

In reaction to the mention of Sam, Amy's face once again shows anger, bitterness, betrayal. Then, suddenly, her rage dissipates and she is calm, collected, and confident.

Sensing that she seems to have thoroughly assessed the situation, Roger asks, "What do you think we should do?"

"I'm not sure yet," Amy answers. "But I do know that we should show this to Sam. We must show it to him, right now. We need to know exactly what happened, his version. Despite it all, we have to trust him. I've never known him to lie, not once."

Roger hesitates. He doesn't want to lose control of the files. They represent his educational passport to a successful career. He speculates that if Sam is deeply involved he will immediately take control of the files, and there won't be anything Roger can do. And that would undoubtedly be the end of his time at UT. But if Sam isn't involved, he could be useful in helping Roger and Amy expose the truth, and stamp his career passport. He also isn't sure of Amy's motives. Does she truly want to expose the evil in these files, or is she more interested in protecting Sam's reputation?

Roger decides to test Amy. "Are you sure? Maybe we should just destroy them. Especially if Sam was as involved as it appears he was. These files are going to cause a heap of trouble for him, Amy," Roger explains.

For a moment Amy hesitates, but then responds with the confidence and authority of a person intent on discovering the truth, no matter the consequences. "I don't know yet what all this means, Roger. I don't yet understand it, but we're going to follow this through, to the truth! This is history, and we can't change or destroy history. It is what it is!"

Roger raises his hands, as if to question, as if to make Amy realize the immensity of the project, the undertaking she is suggesting. "There are ten boxes like this one, Amy. I've scanned a few, so God only knows what is in the rest of them, but from what I've read, there is a very, very troubling and dark history that Rufus and, I'm afraid, Sam played a role in. Are you prepared for that?"

Without hesitation Amy stands, the file in her hands, and she picks up one of the files Roger brought with him. "I don't believe Granddad was involved in the worst of it. He needs to know about these boxes, these files, this information. It's his life too, you know, his legacy. He will want to know, whatever involvement he had, whatever role he played, he will want to know the story these files tell."

"You're that confident in Sam?" Roger asks.

Without hesitation Amy responds, "Yes. Yes, I am!"

Roger tries to think through whether it is better to keep some of the key files for himself or just to make copies. These files are his future, and he cannot risk losing his leverage, in particular, given his social predicament.

Looking for an opportunity to possibly begin to mend his fences, Roger meets eyes with Amy. Roger in his most sincere voice says, "Look, Amy, I'm sorry for all that has gone on, that I've done. I was very selfish and I am truly ashamed of my behavior. And, well, I don't expect you to forgive me, but, it doesn't matter about me now. We do have to do the right thing here, and I'm with you every step of the way." He even, almost, begins to believe what he is saying.

She acknowledges his apparent sincerity with a shake of her head and the smallest of smiles. "Just forget all that for now, Roger. These documents," she says to him, "could determine the future of our country. They are that important. And I've only read in full the one summary file, which outlines the others. The tripartite question is what exactly to do with them, with whom, and when."

Roger smiles, hoping for a return smile, but happy that she doesn't spit in his eye. He is proud of himself for the way he has dealt with the issue but even prouder of Amy. There was no doubt in her determination to find the truth. The depth of her character impressed him, maybe something that was contagious, he hoped. It was an asset he was going to have to develop, sometime, but he was happy that he believed he had just made a good start, at least in her eyes.

"Okay, I understand," he says. "Let's just try to figure this out. I am not sure how your grandfather fits into all this, or how he will react to it. He could have known all about it. He may not know of about any of it. But, Amy, he should have known all about it! And that scares me. And it should scare you."

Amy nods in agreement. "There is no way that I believe he knew of the evil crap that's in these files," she says. "I can't believe that he did. He wouldn't have stood by and allowed them to do this. I know that much about him."

Roger takes the files she has gone through from her. He puts new files in front of her.

"This is scary stuff, Amy. We have to make sure before we show it to Sam that we have a contingency plan. You understand why that's necessary?"

For a moment Amy seems reluctant, confused, but, after a moment to reflect, she agrees.

"You're right. We need to know the facts, the truth. That's all that really matters, as Rufus once said." Knowing at least some of Rufus's involvement from having read the files, they both laugh at the hypocrisy of Rufus's statement. Then Amy continues, "After we make notes and a record of what we have discovered, we'll share that information with Sam. Let's go to your place. I want to read the rest of the files."

Hours later, almost to the point of exhaustion at Roger's apartment, Amy and Roger continue pouring over the material they have discovered.

Several unopened boxes rest next to them, along with empty bags of potato chips and numerous Styrofoam coffee cups and scattered dirty plates.

Roger drops a file from his hand and lets it fall to the floor. He rests back against a chair, exhausted. "The more I read," he says, "the worse it gets, becomes . . . just worse!" Roger begins seeing the true world of political strategy. It is a world he understands. It fits with the way he thinks. For the first time, he actually understands, and is fascinated by learning from history, albeit grounded in deceit.

"Okay," Amy responds, "just share with me what you have discovered so far, the big stuff, the worst stuff. And I'll do the same for you and, and we should both take notes. You record everything I say and I'll record you."

Roger expresses an anguished laugh, with a look of deep sadness and sincerity such as Amy had never before witnessed. She felt, at that moment, that he was being the most genuine with her that he had ever been.

"They knew," Roger says to her. "They knew from the start that it was all a lie. They did it for the power, to get power, and then to keep power. And they sold their souls and the soul of their precious Democratic Party for it. They have subjected minorities in this country to a new form of slavery, to dependence, to manipulation and continuing poverty on a grand scale. They set the stage for the introduction of drugs into minority communities, the break-up of families, the destruction of a social structure. They knew the long-term sociological repercussions of their programs, their Great Society, and they did it for political power, Amy. It is as simple and awful as that: they knew the consequences and the awful, horrible price that many would have to pay, and they did it anyway, eyes open, all for political power, for control! Rufus mapped the whole thing out, in great, well-thought-out detail."

Roger's words have an obvious, troubling impact on an exhausted Amy, and her emotional reaction startles Roger.

"Manipulation! That's something you are intimately familiar with, Roger."

Obviously pained by her words, he looks her straight in the eye, wondering for a moment what to say. Not knowing, Roger points to a single folder titled "Our Great Society Game Plan."

"It's all in there, summed up in that one file," he says, then continues, "the detailed outline of their strategic underpinnings, from some guy named Alinsky, apparently a personal friend of Rufus. The other folders are subject specific. This summary breaks it all down, explains it, exposes it. LBJ's direct comments are there in his own writing. At least I think it's his writing." Roger then takes on his serious tone, thinking this will provide a foundation for their future, and says, "I wish on one hand that I had never been given these files, that I had never read these files, because it is so hard to believe this level of corruption these files disclose." Allowing her to digest how caring and concerned, genuine, he is now, he adds, "How could Rufus have held his head high after doing these things, how could he have masqueraded as a hard-ass, honest scholar, when, in truth, he was just one big, manipulative, power-hungry, political deceiver?"

Amy looks at Roger with newfound admiration. His plan was working. He had slowly begun to once again work his way into her heart; he had begun to find his way back into her good graces.

"There are nine individual thick outline folders and the summary folder," he explains to Amy. It's all there, Vietnam, the addiction strategy and erosion of black culture, the growth of the welfare state, education as a political philosophy tool, Medicare, Medicaid, Democrat dominance through controlling votes, voters, and elections. The sociology of manipulation. All for gaining long-term control of the political process. All to game the political system."

Unable to look up or even acknowledge Roger or his assessment of the files, Amy continues to read the file in her hands.

"You better read this one," Roger says, interrupting her, handing her a color-coded file.

"What is it?" she asks.

"It's a note. It appears to be from the president, LBJ, to Rufus. And it acknowledges what we have come to conclude about these papers. It says, "Don't ever let the nonbelievers get their hands on this shit!""

Amy accepts the note from Roger's hand and reads it.

"My guess," she says after reading it, "would be that the nonbelievers could also refer to people inside LBJ's inner circle, people like Grandpa, true believers that would not have condoned these methods. But there's no proof who wrote it. It isn't signed."

Roger says, "I've read many documents in the presidential library. This is LBJ's writing."

She acknowledges his expertise, then hesitates for a moment, then continues, "Did you read Rufus's correspondence with Saul Alinsky? You know who he is now, don't you?"

"Yes," Roger responds, stretching the truth more than a little, "but let's continue to organize what we have so you can schedule a meeting with Sam."

They stand over the boxes, which are spread across the room, covering the floor.

Amy puts some of the most important, most telling summary files in her backpack.

Roger looks around the room as she begins to leave. "Look," he says, "I'm going to organize these others by topic, just the ones I think are most relevant and important to the Great Society. We can deal with the rest later."

Roger laughs out loud, almost giddy, embarrassed to have sounded so young. But his inhibition makes Amy smile for the first time in what seems to Roger like a very long time.

"This is very exciting, isn't it? Even though it is also a bit frightening, terrifying!" Roger admits.

Amy, her backpack full, leaves Roger standing alone, looking at all the boxes, papers, and files scattered around him, without so much as a "goodbye" or a smile as she departs.

As he stands among the papers, understanding the opportunity before him, and the chance he could win back Amy, he realizes he has never been so happy in his entire life, nor so thoroughly and completely frightened. He did know that Amy was the key to his happiness.

Roger continues sorting through the files, segregating all the Great Society ones into one group, then a second group planning the condemning actions of "necessary tasks." This task is simple, in that "NT" is written in the right corner of these. And the third group just contains inconsequential files that anyone would collect in decades of service.

Roger puts the first group of Great Society files in his briefcase, thinking that Dr. Sam might want to review them. He walks into the bedroom and falls onto the bed with his clothes on. Much to do tomorrow, he thinks, and falls off to sleep.

Chapter Thirty

After dropping off his visitor, Aga drives to the UT campus. He parks his car at his usual place adjacent to the presidential library, exits and begins waking toward his office, only to have Richard call out to him.

"Aga! Aga!"

Aga turns and watches Richard approach. He seems to have been waiting for him, but Aga saw no one as he approached and parked.

Richard catches up, and the two men begin walking together.

"You working in the library today?" Aga asks.

Richard laughs. "I was hoping I would run into you. The discovery of these papers, Rufus's papers. It seems to have surprised everyone except you and me, I guess."

Unsure of Richard's motive, Aga avoids answering.

"Well, I don't know, Richard. The papers are important, I'm sure. But I don't know if we'll ever see them. They may very well get put away for 50 or 100 years, as many presidents do with their personal, political, and confidential papers."

Richard takes a moment, assessing how to continue the discussion.

"Yeah. Well, I hope you still want me to continue my research, my investigation and search for papers involving LBJ's programs. Is there any reason you wouldn't want me to continue?" Richard asks.

"No," Aga quickly and defensively responds. "I still want you to do your work. These papers are important, can help my country in understanding how your country makes decisions, creates programs, get things done."

Richard seems relieved. "Good. I'm happy to hear that. Really, I am happy, as I need the money. I was afraid for a moment there that, that you may no longer be needing to employ me to do research for you."

Aga pats Richard on the shoulder as they reach the building. He opens the door and holds it for Richard to enter. "Don't worry, my friend. I still need you. And I'm sure I will continue needing you for the foreseeable future."

Both men enter the governmental studies building, the door closing behind Aga. As they walk down the hallway past the classrooms, Richard gets to the point, asking, "Is there anything else I can do for you?"

Aga responds, "Not right now, but if there is anything you will be my man. You know that."

Chapter Thirty-One

Roger, Aga, and Richard sit around the conference-room table in the common area adjacent to their offices discussing what Roger had read in the papers. Roger has spent the better part of an hour explaining what he and Amy have discovered, holding nothing back, without any consideration for the sensitivity of the documents. Roger shows them only one note and one three-page summary file that highlights the very nature of the strategic conspiracy he has uncovered. The remaining files pertaining to the Great Society he leaves in his briefcase, thinking that Sam should make the call on exactly what is shared.

Richard seems uncomfortable, nervous, but Aga is more than attentive in Roger's descriptions of various files, asking to hear more. Roger feels he finally is being accepted by his fellow students; yes, he thinks these papers will make his career. He can't believe his good fortune.

Richard looks up from reading the lone paper and barks, "It can't be real. You gotta be shittin' me! Really, it can't be true!"

"Let me read that note again," Aga insists, "the note you think LBJ might have written, let me read it again!"

Roger reluctantly hands Aga the note. Aga reads it and looks up at his two associates.

"Don't ever let the nonbelievers get their hands on this shit?"

Aga continues, "It is so crass, so unsophisticated, so essentially evil and pedestrian. And you want me to believe that the president of the United States, Lyndon Baines Johnson, possibly said that? If it's true, what a conspiracy he put over. What an incredibly evil and base agenda he had." Aga pauses and smiles. "And, ultimately, it is true political genius!"

Roger agrees with Aga, saying, "It is unbelievable, if he wrote it, if it's true. If, if, if it is a truly historical document, then yes, it is true genius, almost devil inspired."

Aga laughs. "It's even better than our family monarchy structure at home. And, obviously," he continues, "you have spent no time around royalty. You have never witnessed what they are capable of, what goes on behind the royal blue curtain."

Aga hands the note to Richard, who reads the note for the ninth or tenth time.

"What's worse, what's so stupid and mundane, the son of a bitch put it in writing. Everybody knows you never, ever put shit like that in writing!"

Roger laughs, and his laugh loosens the tension in the room, causing Richard and Aga to also begin laughing, Richard with the hint of uneasiness, Aga at the thrill of discovery.

"You should both read the four-point strategy this guy, this Saul Alinsky, outlined for Rufus. It is so unbelievable," Roger says.

Richard anxiously scans the three pages in front of him.

"This Saul Alinsky was in grad school with Rufus at the University of Chicago 40 years ago. It's dated right here," Richard says, pointing to the page. "Rufus, evidently, kept this as a blueprint for nine years before he put it to use and shared it with LBJ."

Aga appears confused. "You should let me take some of these files home, to study them, give you an alternative opinion."

"No," Roger says. "They are going to Dr. Sam first."

Aga has difficulty covering up his true disappointment in Roger's response, but changes the subject by looking at Richard and asking, "By the way, how did you discover that Rufus was in school with Alinsky? And who is this Alinsky guy anyway?"

Richard sits up, prepared to answer Aga's question.

"I saw him mentioned in some files I saw in the library a while back. He visited the White House and even was part of a meeting that LBJ attended. I looked him up after I read that. He was a true radical. He published a book seven or eight years ago elaborating a strategy, titled something like *Radical Rules to Create a Socialist State*. He spelled it all out, in detail."

Aga looks to Roger, going back to his centerpiece question.

"When can we see, go through all the files?"

Roger is puzzled by the immediacy implied by Aga's question.

"I don't know." Roger responds. "Later. Amy has them so we can review them with Dr. Sam to . . ."

The telephone rings, interrupting Roger, and he answers it, listens and hangs up.

"That was Amy," he explains. "She wants to meet with Dr. Sam in five minutes, in his office. I gotta be there."

"How about us?" Aga asks.

Roger grabs the one note and the three-page Alinsky file he had shared with them, tucks them under his arm, grabs his briefcase, and answers Aga as he leaves.

"No. Just me and Amy, but you guys stay close. We may need you."

Roger walks down the hallway and into Sam's office. Roger pulls up a chair next to Amy, and they sit waiting patiently for Sam to arrive.

Moments later Sam bursts into his office, passes Roger without comment and sits at his desk. He picks up the summary file Amy has described to him on the phone and begins reading. Within minutes, he seems in a state of total disbelief.

Amy looks at Roger, curious what exactly is going on in her grandfather's mind.

"I already told Sam everything we've seen in the other files," Amy tells Roger.

Sam gestures to his ear, indicating for both Amy and Roger to be quiet as he continues devouring the documents. Suddenly he rises, points to the door, and indicates for them to follow him.

Roger and Amy follow Sam out of his office, down the hall and into an empty classroom.

Once in the classroom, Roger, Amy, and Sam are joined by Richard and Aga, whom Sam has also invited, instructing his secretary to call them as he walked to the hallway.

Standing in front of the group, he waves his hands indicating they should take a seat. Sam places the box of files Amy and Roger have brought to him on the table.

Aga, seeing the box, assumes these are all of the Great Society files. However, to make sure, he asks Sam, "Are these all the files you have reviewed regarding the Great Society, or are there more?" Sam nods, indicating they are all in the box, believing these are the complete set.

Knowing he has the detailed files with him, Roger decides to not say anything. He cannot risk Sam making a decision that would end his career. He needs these papers.

Sam immediately begins, "This could get dangerous, I'm afraid, and I am concerned that the walls of my office could have ears, so we're meeting here. Rufus could very well have planned his exit. I don't know. I am certain he didn't anticipate that Mary would give them to you, Roger. My guess is Rufus thought she would give them to me. I was shocked, frankly, that she gave them to you." Sam cannot help but think for a moment about what he would have done if he would have seen them first. What is in them will likely change the future of the country he truly loved.

Giving his warning a chance to sink in, Sam turns and walks a few steps across the room, speaking as he walks. "Rufus always knew what he was doing. He was a purposeful man and he would have destroyed these papers long ago if he hadn't wanted them to someday be released. And I'm confiding in the four of you because I am going to need your help in the days ahead."

Amy raises her hand, is immediately embarrassed for having done so, and just as quickly lowers it. "Sam, Grandpa, do you really think Rufus wanted us to find his papers?"

Before Sam can answer, Richard poses his own question. "You think there is something fishy in his passing, dying, Dr. Brown?

Sam shakes his head indicating the negative. "No. I do find it strange that he put them in Mary's hands to make the call about who would receive them. He certainly knew she didn't want any part of them. I am surprised he didn't plan ahead better than that. It's almost as if something happened, something he didn't expect."

For a moment, Sam seems in a contemplative fog, confused and yet also on point. "It wouldn't surprise me if the ol' cuss finally realized what our programs had actually done to the country, the negative impact they have had, and will have. And he may have had a bout of guilt over it all. And maybe he finally realized that political control is not the path that the founding fathers had in mind, and that he and LBJ, without my knowledge, operated with extreme prejudice in certain circumstances and employed any means necessary to get the results they desired in many other circumstances, or programs. He always told me, mainly while sharing very late evenings, that the ends justified the means. Maybe I finally understand . . ."

Roger jumps in.

"So, Sam, Dr. Brown, why wouldn't he have told you, warned you of his plan? You two were so close, lifelong friends and all?"

Sam shakes his head and sits on the edge of the desk at the head of the class.

"I don't know," he says. "For me, this is like discovering that your wife of 30 years has been screwing around behind your back since your honeymoon. I don't think, however, that he could face me with some of the things he had done. And I think they took a toll on his conscience over the years."

Aga jumps in.

"Did you know this Saul Alinsky guy? The guy that Rufus was friends with, went to school with in Chicago?"

"No, not really," Sam responds. "I met Alinsky once, and I did know that he and Rufus were somewhat close, though I thought Rufus was just playing him, getting close, seemingly, so he could play him for information, ideas. They did communicate on a fairly regular basis. I knew that."

"These documents," Amy volunteers, "could spell the end of the Democratic Party, Grandpa. They tell a dark, ugly story of their true intent and how they got their programs passed and how they used and kept power."

Sam laughs.

"Sure, like watching sausage being made, right? Hell, they didn't do anything that Republicans didn't do. It's the same ballgame. The plot is always the same, just different players. And the players aren't really congressmen or senators; they are the lobbyists, the full-time guys. They are the ones making things happen. They control the ball game and, most importantly, the rules. Senators and Congressmen, the politicians, are just the equipment!"

No one laughs, and Sam turns away, uncomfortable with his own attempt at a sports metaphor.

"I read a handwritten note by Rufus in the papers," Amy offers. "It was to Alinsky, and it carefully detailed and reviewed their plans and asked for his opinion."

Sam is confused, wondering how she could have read that because all of the files are in the box. As he is ready to ask Amy what she has shared, Amy comments, remembering she had read this file last night, "I read that. Four strategic points: One, to create a welfare state, control the lives, food, housing, and income of blacks so that we can control them, adding to the list of their free spoils, making them a very dependent and thus very a reliable voting block for the party." Amy looks around to looks she has never seen before, of disbelief.

She continues, "Point two was about controlling health care, which also provides control of the masses, that I guess was the basis of the Medicare and especially the Medicaid programs."

Amy looks up to gauge the reactions, then continues, "And point three was debt! Increasing the payments to the poor, mainly minorities, will over generations exponentially increase the cost, which taxes cannot keep up with. This will lead to debt, meaning borrowing money to fund these political bribes. The note at the bottom said this will eventually lead to the government accessing personal savings and retirement accounts, essentially a wealth tax, and eventually gets the country so far in debt that it could no longer govern. He underlined one phrase, 'total redistribution.'"

Amy clearly understands this economic strategy. She looks at Sam, who is looking out of the window to avoid anyone seeing his emotional response to what he is hearing. Sam realizes that Amy must have already shared this file with the others, given her comments, thinking he can't wait to go through all of the files in this box.

After a prolonged silence, Roger adds, "And point four speaks to developing a way to nationally control education through unions, so they would be able to dumb down our society, once again making it easy to control voters. My interpretation of this is that by controlling the unions, they could control the tenure granting and protection of teachers, making sure they become a protected group, which cannot be let go for any academic shortcomings."

The Alinsky strategic points astonish them all.

After maybe 30 seconds of dead silence, frustrated, Roger adds, "What does it all mean? Why did they do it?"

"It means," Sam responds, not wanting to answer his direct question, "the end of the Democratic Party if this information is discovered. You are right, Amy. We would go to a one-party system, with the country having lost faith. It could eventually lead to a totalitarian state."

"So," Richard adds, "our national security would be at stake, could be at stake, if this information gets out?"

Increasingly uncomfortable and obviously becoming traumatized by the events beginning with Rufus's death, Amy approaches her grandfather and looks him in the eyes. "Tell me," she demands, "that you didn't know these things were happening.

I don't believe you could have known that they were doing these things, planning these programs?"

Sam's shoulders slouch, he seems to crumble before Amy's eyes. There is a long pause and he takes a deep breath before he begins to speak.

"I wish that were true, Amy. I always knew something, more than I have ever acknowledged. I knew enough that I should have challenged them, done more to stop them. I should have called Rufus on many of the things he shared with me, but I didn't, honey. I'm sorry, but I didn't. I didn't realize this was all part of a master plan." Sam's uncharacteristic softness catches the three graduate students completely off guard.

Amy turns her back as Sam continues. She doesn't want to look directly at him as he confesses, allowing him at least the privacy of her eyes.

"I knew Rufus wasn't always being completely straight with me, and he knew that I knew," Sam continues. "It was a game we played. A game so that Rufus and Lyndon could have their way, carry on their own private agenda. It had all been done before, you know. FDR winking at Congress after passage of the Social Security Act, letting them know that their river of funding was now ready to begin flowing into their hands so they could spend it on their own self-motivated political pork. And there is a long history of lying to the American public, in the interest of gaining, keeping, and controlling power. I did believe our goals were right, at one time. I did believe we were doing the right things."

Sam walks to the window, looks longingly out on the parking lot, wishing somehow he could be somewhere else, anywhere else. Standing erect, he continues, "I am not a fool, Amy. I knew what was going on but I did look the other way. And, truth is, I guess I didn't really want to know all the things, the reasoning behind what we were doing. I knew there was some dirty dealing going on. And I admit, I did come to believe that the positive ends justified the means. "

Richard sits forward in his seat, anticipating his next question, finally have framed it in his mind so that Sam would be impressed, he hopes. "The stuff in these files, Sam. It is devastating stuff. It will forever change the way many look at the Democratic Party because, many people, my people, hate more than anything to have been played, tricked, lied to."

For a moment everyone is silent. Amy breaks it by asking, "If leaders would lie to their own people so flagrantly, so boldly, then we must expect their lies to have traveled internationally. And exposure of all this will create a lack of confidence in the world, spiraling markets downward. Our future as a society and world leader, world policeman, could literally be at risk. So Sam," she asks, a single tear running down her cheek, "what do we do now?"

Roger, realizing the import of what Amy has just said, jumps in with, "It's the fuckin' end of the world, Sam. End of the fuckin' world!"

Sam, ignoring Roger's unhelpful and basically stupid, yet unfortunately accurate summary of the situation, offers, "I have an idea. Leave the summary file with me and go through all the subject files, pull out all the papers that relate to this summary and we'll meet again tomorrow . . . to discuss and determine our next move."

They file out, Sam heading for his office, Amy and Roger going the other way toward the exit, and Aga and Richard heading back to the grad offices. As they see Sam turn into his office, Aga says, "No more library work. I will call you later tonight. We need these files." With that, Aga turns and goes the other way, heading for the exit door.

Sam walks into his office carrying the box and asks Miss Jones where the nearest Xerox center is located. She tells him she will be happy to make copies here for him. He shakes his head, indicating no. Not knowing what to think, she says, "The closest one is on the southeast corner of campus by Pete's." Not knowing exactly what is going on, she adds, "Do you want me to go make the copies there?" Sam shakes his head again and says, "No, I have to go out anyway; I'll take them with me."

Chapter Thirty-Two

Later that evening at Roger's apartment, Roger and Amy lie exhausted on the floor in the living room, with papers, notebooks, and files neatly placed around them. Amy is reviewing the "necessary tasks" files, and Roger is checking the nonrelevant group, making sure he did not miss an important one.

Roger looks up from behind the box containing the general files, commenting, "Much of this goes back to the '64 election, a period many now consider transformative for American politics. There seemed to be a break there, during that period; the Democrats had become the party of civil rights. And by the end of '65 LBJ had gotten Medicare, Medicaid, Head Start, and the Voting Rights Act all passed. Goldwater didn't have a chance; the Democratic machine was running on all cylinders."

Amy also sits up.

"LBJ said Goldwater had a poor strategy. That he was a 'dumb ass' and his opposition in the election 'not worth mentioning.'"

Roger considers Amy's assessment. "Probably all true, but do you know what Goldwater said, how he summed up his own election strategy?"

"No," Amy responds.

"He said he just didn't believe in the government telling people what to do," Roger says. "Simple as that. That's how he saw it, the Dems setting people up so the government could tell them what to do, the conservatives believing people should rule themselves. What separates the party philosophies is simple: one believes in personal responsibility and the other does not. "

Amy seems surprised by Roger's definitive summary assessment.

"So do you agree with Goldwater?"

Roger holds up a handful of papers.

"Did you know that it was Goldwater who pushed for desegregation of the military? That he was instrumental in getting minorities into the Air Force Academy? While LBJ, as we have discovered in these papers, was an avowed racist until he saw how civil rights could be used to build large voting blocks."

Amy listens as Roger continues and laughs when Roger laughs out loud and says, "Did you know that Goldwater had a six-inch-by-four-inch rubber stamp made and that he stamped any correspondence he didn't like with it, and that all it said was, 'Bullshit!'"

Amy laughs out loud and the two roll on the floor, letting off some of the personal stress and political gravity that had built up.

"I have been such a fool, Amy," Roger confesses, honestly, maybe for the first time in his life. "This experience, the papers, Sam, Rufus, the discovery, revelations, they have changed me. I swear to you. They have opened my eyes, showing me where an attitude like mine will eventually lead. And I swear to you, Amy, I do not want to be like that. After seeing all this, I will never be the same. I never want to be like the men who wrote these programs, who knew all along just how evil it all was, what it had to eventually lead to . . . and they did it anyway, for power, for votes. They used so many people, so blatantly, so calculatedly, so devoid of any true sensitivity to any real cause, other than their own vanity . . . their own selfish goals . . . their own hunger for power."

Amy smiles. The first time she has smiled in Roger's presence since the meeting in Debbie's office.

But she hides the smile from Roger and says, "Grandpa isn't like that, Roger."

Roger stops Amy from continuing and asks, "Do you really think releasing these papers is in the best interest of our country?"

Wanting to avoid where their discussion is heading, Amy gets up and goes into the kitchen. She returns with a bottle of Lone

Star for each of them, sort of a peace offering. Roger accepts the beer without question and smiles.

"I just don't know about Sam, Amy. I believe people ought to know the truth, but I'm afraid of what could happen as a result. I don't think anyone can really predict the outcome of a situation like this."

Amy takes a long drink from her bottle of beer, closes her eyes, and lays back against the sofa.

"I just can't think about this anymore tonight, Roger. I'm exhausted. Do you have room for me to stay here with you tonight?"

Roger thinks carefully, then responds, "Of course." Wanting to show her the respect he knows she deserved, he adds, "You take the bedroom and I'll stay here on the sofa. I want to do a little more reading anyway." With the last comment, Amy thinks things are different. He has changed. She goes to the bedroom thinking again that they may have a chance at a future together.

The next morning, Roger is just rising as Amy is preparing to leave, telling her, "Please take the one big box we put together last night with you, Amy. Maybe try to organize them so that we can review them later with Sam. I'm anxious to see what he has in mind."

Amy picks up the box and smiles.

"I'm going to grab some breakfast at the coffee shop. Maybe Grandpa will be there. Let's talk later."

Roger watches her as she departs, not wanting to take his eyes off of her, hoping and praying he can somehow get her back in his life. He has realized her true importance to him, understanding that she was the most important person in his life, and far more important to him than the miscellaneous, nonrelevant files and papers spread around the room. Their review did, however, discover many other cans of worms, which shed light on the executions of plans motivated solely by thwarting the political competition. These were the appropriately labeled "necessary tasks."

Roger reviews once again, but in much greater detail, the key summary Great Society files he has in his briefcase, about a dozen or so. He begins to catalog the files; then, after looking at his watch, he repacks them into his briefcase, along with the beginnings of his outline. He knows developing a complete outline with a top-line summary will take a significant amount of time, which he cannot undertake until after his class today. Roger throws on a short-sleeve madras shirt he had in high school and heads to school, leaving the file remnants that were originally housed in the boxes on his floor. He can't help but think about where this will take him. And Amy.

Chapter Thirty-Three

Roger, carrying his briefcase still containing the detailed Great Society documentation files, unlocks the door to his office in the grad student offices area of the Government Department. He enters and stands speechless as he views his office having been thoroughly ransacked. His file cabinets lie on the floor, drawers completely taken out so that even the inside of the cabinets could be searched. Manila folders, papers, and books are scattered about. "The place," Roger mumbles as he looks around the room, "looks like a bomb went off."

Roger puts his briefcase on his desk. He steps around overturned furniture and hurriedly calls Amy at her office. He hears her answer and warns her even before she can respond. "Amy? Don't come here! Don't bother! We'll meet at your office; mine has been ransacked, destroyed."

Amy responds, "I just got to my office, somebody has destroyed it too, Roger, even the door was kicked in. I already spoke with Sam. He was at the coffee shop, just like I'd hoped. He told me to tell you to go to his office. He will meet us there."

Roger notes his door was not kicked in, causing him to wonder how they got in. He then asks, "Do you have the box, Amy?"

"Yes," she responds. "It's in the trunk of my car. I'll bring it with me."

Roger hangs up just as Richard and Aga arrive. Richard is aghast at the damage.

"Judas Priest!" Richard shouts. "Are you all right?"

"Do you have the files?" Aga asks. "Are the files safe?"

Sensing there is something off in Aga's question, Roger begins to answer anyway but is immediately cut off by Richard, asking, "Have you spoken to Amy yet? Do you know if she's okay? Do you know where she is?"

Roger answers, "Yes, I just go off the phone with her. Her office was plundered too. She's on her way here to meet with Dr. Sam."

"Let's go down and wait for Amy in his office," Richard suggests.

Roger is curious in regard to Richard's harsh interruption but decides to let it pass, as his first concern now is Amy and, for some reason, he believes Richard may have purposely cut him off for her sake.

Roger grabs his briefcase and goes with Aga and Richard to Sam's office.

Both Richard and Aga appear anxious. Amy arrives shortly after they are seated, carrying the one box under her arm. She puts it on the desk and, for a moment, all eyes in the room are on that second box.

"Sam should be here any minute," Amy announces.

"So what's in this box?" Richard asks.

Amy seems reluctant to answer, though she does not know why.

"Amy and I spent last night sorting through all of Rufus's files," Roger explains, "and this box contains the files that spell out the details of what to Rufus were known as 'necessary tasks,' both their underlying strategy and execution, which were illegally conducted by the full authority of the White House." After a short pause, allowing his audience to digest the term "illegally," Roger continues, choosing his words carefully not to offend Amy, "The ones LBJ strategized with Rufus, and Rufus oversaw their execution."

Richard moves and stands next to the box, seeming to want to pick it up. Just as he reaches for it, Sam enters the room and signals for Richard to pass it to him. Richard hesitates but complies, then looks to Aga as if curious to observe his response.

Sam pulls a chair up to the conference table and the others follow suit.

"They ransacked my office," Roger announces.

"And your office too, Amy," Sam confirms, "but did you notice any other damage?"

Amy assures Sam there was no other damage that she noticed but that her office has been thoroughly "wrecked."

"What other type of damage are you looking for, Grandpa?" Amy asks.

Sam waves off the question. "Okay, look," he says, "we're all nervous, but we are all also likely to have been followed, so don't go back to your apartments. Roger, where are the rest of the files?"

Not willing to share with anyone the files that are in his briefcase, Roger says, "The key ones are all in this box," in response to Sam's question. "They support the summary file you have, Sam. Amy and I sorted through all the boxes, which took most of last night, and the ones here tell the complete story. The rest are all meaningless."

Sam acknowledges Roger's explanation as Amy asks, "How could anyone know anything about all of this so soon?"

Sam moves to a desk and sits, relaxing into the chair, showing only at that moment his exhaustion from having been up all the previous night. In somber reflection, he says, "I shouldn't have made the call. I know better than to do something like that. It was just, with Rufus gone, I needed to share it with someone. Someone I knew, from the old days, and who also knew Rufus. Someone I hoped could help us. Someone I believed I could trust."

Richard laughs. "Yeah," he says, "good luck with that."

Sam glares at Richard, but he quickly sees that Richard's comment has broken the tension in the room, and they all share a smile and a nervous laugh.

"So, please Sam," Richard asks, "explain what's going on here."

Sam hesitates, but complies. "I called a very senior guy in the NSA, just to let him know what we had, what is going on here."

"NSA?" Roger questions.

"It's a spy agency," Sam explains. "A super spy agency."

Richard seems unimpressed and asks, "So what happened with your guy, the guy you called?"

"He said," Sam explains, "that he would look into it and get back to me."

"Is that it? Is that all he said? Richard questions Sam, in a strange and challenging manner. "Did he mention when he would get back to you?"

Aga also becomes curious and questions Sam. "And was that your only call? The only call you made, Sam?

Sam seems suddenly surprised by their rapid questioning, troubled that he wasn't in control, but then also suddenly alert.

"No," he responds. "I called one other senior guy at the FBI, a friend, a guy I felt comfortable calling, sharing all of this with, word by word from some of the documents."

Amy has been growing increasingly nervous with Sam's responses, and with his steadily growing discomfort in answering the rapid-fire questions from Richard and Aga in succession.

"Grandpa!" she blurts out. "How do you know all these people? Are you sure you can trust them?"

Sam smiles at Amy. "They were among my closest friends in Washington. They are honest guys. They care about the country, and I believe they put country first. And, well, I needed advice, and I suppose I also needed to hear some friendly voices."

"So what'd the FBI guy say?" Richard asks.

"He said," Sam explains, "that these papers are potentially very dangerous, depending on who knows about them, what is in them. He said there have been rumors about such notes, such files for years, though no one wanted to believe their existence could be true. And he said he would help me and send agents down in a day or so, and to just hold onto the files, all of them, until his agents arrive."

There is an uncomfortable pause when Sam finishes his explanation, which Roger breaks when he asks, "There is something you should see, Sam. A file you should read, review, study. It's titled 'Addiction Strategy' and it's more or less a detailed blueprint for corrupting the social structure of the United States." Roger reaches into the file box and pulls out a file he had previously marked. "It reads like a grand sociological, totally destructive, long-term strategic master plan, including eliminating obstacles." Roger doesn't choose to be any more specific at this time.

Roger hands the file to Sam, who immediately begins devouring it at a speed-reading pace. It includes a note from Saul Alinsky that is attached to the back cover page.

"This note," Sam explains when he reaches the back page, "definitely is from Saul Alinsky and written to Rufus. I thought Rufus saw through the crap Alinsky was selling back in the old days, his 'Rules for Radicals' bullshit. But evidently, Rufus must have bought into it, some of it, anyway. More than I would have believed."

"I know about Alinsky now," Aga offers. "I've been reading about him since his name first came up. But what was his grand plan? And what is this 'Rules for Radicals' crap he wrote about?"

Sam takes the note off the file and waves it in the air.

"Rufus always claimed that Alinsky was an 'organizational genius,' and he liked to say that he was the flip-side of Machiavelli, the manipulative founder of political science. Machiavelli's classic work, *The Prince*, was written for the 'haves' on how to hold power, and Alinsky's 'Rules for Radicals' was written for the have-nots as a step-by-step guide on how to take power away from the powers that be. Basically, he was interested in collapsing the system. Destroying it! So, he wrote a how-to on just that, how to collapse and destroy the system! The specifics were in reference to the United States, using our democratic system as the target."

Aga laughs out loud and in a dismissive tone comments, "So, socialism? That's what we're talking about?"

"It's hard for me to admit," and after a lengthy pause Sam angrily reflects, "but Rufus has obviously lied to me all these many years. My best friend kept the real truth from me and used me to execute this plan. Shit, I guess he really did buy into the crap Alinsky was selling, to overload the welfare system by creating a guaranteed income for everyone possible in our society, which will in the long term bankrupt the system, our government."

Sam hesitates, as if not wanting to continue, but continues anyway. "It's hard to let all that stuff go, to admit that it was all just about manipulation," Sam explains as he passes each page to Richard who, in turn, passes each page to Aga. "But," he continues, "we will have to decide now what to do with these papers, this information. And I do believe, at this point, that this information must be exposed."

Aga looks at Richard, then appears to agree with Sam, while nodding appropriately and looking at each of them. He adds, "Sure, Sam, but you, we, none of us, have exposed, released, shared any of this information yet, with anyone, right?"

There is no response; everyone just nods their heads, seeming to indicate they hadn't. Which leads Roger to ask, "Obviously, these records are going to hurt the party; they will most likely hurt the entire country, for a while at least, and maybe for a long time to come."

Aga begins to question Amy but Roger interrupts.

"Who do you think is after these papers, this information, Sam, the NSA, FBI . . . ?"

Sam answers quickly, purposely, before anyone else can speak. "Hell, I don't know, maybe all three. But the NSA may not have an interest because they're not international—or are they?" Sam is clearly thinking about the possibilities, that the release of the information in these files represents a potential windfall of inside information to enemies of the US. He decides not to go there, or attempt to explain in any more detail to his assembled group. And then he looks at Amy and seems to change his mind, realizing the role he has played in all of this, and believes that his granddaughter deserves, needs to hear some explanation from him. So, speaking softly, he shares, "Honey, you think this isn't international in scope, or in the impact it could have? But another way to look at it is, just to let the system collapse from the inside, let people see the negative impact that the government planned to create through dependence, all just for political gain. This weakness and corruption in our system will embolden our enemies. We cannot fight both an internal war and international aggression. Who would follow our leaders if such chaos were to be revealed?"

Richard looks away from Aga, then jumps into the fray with "Suppose another government got hold of these papers, this information, Sam? Imagine the power they could wield over our foreign policy?"

Sam shakes he head as a response, having already realized the answer to this devastating question.

Roger says, "Jesus Christ," indicating the implication of this had only at that moment finally entered his mind. And with his expression, the sides of Aga's mouth turn upward slightly, almost into a smile, a reaction that does not go unnoticed by Roger.

"This is a wake-up call for America," Sam offers.

"Yeah," Amy adds, "I guess it would have to be."

"Did any of you speak with anyone about any of this, make any calls?" Sam asks.

The group stands silent.

"Okay," Sam finally responds, after several seconds of hesitation. "It's not worth the risk for any of you to be involved any more than is absolutely necessary. I'll take this box with me. Be alert and be careful. Amy, why don't you stay with me?"

Amy nods her head. With that, the meeting adjourns.

As Roger walks out with Amy, he can't help but think that Sam has both boxes that contain all the files to indict LBJ's Great Society, the legislation he was directly a part of getting done. They walk out in total silence.

Chapter Thirty-Four

Aga and Richard walk out of the building toward the library, where both of their cars are parked.

Richard turns to Aga. "So, did you find anything, anything at all?"

Aga answers, "Nothing. But it is obvious that Sam has the key files we need in his possession. Sam has two boxes of files, one specific to the Great Society and the other outlining the clandestine operations of the LBJ White House. And the other crap files are still with Roger, and those are not important to us." Aga stares at Richard, obviously making a judgment to determine if he should continue; how much he should share with Richard, how much he can really trust him.

"Okay, Richard. Here it is. You know that I am a member of the Kuwaiti royal family. And you know that we, our country, exist in the center of several unstable governments. You only have to look at Iran and Iraq. We are constantly on the alert, and I am on a mission, as are many others. Our mission is to gain leverage on the world stage, to ensure our national security. We must have information. Information that can be used in our support, which can be used in assuring military support if the time comes! This is the funding behind your work for the last three years, why I have been willing to pay you, to be so generous with you. The information in these files will help to protect our country from any of our crazy friends in the Middle East, even Asia if the bear gets hungry for more oil.

Richard asks, "How can that be? How would the papers help you protect your country?"

Aga responds, "Look, if the US knows we have them, they will defend us. If the Russians know we have them, they will defend us. And, most importantly, they both will continue to fund us. There is great power in these papers. For my country, for you, and for me."

Richard says, "Okay, what exactly is our deal if we can get them?"

Aga responds, "You have an opportunity here, Richard, that is beyond your wildest dreams. You may never have to work again, Richard. You and I have become friends here at this university. I believe you are someone I can trust; you have protected me. And I need you now. I need your help, and I promise you that you will be rewarded greatly if you help me."

"Okay, what do I have to do," Richard questions, and adds, "and what other information beyond the two boxes of summary files do you need, is of value to you?"

Aga answers quickly, anxiously, exposing to Richard for the first time his real level of commitment and interest. "These files contain certain information, information that we need, to better know our friends and our enemies. They could give us insight into the strategic plans regarding the entire Middle East. They will likely have country-specific information regarding personnel, spies, people who have been placed in important, key positions. This information is vital to the security of my country."

Richard appears confused. "You seem to know a lot about these papers, Aga." He hesitates but then continues, "Okay, Aga. I'll help, as long as you don't expect me to do anything really wrong. I don't want to get in any trouble. I don't want to betray my country, and, with what Dr. Sam just explained, the entire US government likely knows about these papers and that they are in play now. It will be dicey how to avoid being caught."

Aga momentarily appears startled with Richard's use of the words "in play now," but answers anyway, "Yes our time is short, but the papers are here, we are here, on the inside, and they trust us. I am sure we can just talk to that dumb shit Roger, he'll be able to get his hands on them and let us read all of them, then we'll know for sure where the papers are located and we can get them. They will be all mine—I mean ours. And you don't have to worry about trouble. No one will be harmed, and no one will ever even know what has gone on here. If we can get the papers, that is all there will be to it. That is all anyone ever needs to know about it."

Aga watches Richard relax. He smiles to himself, believing he has Richard in the palm of his hand.

As Aga begins to climb into his car, Richard asks him, "So what is it? What is your plan, Aga?"

Aga gets into his Mercedes, starts it and puts it in gear before answering, "Don't worry about that now, Richard. I have a plan, and I will share it with you later. For now, I just needed to know that you are my friend, that you will help me, and that we can work together."

Richard looks Aga in the eye and says, "I need two things: I need to know the exact specifics of the plan, including who is involved and the entire game plan, and" now smiling, "what exactly is my reward for being your loyal teammate in this affair?'

Realizing Richard's loyalty can be bought, Aga nods and says, "Will do." He rolls up his window and quickly drives away, leaving Richard standing alone in the parking lot.

Chapter Thirty-Five

Roger is trying to think through where this discovery will lead as he walks into a classroom unprepared, not surprisingly due to the circumstances, for that morning's lecture but, he is also, for the first time, oddly relaxed, even anxious to face his students. Unaware why or how he has suddenly acquired this newfound confidence, he is enjoying, at least for the moment, the feeling of it.

Somewhat startled at his newfound assurance as he prepares to speak to his class, Roger opens with, "I am changing my original plan for today's lecture." He looks at his class of assembled students, realizing they are interested, positively expectant for the information he can share with them. This reversal in attitude is a direct result of their last class. And, for the first time, he wants to give them something, rather than just fill his hour of responsibility to lecture them, really just asking a series of questions, then escape. Roger's entire orientation, toward everything, has changed.

"I realize that this change will require a compelling rationale," he begins, "and this change in plan is due to some students that came by my office asking about the long-term implications of Great Society programs, brought into being by LBJ and two of our major professors here at UT." Roger knows this setup will get their attention, and he continues, "So, I thought this would be a great time to discuss the potential implications, starting with creating national welfare programs. What was the explicit and implicit strategy behind creating these programs, which provided food stamps, general assistance, Head Start? And what will likely be the long-term results of these programs?"

By framing such a thought-provoking question, this proved to his students that he had actually listened to their questions and was now willing to bring the perspective of their legitimacy to light, yielding an attentive response from his audience. His idea worked. The students actually sit up, move forward in their seats, ready and anxious to pay him attention. It is as if some almost electric charge has ignited their desire to listen, think, and learn.

Roger initiates the discussion by reversing the order of his initial planned questions, asking, "These welfare programs were announced, presented as systems which would accomplish great things, elevate many people, and change the very structure of society in our country. Did they?"

Every student in Roger's class was obviously challenged, most for the first time, curious and genuinely interested in his thought-provoking question.

After giving his students some time to ponder his question, Roger asks, "Okay, let's start with some more basic questions."

His students, Roger realized, sat wide-eyed, interested. Even those who had been so skeptical of him were anticipating his words. It was a new experience for Roger, and he loved the feeling of power and the rush that came with it, making him think that maybe it is possible that political science is not a misnomer.

Roger looks over the class and proceeds, "To begin, I will put a seemingly simple question to you: why do we have welfare in this country?"

A student is so anxious to answer that he doesn't even raise his hand, "We provide it to help those who need a helping hand, to provide food and education for their children until they are able to provide it on their own."

Roger continues his questioning, anxious to maintain the energy in the room. "So, why is this important, what problem could this help solve?"

Another student in the back of the room asserts, "Equaling things out, eliminating poverty."

Roger follows with, "Is that what the long-term outcome will be?" And as the students try to think through where his line of reasoning is going, Roger continues, "Let's consider two implications, sociologically first. What is likely to result in future generations if welfare becomes a way of life, rather than just an economic support system?"

A female student in the front row responds, "No negative effect or harm, really. It's a great positive. It just helps folks who need it, when they need it. So it is a way of giving folks a hand up. And it exists because we, as a society, care." Most of the class, especially the females, nod in agreement.

Roger asks, "Are there any other points of view?"

The male student friend of Ms. Pyramid, who disdains Roger, contributes with, "I guess it could become a way of life. It could feed on itself, grow, take away the fundamental notion of having any real 'personal responsibility' for one's life, one's family, and to be on one's own."

This perspective obviously strikes a chord with some of the students, with another suggesting, "I can understand that folks on welfare could get used to it and lose their drive to get ahead in the world."

Roger smiles, then asks, "And what would be the likely long-term result of relying totally on welfare for one's family?"

It is clear at this point the students are trying to put themselves into this situation, to think about how they would react if subjugated to such conditions.

The first female student, who had voiced the "caring" label for welfare, offers, "Well, I can see how, over time, welfare could become a way of life, just part of it, you know. You would come to expect it, and without a reason to go out and do something, you could just learn to rely on it."

"Okay," Roger responds, "who agrees with this possibility?" More than two-thirds of the student raise their hands in agreement. Holy cow, Roger realizes. They got it. They actually got it, and he goes on with the question, "So what should we term this result, this psychological state created long term by a welfare society?"

Ms. Pyramid, as always sitting in the front row, answers, "It would result in creating a state of dependency, and condition future generations to this end. Dependency would be the likely result, for some if not many, of these governmental welfare programs. It would supplant the most fundamental human motive of survival, which is to live."

Using this as a basis, Roger now goes back to his original question, "So, with this enlightened perspective, what do you believe will be the likely long-term consequences of welfare systems, say, after several generations, maybe three or four? Will this become institutionalized in the thinking of those who are raised in such conditions?"

After 30 seconds with no response from his students, Roger concludes there is no longer any opposition to his summary, and, knowing now he is right given the files he has read, he continues, "So could this be an intended outcome?"

The students look at one another virtually in a state of shock, asking of themselves, could this actually be possible?

Wow, Roger thinks, I got them! And he then asks, "So, given this is a political science class, if you wanted to create dependency, why would you have these programs?"

A female student in the second row, wanting to reject the question or even the consideration of its viability, asks, "Are you really saying that our country would develop a societal framework where freedom can be translated into a 'right not to work'?"

This fundamental, crystal-clear insight launches a wave of hands immediately rising into the air. Not waiting to wait to be called upon, several students begin to voluntarily answer at once. Roger takes this in for a second, basking in his success, and then finally coming to the realization of the true joy of teaching and sharing ideas, ideas that can actually change the way people think.

Roger continues, "Okay, we all see where this is going. So answer me now, what is the political implication of the potential outcome you have come up with, what is the likely outcome, the end result of creating a welfare-based society?"

A student who has never before spoken out in Roger's class blurts out, "It's obvious, it would result in the building of a voting constituency and a voting bloc, a dependency-driven voting bloc."

Roger smiles, and the class grows suddenly silent as students ponder this pronouncement.

Taking the silence as an indication he has won the day, Roger now asks, "If you take out 'personal responsibility' for a major portion of our society and harvest this segment of the voting population as becoming completely dependent on the government, what will be the likely outcome?"

Two students, independently, but in unison, shout, "Political power!"

Roger points to the one immediately to his right and asks, "So, how would this work, how would it manifest itself?"

The student he pointed to excitedly responds, "Yeah, I can see how it would work. It's going on right now. The simple idea is that you keep promising more and more to get yourself elected and then reelected, which creates more and more dependency, creating a larger and larger voting bloc you are always able to count on."

Roger nods and says, "Very good! And what does that do to budgetary economics?"

The student sitting right in front of him says, "It's easy: more and bigger welfare programs. The more the better, if you are a politician. That's how you keep your job."

Ms. Pyramid then adds, "Think about the key factors. What will the likely result be to the high school drop-out rate if students believe the government will take care of them, no matter how poorly they perform in school? Housing subsidies? With lessening personal responsibility, out-of-wedlock births, further leveraging the welfare system, one entitlement piled on another? It could be never-ending dependency, a true welfare state!"

Roger's lecture is interrupted by a knock on the door. It is Aga. Roger excuses himself from the class, and, once he is in the hallway, Aga demands they have a meeting with Richard immediately after his class to "discuss the files." Roger is confused by Aga's sudden and extreme interest, surprised that he would even consider interrupting his class.

"Look, Aga. I can't talk now. I'll meet with you later. I've got to get back to my class."

Roger walks back into his class and goes to the blackboard, first taking a deep breath, then offering, "Let's summarize where we are." He lists in order the following points:

1) Institutionalizing government broad-based welfare will create a dependency on government to live a normal life

2) The sociological effect on American culture, if dependency is created, will move us from personal responsibility to complete government dependence, primarily targeting poor minorities

3) Dependency will create economic problems, with an increased burden on budgets, forcing ever-increasing deficits because tax income is also reduced

"Is there any disagreement with these three points?" Roger asks. And, when it is obvious there will be no response, he continues, "So what could all this likely mean to the two-party political system in the US?"

Ms. Pyramid again wants to insert her insight, raises her hand, and without being recognized begins, "There will likely be two orientations, one driven by a rational notion of fiscal responsibility, and the other operating under the 'caring' rationale for enlarging welfare. This obvious endgame for the latter being the creation of a voting bloc that will let them keep their political jobs. This will ensure the long-term success of their party, as the dependency factor becomes integrated into the entire culture."

The class sits, mesmerized, completely absorbed in the discussion.

Roger writes on the board.

4) Two political orientations: Fiscal responsibility vs. Welfare state, driven by the posturing of "caring"

Roger then adds, "Okay. Super. What is the likely political result?"

The student who had offered his first-ever comment raises his hand, and asserts, "Again, I think it is obvious. The welfare system 'have nots' will grow over time. Eventually they will become the majority and win out, which will bankrupt the government. It may take four, five, or six generations, but it is inevitable."

With that straightforward statement Roger goes again to the blackboard and writes his last point:

5) There will come a 'tipping point' in such a dependency-driven society. There will be no going back, bankruptcy must follow, which will effectively result in a total redistribution of wealth.

Roger turns to the class, remembering reading in Alinsky's writings, realizing that he and likely Rufus had it all figured out many years ago. And so he continues, "Wow. Look at how smart you all are? How smart you have become? And in such a short time."

Broad, self-congratulatory smiles emerge from the students, some laughter but, most surprising to Roger, a celebratory round of scattered clapping also results.

Roger calls for quiet and continues, "Having this welfare perspective as a basis, consider for our next class how the idea of a death tax fits within the political strategy of this framework." Roger smiles. "Okay, good thinking! Class dismissed."

Roger receives several compliments as students file past him on the way to the door. Ms. Pyramid, realizing all the nearby students can hear her, pronounces, "Oh, Professor Forsell, this was just great. I really enjoyed it. Really, I mean, really."

Roger smiles, and then asks, "How would you like to do something for me?"

She jumps at the opportunity and Roger gives her a handful of file folders which he pulls from his briefcase, previously wrapped and ready for mailing. He also hands her a ten-dollar bill and an address, with the request, "Please take this to the post office for me, will you? And mail it right away, today. Can you do that? Will you do that for me?"

Ms. Pyramid accepts the file folders and the money, obviously thrilled to be helping Roger in any way she can. She smiles and walks out, anxious to show her newfound appreciation.

Roger grabs his now empty briefcase and proceeds down the hallway. He thinks about calling Amy but decides he just will visit the Longhorn for a cold one first, some time to reflect, then go home and call Amy and, hopefully, take her to dinner.

Chapter Thirty-Six

It is just after 5:00 p.m. as Amy walks up the cement steps to Sam's house and pulls a key from her purse. She opens the door, enters, and calls out Sam's name.

"Grandpa, Grandpa. I'm here. It's dinnertime."

There is no response, and the silence immediately becomes frightening to her. She steps toward the guest room at the end of the hallway but suddenly stops, frozen in place by the sound of another door opening. Suddenly she smells the familiar odor of musk and a man, dressed in black and wearing a stocking cap mask, looks directly into Amy's eyes from across the 15-foot expanse separating them. She realizes she is cornered, that she has no way out, no way to get around the man or to escape him. Before she can even scream, another man, similarly dressed, appears behind her. In a flash, he is on her, covering her mouth with a cloth while grabbling her from behind. She cannot even scream and goes limp and quickly unconscious after hearing her attacker voice a single word, which sounds like Arabic.

An hour later Sam arrives at his house and sees Amy's car parked on the street instead of in his driveway. He immediately thinks it strange that no lights are on in his house, parks his car in the usual spot, and walks to the front door.

He is immediately alerted as the front door is open, slightly ajar. He walks back to his car and gets his .45 semiautomatic Colt from the glove box, where he had put it yesterday, just in case. He cocks it and walks slowly, carefully, and silently into the living room. Where is Amy? he wonders. It is all that is really on his mind.

It is apparent as he looks into the living room that his house has been ransacked. As he goes from room to room he sees that every area has been searched. More importantly, there is no sign of Amy, and he is very worried. And his worry quickly turns into anger.

Real, genuine terror floods Sam's mind and registers across his face, as he thinks about what could have happened or what could be happening to her. His fear quickly reverts to pure anger. Then, suddenly, he feels sick, realizing this was not just an obvious military mission; this wasn't about people he didn't know—this was about his own granddaughter. And the entire event has the smell of more than espionage. It has the musky smell of war and the feeling of doing whatever is necessary to win, to get what is wanted.

Immediately, Sam determines he will be more determined, more cold and calculating than anyone who opposes him. He goes into the living room and picks up the phone, where he notices a note on the table. He reads it, looks in his address book next to the phone, and dials.

"Roger, they've got Amy! Don't ask questions; just meet me at Pete's coffee shop. Now, Roger, right now!"

Sam walks to his car, gets into it, and drives off.

Chapter Thirty-Seven

Sam sits alone at a table in Pete's coffee shop, going over the events of the past couple days in his mind, trying to put the pieces together since Rufus's death. Who was it that took Amy? And why? Sam never thought to analyze which government agencies may be after them, or which would be desperate enough to kidnap Amy. He knew the Democratic Party itself would do almost anything to keep the secrets hidden away in Rufus's files from being exposed.

And yet there was even more to it than that. So many things were wrong about it all. Why hadn't Rufus come to him? Was it a heart attack that killed him? Was he killed by someone desperate to get the documents? But most of all, now it had come down to Amy, just Amy. That made it simple for Sam. Nothing else really mattered any more to him. He had nothing to fear from the documents. Whatever was in all of them, whatever came out, made no difference to him at this stage of his life. No, it had become simple for him. This was about his granddaughter having been kidnapped. He had the note to prove it. And he was going to get her back, safe. That is all that matters to him now. All he cares about.

Roger enters the coffee shop, notices Sam at a table near the back, next to the only other door, an exit door, his back to the wall. He walks toward Sam, noticing that Sam doesn't look up until a moment before he arrives at the table, but also realizing that Sam has been cognizant of his every step and movement since entering the restaurant. He could tell that Sam had been watching his reflection in the glass, while at the same time, checking through the plate-glass front window outside for any strange movements. Sam's obvious ability and training is a realization so specific, so purposeful, that it startles Roger, makes him feel as if he has been put on notice, though he knows not why. And it makes him understand that Sam is far more of a force than he has ever thought.

Roger, now deathly aware of Sam's demeanor stands next to the table, looks across at Sam and says, "So?"

"Sit," Sam commands Roger. "They got her. They have my Amy."

"They? Who is they, Sam?" Roger asks as he seats himself, never allowing his eyes to leave Sam, experiencing a feeling he has never had before: true fear of losing someone he loved.

Sam reaches for his coffee cup and with growing frustration repeats Roger's question which, in his mind, summarizes the problem, "They, yes, they! Them! The guys who once were good guys, white hats, but now are the bad guys, black hats. My old friends, one-time comrades, my buddies! Or someone else. Who the fuck knows?"

"So it could be government guys?" Roger asks.

"I can't think of anyone else it could be. Maybe a question of which government guys? But, yeah, government," Sam responds. "And they left a note."

"Maybe FBI then, if they left a note?" Roger questions.

Sam smiles, sips his coffee. "Why in the world would you think that, Roger?"

"Well," Roger responds. "I thought CIA was international and FBI was national."

"Okay, good thinking, Roger," Sam responds. "The FBI is responsible for what goes on inside the country, espionage included. But it could also be NSA, could very well be . . . the more I think about it. Good old NSA. A more sinister bunch God never allowed since his own angels were corrupted, since he kicked their sorry asses out of heaven. Yeah, NSA, those are the kind of guys we're going to be looking for."

"So?" Roger questions, though unsure of what to ask next, where to go with any further questioning, finally feeling enough confidence to trust Sam and sit at his table, confident Sam does not include him as a suspect.

"So," Sam responds, "it could be a new group, new agency, new bunch of dressed-in-black, no-soul assassins . . ."

Sam stops in midsentence, adding "It could even be a private national group, or a group from another country."

Roger appears startled with this revelation. "Really? Like?"

Sam sips his coffee, then says, "Like the DNC, or terrorists!"

Roger appears more confused than ever. "I don't . . . the DNC? Really, Sam? Why would the Democratic National Committee be involved?"

Sam laughs.

"This discovery would end them." Sam continues, "It's big business, the most power-driven business. You ever been in DNC headquarters in D.C.? Down in the basement, one of those small rooms, private meetings with you and just one or two of the big boys or girls? Where they lay out just what favor contributors get for their generous support. Fifty grand gets you invited to the first ball after the big election. One hundred grand gets you an invite to both the first and second ball, both black tie, of course. But two hundred grand, now we're talking. That gets you invited to all the balls, which you don't give a shit about attending, but also includes your participation in an extremely private Oval Office ceremony after all the balls, all the bullshit. And there, right in the Oval Office is where you are asked which country you would like to be ambassador for, if, of course, you ever had such an opportunity, idea, such an interest in mind? And if such a chance were ever to be offered you, this would run $1,000,000 or more, with the check written to the DNC."

"Now," Sam adds, "if you are a lobbyist and you want to talk turkey, the prices go up dramatically. And where does the money go? To fuel the political machine."

Sam smiles at Roger, who is aghast, unsure if Sam is telling an out-of-school joke or sharing a dark, secret, intimate truth about how the world really works.

"Of course, the best roles, the ones that mean the most, are the ones where you are simply labeled an advisor to the president. A come-and-go-at-will position, a meet with the 'man' whenever you desire, with just you and the man in charge, just two good buds, sharing a drink, sharing a few laughs, but on a strict, 10-minute timetable. That kind of influence can be purchased."

Having not yet been served, Roger takes a drink from Sam's water glass, as Sam continues.

"Really, Roger? You need to ask why would the DNC be involved? Come on, you're smarter than that. Think! Who is going to be hurt the most by disclosure of these documents? What will people think? What will blacks think of the party they have so blindly supported since Roosevelt?"

Roger leans back in his chair, intrigued by the revelations Sam has presented, but also terribly confused as to why Sam would share such secrets.

"I don't understand, Sam. And you mentioned terrorists?"

"It is not above the DNC to hire terrorists. Bad guys do one another's bidding, when it's convenient, when it serves their own purposes. It could even be the other way around: there are a bunch of well-known senators, congressmen, big players in D.C. who have associations with the big oil players in the Middle East."

"Aga?" Roger asks.

Sam doesn't answer but hands the note to Roger. After reading it, Roger looks up, straight into Sam's eyes. "Why would someone have booked you on a Southwest flight to Dallas tomorrow?"

Sam smiles. "That's only the first leg of the trip. Final destination on that ticket is Chicago."

"Chicago?" Roger questions, still not in full control of his feelings, knowing Amy is his life.

Sam finishes his cup of coffee.

"Yeah, Chicago. Somebody wants me in Chicago and planned far enough ahead, before grabbing Amy, to buy me a ticket and leave it with the note. But don't worry, Roger. We're going to get her back. I don't give a damn about the files anymore. Their only importance is to help recover Amy. She is all that I care about at this point. And I promise you, Roger, that I will personally pave the way straight to hell for anyone who gets in the way of my getting her back. Whoever took her is dead! And that is a promise!"

Roger smiles, feeling better, and perhaps, the most confident moment Roger has ever experienced with Sam.

"I'd like to play a hand in getting her back. If you'll allow me, trust me, give me the chance. I will do whatever it takes, Sam. I swear! I'll do whatever you say."

Sam pulls his wallet out of his back pocket, drops a five-dollar bill on the table to cover his coffee and stands up.

"Okay, Roger. I'm going to let you in the game, back in Amy's life. You have a chance to do the right thing. So let's go back to my house; I don't want you out of my site. Just leave your car here. We'll pick it up later."

Chapter Thirty-Eight

Sam drives his Ford Galaxy 500 slowly toward his house. He and Roger view Sam's darkened house just as a flash of light erupts from inside the study. They drive by without slowing down, and both Sam and Roger notice a car with a man sitting in it a block and a half south of Sam's home.

"Who could that be?" Roger asks, expecting no response from Sam and getting none.

Sam stops at a stop sign at the next corner, after driving around the entire block to check for other cars. He passes several parked cars and then parks his car far enough away to be out of the sight of the mysterious man parked a block away from his house.

"Okay," Sam begins instructing Roger, "here's the game plan. Give me four minutes. Then pull in front of my house. Make a little noise, then go the front door like you plan to enter, but don't go in. Just stand at the front door and wait."

"Wait for . . ."

"Don't worry about what for," Sam anxiously instructs Roger. "Just wait. Now look, I'm counting on you here. And I am convinced you are genuine in wanting to help Amy and that you're willing to risk your own life to help her. Am I right?"

"Yes, yes," Roger insists. "Okay, Sam! Whatever you want! I'll do whatever you want!"

Sam gets out of the car, quietly closes the door, and Roger slides across into the driver's seat. In only a moment, Sam has disappeared.

A minute later, Sam knocks on the window of the car they had passed minutes earlier with the butt of his .45 while pointing it in the driver's face. The startled and surprised driver timidly opens the door and gets out of the car, where he is met with the butt of Sam's weapon on the back of his head. Sam takes the unconscious man's wallet and discovers the man is carrying a gold FBI badge.

"Shit!" Sam says, expressing his frustration at having just knocked an FBI agent unconscious. He puts the badge in his pocket, takes the agent's weapon and his keys and opens the trunk of the car and deposits the unconscious agent into the trunk. He leaves the keys on the car's roof, driver's side.

Roger, driving Sam's car from the opposite direction, arrives at the front of Sam's house, slams the car door shut, and walks to the front door. While wrestling with the keys to unlock the house door, he hears a gunshot from the rear of the house. Roger runs to the back and finds Sam pointing a gun at a man on the ground, about 20 feet from the back door. The man is bleeding from a bullet having just grazed his leg above his knee. His screams are muffled, primarily by a constant series of highly descriptive four-letter words.

While pointing the gun at the wounded man, Sam explains the events to Roger, while the man on the ground groans in pain, his most frequent utterance being "mother fucker."

"I told the son of a bitch to halt. He didn't, so I had to put him down. So go through his pockets, Roger."

Roger grabs the man's wallet, opens it, and shows the contents to Sam. The contents include an FBI badge identical to the one of the agent in trunk of the car.

"Look, you stupid piece of shit, you best get me to a doctor and fast! I'm an FBI agent you ignorant shit!"

Sam smiles. "Well," he explains, "you and your partner need a little more training. A 75-year-old college professor just got the goods on both of you."

The agent looks up. "Is my partner okay?"

"Don't worry about your partner. He's fine. Better than you," Sam laughs.

Lights go on in a nearby neighbor's home, as someone has heard the shot.

"Who sent you? You have five seconds before I shot you in the other leg," Sam threatens.

The FBI agent delays answering, but only for a moment, realizing that Sam will follow through with his threat and shoot him in the other leg.

"Okay, okay. Just relax. Special Agent Rogers sent us."

"And who is Special Agent Rogers?" Sam asks.

The agent presses both hands on his wounded leg to slow down the flow of blood. "He's head of the Organized Crime Division out of New York. Undercover group."

Sam and Roger look at one another, confused. "And who does Agent Rogers report to?" Sam asks.

"Washington, directly to Washington," the agent responds.

Sam smiles. Roger also nods his understanding. "Okay," Sam says, "now we're getting somewhere."

Roger starts to question the agent, but turns to Sam instead. "If the FBI had her, why would they come here?"

Sam nods in agreement, and he and Roger begin walking toward Sam's car.

"What about him?" Roger asks.

"Fuck him. It's just a flesh wound. He can use his belt as a tourniquet and drag his sorry ass back to his car, let the other sorry ass out of the trunk and drive to the hospital."

As Sam and Roger walk away, the wounded FBI agent screams out to them. "Hey, hey, what about me?"

Sam looks back, "Put a tourniquet on it you stupid fuck. Where'd you get your training anyway, you fuckin' Cub Scout? Your keys are on the roof of your car and your partner is taking a nap in the trunk."

Roger laughs. "You learned to be like this in the Marines, didn't you, Sam?"

Sam looks at Roger. "Don't worry about it, lover boy. Before this is over you'll be doing some work of your own."

Minutes later, Sam and Roger arrive at Sam's car, get in, and drive away.

Inside the car, Roger laughs. "That is one pissed-off, sorry-ass FBI agent."

Sam waves his hands in the air. "So," Sam tells Roger, "we need to determine who actually kidnapped Amy, and I guess we can eliminate the FBI."

Sam pauses, then continues with his train of thought. "Kidnapping isn't really in the FBI's playbook. NSA would do it without hesitation, but not the FBI. But I also don't think this is NSA's kind of business."

Confused by it all, Roger asks, "So the NSA does this kind of shit?"

Enjoying disclosing such information to someone as naive as Roger, Sam continues with his explanation. "Lyndon formed the NSA back in '52. It was supposed to deal with, monitor, and decipher any and all questionable communications, domestic or other. The old man saw it as a control mechanism, a division for maintaining political control. It's the largest agency in government, and their design is specifically to protect the power elite, and few even know it exits. And even fewer others know what it actually does."

"So," Roger asks, "you think maybe they are behind or involved in some way in all this?"

Sam smiles at how quickly Roger is catching on and responds, "Could be, probably, definite maybe, but . . ."

Turning quickly to look at Sam, obviously confused, Roger asks, "But?"

Chapter Thirty-Nine

Sam and Roger sit in an office two doors down from Sam's office. Sam is talking on the phone but suddenly finishes his call and hangs up.

Roger sits at a small conference table across the room, a glass of bourbon in his hand. Sam takes a long drink from his glass, surprising Roger with the amount he is able to consume in one swallow. Then Sam gets up, goes to the bottle in front of Roger and refills his glass.

Carrying his drink in one hand, Sam walks to the door and motions for Roger to follow.

"My friend on the phone," Sam explains, "invited us to a meeting down the hall."

Roger glances around the room, realizing that Sam has just indicated that this office has also possibly been bugged. There is no meeting.

The two men pass several students in the hallway as they walk into an empty classroom one floor down in the Department of Government area.

"That phone call was from my old friend at NSA. He confirmed in a roundabout manner that all the occupied offices in this building may be bugged from top to bottom. I suspected as much. So tell me, what do you really know about Aga and Richard?"

Roger seems confused by Sam's question. "Well, they're both smart. Smarter than me, which you probably have already surmised."

Sam smiles. "Background, I mean."

Roger stumbles over his words as he tries to express himself. "Honestly, Sam. I don't know much; neither of them has ever been very forthcoming."

Sam pats Roger on the shoulder. "Well, let me tell you, son. Aga is part of the royal family in Kuwait. Richard is a

Vietnam vet, a highly decorated Marine, and is currently in the employ of our government. Not sure which division he works for yet, but he's in there somewhere. My contract was not forthcoming in this regard. Professional courtesy, I guess."

Roger appears dumbfounded. "Aga, well, no real surprise there, I guess. He has money and likes everyone to know it. Richard looks like a Marine, but why would he be here? Why would either of them be here?"

"The papers," Sam offers, "it's all about Rufus's papers. The government knows how critically important they could be, so to have one, maybe two, undercover operatives here for the past couple years makes sense."

Confused by it all, Roger asks, "I don't understand, Sam. How could anyone have known? We just discovered the papers and files when Rufus died."

Sam laughs. "Oh, they knew that Rufus had the papers. They just didn't know where. I think that's why they were here, looking for them, and that's why there's trouble now."

Roger seems in a state of disbelief. "So, Sam, you think Aga is mixed up in this? Is involved in this?"

"He's got to be," Sam responds. One way or another, he's involved. It wasn't just NSA and it wasn't just FBI. There are major spooks, and God knows who else is in on this deal."

"So," Roger questions, "the two agents at your house. They were both FBI, so we know they're involved."

Sam concurs nonverbally, but then confirms it again. "Yeah, and my friend believes the papers, Rufus's papers, are way more important to some folks than we realized. More important than my friendship with Rufus. More important than Rufus's relationship with anyone, including Mary. You know there is some really bad shit in the files. But why would Aga be involved? Why the Kuwaiti royal family? I understand Richard, he's a fairly typical operative now that I think about it, but Aga?"

Sam motions to Roger that it is time to leave, knowing the question has no immediate answer. As they walk down the hallway, almost on cue, Richard approaches them from the opposite direction. Sam opens his sport coat, revealing his pistol for Richard to see. As they come together, Sam speaks first.

"So, Richard, what's the truth here, Gyrene?"

Sam opens the door to an unoccupied seminar room and directs Richard inside. The three men sit at the conference table in the middle of the room.

"So," Richard begins, "you know about me? You know why I'm here?"

Sam nods in the affirmative, leaving Roger confused at the end of the table, which is what Sam is hoping for.

"Okay, Sam," Richard begins, "I'm deep undercover. Been here almost three years with a special group of the NSA that tracks foreign nationals attending American universities. There are, presently, 14 well-funded Arabs, mostly Saudis, in grad school in Texas alone. And all of them have a tag-along special ops team following them around, shadowing their every move."

Sam and Roger now know who Richard is with, the NSA.

Frustrated, Roger can wait no longer. "What about Amy, Richard, or whoever the fuck you are? Do you know who kidnapped Amy?

Richard smiles, relieved to finally be himself to Sam and Roger. "Yes, we have a good idea, Roger. But we're not sure, not sure enough to make a move, not yet, anyway."

Sam and Roger stare across the table at one another. Then Roger turns to Richard. "One of us, Sam or me, is going to shoot you in the next minute if you don't get more specific than that. Is Aga involved? Is he part of some organized group that kidnapped her?"

"Look, Roger, Sam, we know they have a long-term game plan revolving around control of the global economy, oil, specifically, and we know they are looking for things or people of value to use in bartering for power. Somehow they learned about the papers. We don't know how. But Amy was just a convenient hostage. When she showed up at your house, Sam, they decided to take her as bait, likely to ransom."

"Why are the documents so important?" Sam asks, opening his coat, his hand now on his weapon.

"The documents are real national and international game changers, Sam," Richard says. "And I think you already suspected that. They can be used to ransom and own Democratic Party leaders. If the information in these files gets out, it would kill the Democratic Party forever. It would also jeopardize the two-party system in this country, undermining belief in the system, especially by the minority communities, most especially by my people."

Roger sits forward at the table.

"Yeah, okay, I got all that. And the Republicans could benefit immensely, for the short-run, if the files got out."

Richard shakes his head, as if Roger's assessment made no difference at all, forcing Richard to continue in his explanation. "Of course, the Republicans would love it, but that's not where the control comes from. Given that the Democrats will continue to follow the strategies outlined in these documents, my fellow blacks won't care, as long as they stay on the government tit. After all, they've worked marvelously well for them for the past fifteen years, and do seem to get better every year. But they could well give the Arabs a hammer hanging over the heads of the power elite, and they could drop it, or threaten to drop it, anytime they wanted. It's a gotcha, isn't it? It gives them the power to change our political system for their benefit, granting them oil rights, taking rights away from American producers. The Arabs could operate at their convenience, dictating to our government the prices, the flow of oil from whatever direction they want it to travel, and who gets to produce it, store it, and move it. It's brilliant!"

Roger doesn't seem quite as convinced. "Yeah, but they only have the power if they have actual proof, which they believe is spelled out in Rufus's papers, the documents."

There is a prolonged silence.

"Yeah, unfortunately, that sounds right," Sam finally blurts out.

"I believe," Richard continues, "that our number-one priority should be to get Amy back, safe and unharmed. Number two is to protect the documents and to take care of the shitheads that kidnapped your girl, Sam, and for you Roger. And, you should know, before you shoot me, that I have received clearance to do just what I have explained."

Sam quietly considers Richard's pitch, then says, "I don't believe you really put Amy first, Richard. But you should. You'll pay one hell of a price, I promise you, if we don't get her back safe. Now, what intel do you have? And did you know the FBI has already gotten involved in this case?"

"FBI? No. When did they get involved?" Richard asks.

Sam smiles, Roger looks away. "They paid a visit to my house," Sam says.

Richard looks for answers in Sam's expression but reads none. "And so, what did you tell them, Sam?"

Roger laughs. Sam shoots him a keep-your-mouth-shut look, but Roger keeps talking. "Sam just pointed them in the direction of the nearest hospital, which they were in need of, so to speak."

Ignoring Roger's remark, Sam presses Richard. "Intel, Richard. What intel do you have?"

"Aga rented a plane last night," Richard informs Sam, "and filed a flight plan for St. Louis, with continuation to Chicago. He has flown to Chicago three times in the past two months. I'm sure Amy was on the plane with him. Now, look, Sam, for helping you, I'm supposed to bring the two boxes of files with me. I assume the three of us will be going to Chicago together."

Sam relaxes his hand off his pistol. He buttons his coat. "That all fits with Aga. They booked me already for a flight to Chicago tomorrow morning, and I'm supposed to bring the files with me, to exchange for Amy. They instructed me to check into the Palmer House until the actual exchange can be arranged."

Roger jumps in asking, "Why Chicago?"

Richard, happy to move the conversation away from Sam, jumps on Roger's question. "There is a South Side mosque that operates as headquarters for militant Muslims and a group of radical Black Panthers. It is also headquarters for the Arab grad school group that we have been monitoring the past two years."

Roger is elated with Richard's knowledge. "Jesus, Richard! What kind of alliance is that, in Chicago, at the mosque?"

Richard shakes his head. "It's an unholy alliance, Roger. But that doesn't make any difference, really. The people involved with this group would kill without hesitation to get their hands on Rufus's files."

Richard looks to Sam. "We need to stop these guys, Sam. I know it's more important for you to get Amy back, and we're prepared to do that, to make that our first priority, if you will help us. But we must have your help; you have to guarantee it—we need those files. And we need your help, Sam. No one knew Rufus better than you, and no one knows Aga better than you and me. If we help you get Amy back, safe, will you agree to turn over the files, all of them, to us?"

Without hesitation Sam stands. "Agreed! Let's go, Marine."

Richard smiles, laughs. "You don't mind if I don't salute, do you, gunny?"

Sam also smiles, for the first time since meeting Richard in the hallway. "No, as long as we get Amy back safe, your ass is safe with me."

Both Sam and Richard stop smiling. Unaware of the actual tension between Sam and Richard, Roger smiles. "Okay, let's go to Chicago," Roger says.

They shake hands. Richard tells them he will ride to the airport with them; their plane is waiting.

Chapter Forty

Sam, Roger, and Richard board a Lear jet at the private FBO located in Austin-Bergstrom airport. Sam carries a black duffel bag and a large briefcase that he holds close and places under his seat. Roger carries a small gym bag and two boxes of files, wrapped completely in duct tape that Sam has given him, which he places on the open seat directly across from him. Richard carries only a small, hard-shell suitcase.

The small aircraft has only four passenger seats. Richard has appropriated the front-facing window seat on the right, forcing Roger and Sam into the two rear-facing seats, with Sam electing to seat himself directly across from and facing Richard, as Roger has commanded the extra aisle seat for the files.

The pilot approaches and speaks directly to Richard. "So, sir. There will be only two guests flying with you this evening?"

"That's affirmative, captain," Richard responds, in a crisp military manner, and immediately follows it with "What is our expected ETA, captain?"

"That would be 23:20 hours local time, sir," the pilot responds and then follows with "There are storms we will need to finesse our way around, sir, but I don't anticipate our arrival will be delayed."

Sam notices that the pilot, though obviously military, wears airline clothing, and he is curious of the pilot's specific use of language and the military manner with which he speaks. He thinks both are odd, off-putting, and make him uncomfortable with his back to the front cabin.

The pilot semipivots and quickly reenters the cockpit, taking the extra baggage with him. He tries to take the file boxes but Sam tells him no. The pilot says something to the copilot that neither Sam nor Roger are able to discern. Roger shakes his head in frustration, indicating to Sam he can't make out any of the conversation, as Richard looks out the small circular window.

Sam can hear both the pilot and copilot buckle up and begin communicating through their headsets.

As the plane taxis the runway, all three men buckle their seatbelts in anticipation of takeoff, and Sam notices a file labeled "NSA TOP PRIORITY" close to Richard in the seat pocket just below the plane's window.

A moment later the plane climbs at 45 degrees vertical for several minutes, then levels off. Roger sits, nervously exhausted from a combination of the steep takeoff, his seat facing toward the rear of the plane and a lack of sleep. Not a good mixture under the circumstances, he thinks.

"Coffee?" Richard asks, attempting to cover for his discomforting and disarming feeling, which is the result of Sam's ability to read him, and which Richard knows Sam is well aware of. Both Sam and Roger accept Richard's offer of the hot beverage.

Richard rings for service using a buzzer alongside his right armrest and, moments later, the copilot arrives. "Three coffees," Richard orders the copilot, who, after taking the order, begins a fresh pot of coffee in the galley between the cockpit and the seats.

For several minutes the three men sit quietly, until the coffee is served. Sam keeps his eyes diverted from the file under the window, but Roger cannot keep his eyes off it.

As the copilot serves black coffee, assuming none of the three men desire cream or sugar, Richard offers something extra. "You want a shot or two in that, either of you?" he asks. But both Sam and Roger decline, and Richard waves the copilot off, saying to Sam, "I thought a shot or two would be right up your alley, professor." Sam ignores Richard's comment and blankly stares out the window, hoping Richard is unable to notice his exhaustion.

Moments later, Sam turns to directly face Richard while sipping his coffee, then confronts him about his game plan. "How is this going to go down, Richard? You want to fill us in on your plan?"

Richard smiles in a relaxed and comfortable manner, as if filling the two men in on his plan was exactly what he had in mind. "We're going to meet up with our Chicago team when we land," he explains. "I phoned them earlier, back at the gas station, and they will give me a full briefing upon landing. The good news is we will have the element of surprise. We know our Arab friends' possible locations, of which there are very likely only two."

"Do you know where Amy is?" Roger demands in the guise of a polite question.

Richard shakes his head to indicate the negative, then responds, "No, not yet. But we have a good idea. The Kuwaiti group has used the same safe house for the past two years. The only other possible option, we think, is a mosque, which they use as their headquarters."

Sam seems disturbed by this information, saying, "Headquarters I understand, but one safe house doesn't sound right, Richard. No professional group would make the mistake of only having one safe house."

Richard agrees with Sam. "I know, Sam. It doesn't make sense. These guys are more or less your typical garden-variety terrorist types, so they are not that well trained. And a bigger problem for us right now is the FBI, my team tells me. They seem to be much more than a little upset with you, Sam. You sent a couple of their own to the hospital. Don't underestimate them, Sam. They are formidable, good men who, when they put their minds to it, can get the job done. We need to know their plans by the time we land in Chicago to avoid a direct conflict."

"If they are so pissed, how will this happen?" Sam asks.

Richard answers in a matter-of-fact manner and with a compelling tone in his voice. "Because we have a mole in their camp and we should know their plans regarding Amy by the time we land. And," he casually and comfortably continues, "because we bug their phones."

Roger cannot believe what he has just heard, and immediately questions Richard, unable to suppress his disbelief, "Did you say that you bug the FBI?" Richard nods in the affirmative, but Roger is still unable to believe what he has heard. He is also frustrated, noticing that Sam isn't curious and has readily accepted Richard's revelation as fact. So Roger leans back, deciding to accept that what he has heard must be standard operating procedure for the NSA.

Sam seems satisfied for the moment with the news about Amy, but Roger cannot resist asking another question. "So, you guys spy on one another?"

Both Richard and Sam laugh, unable to resist.

"The NSA," Richard explains, "spies on everybody: CIA, FBI, individuals, important people, celebrities, nobodies, anybody, everybody! For good reasons and for no reason at all."

Still curious, Roger asks, "I thought the NSA could only spy outside the US?"

"No," Richard answers, "the CIA is supposed to be restricted to outside the US, but the NSA can go anywhere, everywhere." After a brief pause, Richard continues, "The wild card in this is the Black Panthers. My guess is that, given they are in bed with the Arabs at this point, they will know about the documents and the potential power they offer. These documents are truly a get-out-of-jail-free card that can guarantee, no matter what they do, they will not be prosecuted."

Roger stays on subject, asking Richard, "So what exactly is at stake here? Why were they so desperate that they would kidnap Amy?"

"At stake," Richard responds to Roger's insistent questioning, "is control of the United States government. It's that big. The Kuwaiti's care about controlling our foreign policy, especially in regard to energy, and even more especially given their direct link to Moscow. The leverage Moscow could gain here is incredible, incredibly bad for the US. The Russians would have unopposed leverage over our government's leaders, which would open the door for all sorts of side deals and likely ramp up their covert spying operation. And to round out the opposition, the Black Panthers stand to gain control of our government's domestic political agenda, with, as I mentioned, complete immunity, and perhaps opening the door to get some of their own people out of jail and into power positions in the government. And the wild card in this is the FBI, which is either motivated by protection of our government or by a particular individual's attempt to gain power and control of the political system. It could be either. It is more than likely both."

Richard's description reminds Roger of the dialogue for Abbot and Costello's baseball routine, specifically trying to sort out "Who's on first?" But, not wanting to add a comic element or make light of the situation, Roger asks, in regard to Richard's FBI explanation, "What, what type of individual?"

"My sense," Sam comments, looking directly and with a hint of frustration at Richard, "about the FBI is that the individual you're talking about is not Civiletti, the attorney general, nor is this linked directly to Carter. Carter is too loyal to the country. He is a patriot, misguided and inept as he may be."

Richard smiles and nods in agreement. "Yes," he says, "I believe Carter is loyal, as is his AG. But wouldn't a leader who really cares about his country protect it by making sure these papers never see the light of day? There is just too much at stake here, Sam. And none of these guys, agencies, are willing, or can afford to lose any power, or give up any power to another agency or, God forbid, to a foreign government. So what we have here, gentlemen, in that big wad of duct tape Roger keeps so close to his side, is what they all want most in all the world, access to true power. The power to control political agendas, both domestic and international, for the coming generations."

Richard pauses, glances at Roger but looks Sam straight in the eye, declaring, "And it's not just these groups we're worried about, Sam. There are some individuals, big players that could also be involved. Yes, there is potentially world-changing power in these documents. The type some people would do anything to get their hands on. There are billionaire naive big boys and very organized, disciplined nut jobs who believe they should be the new dictator on the block. The bottom line is we need to know who is pulling the strings behind all of this. My guess is that it more than likely involves multiple, very highly interested and invested factions."

Sam sips his coffee and reflects on Richard's insight, saying, "You're right, we're between a rock and a hard place. There is no safe haven, or so it would seem. People since the end of WWII have decided to get power by any means necessary, and now that that door has been opened, now that they've gotten away with keeping our people as hostages in Iran, everybody's going to get in on the new game in town."

"It's a mistake we will all pay for," Richard reflects, "for years and years to come. Once our enemies know we are weak and not committed to protecting ourselves, they will continue to threaten and attack our way of life, and our people, whenever and wherever they can."

Sam looks out the window, pondering the future Richard has laid out. Richard allows Sam a few moments to reflect on the scenario he has described, then continues, "And Iran is the first installment that sets the world stage for this international cluster fuck."

Too frustrated to sit silently by any longer, Roger unbuckles his seatbelt and stands, brushing his head against the ceiling of the small jet, and expresses his sole concern, "Let's just focus on Amy, okay? We need to focus on the most important issue at hand here, and that's Amy! Getting her back, that's why we're here, right, Sam?"

Sam smiles. "Yes, you're right, Roger. They took Amy because they knew it was the one card they could play and that I would have to respond to. So let's focus on Amy, getting her back. We'll deal with the rest of this shit later, or you will, Richard."

"Semper Fi, Marine," Richard comments back to Sam.

All three men gaze out the windows of the plane, occasionally observing brilliant groupings of lights below as they pass over seemingly endless miles of Texas landscape. Richard pulls out the NSA file from the window pocket and begins reading.

A little over ninety minutes later the plane begins its approach into Chicago. Looking up from the file on his lap, Richard carefully examines Sam and questions him, "Before we deal with this crap, I'm curious about a question that was on our doctoral exam." Richard cannot help but break a smile and continues, "Just out of curiosity, Sam, and as it appears that my academic career has come to an end, share with me your scholarly view, sincerely, what do you think will be the long-term outcome or implication of our country having stopped the draft?"

Sam is only too happy to enjoy the return of his academic authority as Richard and Roger's professor, at least for the moment, and offers a historical framing, "Your answer on the exam was by far the best of the three, Richard. Bottom line, Nixon walked right into the Vietnam trap, following Kennedy's and LBJ's lead, didn't learn a thing from their failures, or didn't want to learn anything. He did it with the same reasoning as dropping us from the gold standard, political expedience followed by what his dumb shit advisors fed him."

At that moment, the plane touches down.

"What Vietnam trap?" Roger asks.

Richard concedes to Sam for a response to Roger, and Sam jumps on it. "Nixon had to stop the draft because of the almost unanimous discontent with the war. But he didn't foresee what stopping the war and, subsequently, the draft, would do. Same as gold and the dollar."

Anxious to respond and append to Sam's perspective, Richard explains, "On the exam I answered that there were basically four benefits of the draft which were negated by stopping it. First, getting the poor, white and black, out of their dead-end ghetto surroundings, essentially giving them a chance to change their destiny. Second, military experience, at the very least, taught personal discipline, respect, logic, and for many a first chance for good health care. And third, to create a foundation for all, the military gave all the opportunity to finish their high school education, and maybe even further their education later. It offered a way out of the ghetto and poverty, and military experience offered a better future for all, potentially, anyway. And fourth, maybe most importantly, going into the service broke down racial stereotypes. Having to work on the same team with those of different color, ethnic background, and religions created an acceptance and understanding that our country's founders originally had in mind. We are all one nation."

Sam agrees with Richard's conclusions, adding, "Vietnam, as dumb as it was, was the first war we ever fought where all men were treated equally, at least more equally than ever before," Sam reflects.

Roger appears excited from this new insight and adds, "I can't imagine getting drafted, having to serve, being forced to serve. Really, that's a real load. But I think I finally understand the question. What became the most important implication of the war? It was teaching all our young men and women the history of the US, the true cost many others paid for our freedoms, and the opportunity that could be available to all."

Richard looks at Sam as mild shock registers on his face. Sam then turns, looks at Roger, and nods in agreement. "Go on, carry that thought out, Roger."

Smiling widely, Roger continues, "The real difference is the value system that they left the military with, an understanding, a belief that country was more important than self. That it is worth fighting for! I didn't understand this when I first read Rufus's files. But, by getting rid of the draft, the country, on a long-term basis, will take second place to self, setting the stage for a self-oriented culture, which leads to dependency."

Sam and Richard exchange looks with more than a bit of amazement as they prepare to exit the plane. Roger seems incapable of containing himself from his newfound intellectual accomplishment of understanding how, for perhaps the first time, to connect the implication dots.

Sam, picking up his duffel bag and briefcase, turns back to Roger and says, "Bring those boxes along, Roger. Your education could actually be starting to pay off."

Chapter Forty-One

The Lear lands at Meigs Field with Lake Michigan directly on their right and the Chicago skyline to the west and north. The plane comes straight in from the south and west, banking to the left to head due north as the runway is in sight. Roger's first sight of his inaugural visit to Chicago is the dramatic skyline, whose bright lights are mirrored in the waters of Lake Michigan.

It is near midnight as a black Chevrolet Suburban pulls up alongside the plane and the three men exit. Richard turns to Sam. "Are these boxes Roger is carrying the only ones Sam?"

Sam laughs at Richard's awkward question. "Maybe, Richard. Could be." Sam smiles and continues, "Actually, those are the only two, one has the Great Society docs and the other the covert ops docs." Richard is satisfied with Sam's point blank response.

The three men get in the black Chevy Suburban, putting their luggage in the back door, but Roger keeps the boxes of files next to him on the floor. There are front and back facing seats behind the front seat in the limo-like Suburban. Richard sits across from Sam and Roger, while another agent sits next to Richard; two other agents sit in the front seat. All three agents are identically dressed, all in black pants, shirts, and sport coats. The Suburban pulls up to the airport security gate and is waved through.

The agent sitting next to Richard hands him a file. Richard speed-reads the first page without looking up. Sam notices the cover reads, "TOP SECRET."

"Neither of you have ever suspected Aga?" Richard asks, still not looking up from the paper he has been reading. "You never noticed anything about him that seemed odd, out of place? Perhaps, maybe he was a little too self-serving?"

Roger quickly replies, "No. Not really. I thought you were his best friend. We all thought so. You sure did a lot of work for him, research . . . at the library."

Richard smiles. "Sure. Keep your friends close, and your enemies closer. Right?"

Sam momentarily considers Richard's response, seems to dismiss it as insincere and evasive, and questions him, "What are you really looking for, Richard?"

Richard again looks up from the paper, determining that Sam has not been put off by his evasion and responds, "It's just odd, isn't it, Sam? Aga is all about power. Power of the ruling class, his class, his family. About how to extend their reach, their base. It's well known the Kuwaitis, and Middle Easterners as a whole, are most like Nazis in their hatred of non-true-believer groups, like Jews, for example, and Christians, and blacks. They're prejudiced, yet they expediently elect to work with a black terrorist group in Chicago?"

Sam wastes no time responding, "The enemy of my enemy, Richard. Besides, I'll admit that Aga kept a pretty low profile, except of course for his high-rolling accoutrements."

Roger understands Sam's reference to "high rolling," but can only guess about the definition and meaning of accoutrements.

"Yeah," Richard replies, "Aga appreciates nice things, enjoys the life here, and his backers are patient, their horizon long-term, like the Chinese. Twenty- to fifty-year agendas are no big deal to them."

Sam smiles. "Sounds like you boys are following a lot of Aga types around the country, Richard?"

Richard answers directly, surprising Sam. "We are, yes, all over the world in fact. And these groups of Arabs believe in religious superiority, domination, power. And they're happy to martyr themselves for it, Sam. Long term, they may be an even bigger threat than the Russians."

"Maybe," Sam replies, "but, well, I think Aga liked it here. Hell, I believe he came to like it too much to want to give it up. He lived a damn good lifestyle. Being here was definitely growing on him, Richard."

Richard seems pleased with Sam's assessment of Aga, commenting, "Well, yeah, he did like it here, but think about the power, personal status, and female sex slaves, young and mature, he could have back home. He often expressed that was the real virtue of being a royal Muslim, or just being a Muslim for that matter, that women are nothing more than slaves in his country. Hell, he didn't do so well here, wasn't very good with the ladies. He had to buy sex here."

Sam realizes he has not been reading the Aga situation accurately.

"Regardless of Aga," Richard goes on, "the people calling the shots, no matter who they are, have a power goal for themselves that will result in a dark future for our country. They have a well-thought-out plan, and the stakes are very high. It is virtually control of our country, in many different ways, that is at stake here."

After a short drive, the Suburban pulls up to a South Loop all-night diner, filled with mainly young people eating large meals to ward off that evening's alcohol consumption. Richard, two of his cohorts, and Sam and Roger seat themselves at a table. Richard pulls a menu from behind the condiments gathered in the center of the table, making clear to Sam that he is familiar with this particular restaurant and its location in the city. Roger sits next to Sam, clinging to the files, placing them on the floor between his feet, growing increasingly nervous as the protector.

"Why didn't your other guy, the driver, come in with us?" Roger questions Richard.

"He's staying with the car," Richard responds, with a hint of sarcasm in his voice and a smile escaping his lips. "This is Chicago, after all."

Richard hands the menu to Roger, who accepts it with one hand, the other keeping a tight lock on the box.

"Okay, Richard," Sam demands, "We need to hear the game plan."

Richard glances at his agents, as if signaling them not to respond to any questions. "The game plan," Richard says, "is Amy! Just Amy as far as you need to be concerned."

The agent sitting next to Richard fixes his gaze upon Sam, adding, "You boys really created quite a mess when you discovered those files in Austin."

Richard elbows the agent, saying in a commanding voice, "Pay attention, dick head! Just give us the latest info you have on Amy."

In an attempt to save his fellow agent embarrassment, the second agent speaks directly to Sam, "We can clean this up quite easily, Dr. Brown." Having not been introduced, Sam is mildly impressed that the agent knew his name and title.

Richard shoots a sordid, silencing look at the second agent, knowing where the agent's comment is headed, insisting with his glare that the agent had better learn to hold his opinion and learn to listen. And thus Richard begins to outline the plan for them all, explaining, "We are here, first of all, to get Sam's granddaughter, Amy, safely back from the bad guys. That's our mission as far as anyone here is concerned! The files Sam has, that he is willing to trade for our assistance in recovering Amy, are secondary."

Richard allows his words to sink in, then adds, "As you know, these are the same files formerly controlled by Dr. Rufus MacIntosh, the same files that all of our work has been pointed toward for the past several years. Do I need to make this any clearer to you, gentlemen?"

Richard's obvious exclusion of Roger in reference to the files does not escape Roger or Sam, and both of Richard's agents express themselves to him with nonverbal cues, making it clear they understand Richard's directive in regard to the importance of the papers as well as doing what he commands, no commentary required. Also communicated is the fact that Roger was expendable to the mission, if necessary, while Sam is the key and necessary asset. They both question why Richard just doesn't take the files, but realize he must have a good reason.

Roger assesses the situation, understanding Richard's plan, appreciating that both agents are in top physical condition and carry hidden weapons, which they have made little or no attempt to hide. It is clear that they are there to do business, to accomplish the mission they have been assigned, with Richard clearly in charge. It is also clear that after the files are recovered, all others are expendable, collateral damage, so to speak. Amy is important only as an asset to trade for the files.

For the first time since their arrival in Chicago, Sam shows the effect of his exhaustion, frustration, and age, but expresses clearly to Richard, "I am aware of your real priorities, Richard."

Richard shows anger and true feelings for the first time since their arrival in Chicago, unable to hide them from Sam, just as the waitress arrives to take their orders. Sam waves her off, gesturing that they need more time before ordering.

"Just coffee for now," Sam tells the waitress.

Sam, defusing the situation with Richard, leans across the table to speak directly to the second agent, "Careful with the waitress. You screwed up when you leaned forward and she saw your gun."

The agent grabs at his belt and pulls his jacket across to cover. Sam smiles and looks at Richard, as Richard shakes his head in frustration.

"I wasn't certain who you boys were really working for, but I had pretty much ascertained you were bottom-feeding NSA scumbags even before you screwed up showing off your hardware," Sam tells them, with more than a hint of sarcasm in his tone.

Realizing there is nothing he can do at this point, Richard turns in the direction of the waitress, who is now behind the counter, and orders five cheeseburgers, and points to the coffees indicating refills are already needed.

Frustrated by Sam's maneuver, the second agent takes another shot at Sam with "Why did you ever let your granddaughter out of your sight once you knew the shit had hit the fan? You must have known she was the only real bargaining chip available to them?"

Sam responds with a look of coldness, a deep anger and frustration, mixed with determination that neither Richard nor Roger had ever previously witnessed.

There is a silence, then Richard jumps in before any action can result.

"Lighten up," he says. "This Marine has killed a shitload more scumbags than you two have, or probably ever will. I just read part of his record, about his involvement in a Shanghai expedition 50 years ago."

The first agent jumps back into the conversation saying, "You guys have unleashed a shit storm with groups across the country, but especially here in Chicago. You do realize it could be pretty messy here?"

Richard turns to Sam and follows with "I'm assuming there are other files, other copies than the ones Roger has?"

Sam smiles and avoids a direct response. "Of course, Richard, there are other files, but the ones here are key, the others are pretty meaningless stuff."

Richard sits forward at the table, "I'm asking, Sam, are there multiple copies of these key files?"

Sam keeps smiling and tells Richard what he believes he needs to hear. "Well, of course. And when I get Amy back, I'll let you know where all of them are, where all of them are located and how to get them."

The other agents wait for Richard to respond, but seeing that Richard appears satisfied with Sam's answer, they decide for the moment not to question Sam further.

Sam, seeing he has passed scrutiny with his response says, "Listen, I don't really give a rat's ass about you, the NSA, any of your programs, or the files. My only concern is Amy. Is she unharmed?"

Richard looks at his agents and the one nearest him responds, "We believe we now know where she is being held and where Aga is. We think your granddaughter is okay at this point, as of now. They can't risk harming her and losing their leverage to get the files. They got you on strange turf here in Chicago and think they have home court advantage."

Richard looks at his watch, wanting to change the subject, saying, "The flight they scheduled for Sam is supposed to land at Midway in about 10 hours. Upon arriving he would be taken to the Palmer House, where he would be contacted to set up a trade. That gives us a few precious hours before they realize we are on to them."

Sam asks, "And, am I on the plane?"

As Roger tries to sort out the meaning of the question, Richard answers, "Yes, you are on the plane, at least the best I could do for a doppelganger for you on such short notice."

Roger shows his relief, believing he now understands the reference to Sam's having been on the plane.

Sam sits up as if to emphasize the importance of his next question: "If these terrorist spies value the information in the files so highly that they would kidnap and ransom my granddaughter, then we both know that they don't plan on leaving anyone alive who has read the files or who could tell the story."

"That's right," Richard comments, "they want the information to gain control over our country's leaders and you and Amy are just collateral damage to them. They all have one true goal, one purpose."

The waitress arrives and finally delivers more coffee along with the cheeseburgers. Sam sips his coffee and gets back to basics, asking, "Now, Richard. Explain to me, who and where are your local assets? Is this it?"

Richard no longer hesitates in answering Sam's question. "This is all we need. We're all Marines, Sam, and all now work for the NSA. Our job is to resolve situations by whatever means necessary. This time it's Kuwaiti foreign agents enlisting the support of Chicago South Side black militants, masquerading as community organizers, leaders; they are our target here in the Windy City. Our mission has been to establish connection, identify their leaders, monitor them, and to minimize them when necessary. My work in Austin these past several years was to connect with Aga and follow him, learn his plans and to identify the leaders in Chicago and to learn whatever I could about Rufus and his papers."

Sam looks at Richard and his agents. "Explain the game plan for tonight."

"First," Richard explains, "is to get Amy back. You hold the cards, Sam; I need to know you believe that."

Richard waits for a moment, until Sam finally nods agreement.

"Second," Richard continues, "we will deal with Aga and his friends. Their party has gone on long enough. Third, we will execute our plan on all involved with extreme prejudice, and this extermination plan has been enthusiastically endorsed, off the record of course, by the big boys in Washington. This is, remember, the NSA."

None of them have touched their food as Richard waves for the check. Their experience tells the agents it's not good to begin an op with a full stomach. Richard drops enough money to cover the bill with a generous tip on the table, and they all head for the door. Roger starts with them, then turns back, grabs his cheeseburger and rushes to catch up. As he reaches Sam, he whispers, "So, Sam, what do you think he meant by 'all involved with extreme prejudice?'"

Sam smiles and whispers back, "Roger, my boy, you may just come out of this with a doctoral degree in survival."

Chapter Forty-Two

Inside the Suburban, two of Richard's agents begin opening large bags, removing weapons, ammunition, night-vision goggles, vests, communication headsets. Sam and Roger watch as the men unload their cargo, anxious to learn the next step of the mission.

Richard is focused as he prepares his weapon. "We're going to visit the boys soon," he says, passing a small bag to Roger. "There is an automatic weapon in this bag, Roger. Get it out and get familiar with it. It's your new best friend, your sweetheart for this evening, as I believe you are about to be called into an active military op."

Roger holds the military commando submachine gun in his right hand. It is equipped with a silencer and night scope, neither of which he has had any experience with. Roger is obviously unfamiliar and not comfortable with the weapon, but also appears to enjoy having the opportunity to handle it. Richard shows him quickly and with little explanation how the parts fit together and function.

Turning his attention to Sam, Richard explains, "There's another one in here for you, Sam."

Sam refuses a weapon when Richard attempts to hand it to him. Holding a .45 army-issue Colt in his right hand, Sam raises it in the air and explains to Richard, "My old 1911 is all I've ever needed or required for this kind of work over the past 50 years. So, thanks, but no thanks."

Richard smiles but is not amused. "You do realize, Sam, our friends will have automatic weapons, more firepower than you'll be able to return. And it's likely gonna get a bit noisy."

Sam laughs. "Shit, Richard. This is Chicago, right? You really think the sound of gunfire is going to wake anybody up on the South Side? They hear gunfire here on a regular basis."

Richard turns his attention back to Roger and begins showing him the intricacies of his weapon and equipment. "This is a lot to learn in a small amount of time," Richard explains, as he verbally reviews the functionality of the machine pistol, making sure Roger comprehends, and in a systematic step-by-step manner that is militaristic in its specific details. Following each step, Richard questions Roger to see if he understands.

Roger monitors the agents as they begin taping extra ammo clips to the handles of their weapons, and he follows suit.

Sam pulls a helmet and night goggles off Roger's head and commands him to listen carefully. "You won't need this head set, but I want you to listen to me, Roger. It will make the difference in saving Amy and you walking out alive, or neither of you walking out alive. There won't be time for you to think when things light up where we're going, once we're on the inside. This isn't a bullshit PhD prep course. There is no deep thinking on this problem. You're just going to have to act, act first, act with extreme malice, before the other guy. When we go in, you shoot anybody and everybody you see. So don't hesitate! If you hesitate, I promise you, Roger, the bad guys won't, and you'll be dead."

Roger seems perplexed and worried. "But, Sam," he asks, "what about Amy?"

"Amy won't be anywhere near the action, or the entry point. So don't worry about her. She'll be in a back room or basement. You can worry about her after the shooting stops. You got that, Roger? You understand?"

The tension appears to leave Roger's face as he listens to Sam's instructions. He becomes suddenly confident, comfortable, not believing himself some great overnight commando, but with the realization that he will do what is necessary, that he will gladly give his life to save Amy's.

Sam recognizes the calm that has overcome Roger and smiles, patting Roger on the shoulder, and whispering, "This is a test, Roger, to see if you're ready to take care of Amy. And I think you'll do just fine." Roger smiles, knowing he has finally gained Sam's trust.

Minutes later the Suburban pulls to a stop, letting them all out, with the exception of one agent who stays with the van.

Sam and Roger step out of the van and walk side by side down an alley, following the path laid out for them by Richard from the map of the area. They approach a house where Richard has assured them Amy is being held. It is a small, World War II–vintage bungalow, with an attached carport on the left.

As they approach the house from the street, Sam signals Roger to follow him, slightly behind and to Sam's left. Sam carries his .45 in his right hand but they stop and watch from the sidewalk as Richard and one of his agents go in the front entrance to the home, kicking it in, just as two other agents enter the rear of the home. Their entry is simultaneous, perfectly planned and timed and Sam is impressed as muffled gunfire can be heard.

Moments later Sam and Roger also enter the home, guns drawn, and search room to room, including the basement, but, to their dismay, Amy is not there.

Sam turns to Richard and, in a mocking and scolding tone, asks, "Nice intel, Richard. So where's Amy?"

Richard takes the headset off to respond to Sam. "We had to start here to make sure. According to our headquarters, the safe house was the most likely of the two places. So Aga has to be at the mosque. It's just down the street a mile and a half. So let's go there and have a talk with our boy. I assure you, if she is not there, he will know where Amy is. And I'd like to see my employer's face when he sees his library lackey hold a gun on him."

As they leave, the NSA agents set timed charges. And as they leave, passing the home in their Suburban, the house erupts in a nearly silent ball of fire. While there seemed little or no sound, there was a concussion that made the Suburban lean and they could feel the heat as the bombs exploded.

Richard turns from his seat in the front of the Suburban to inform Sam and Roger, "Sorry, gentlemen. Just another Commonwealth Edison gas leak on Chicago's South Side."

The other NSA agents chuckle at their leader's humorous description of a ruse they have often employed in Chicago. It's one of the perks of being in the NSA.

Chapter Forty-Three

Ten minutes later, the men sit in their Suburban across the street and a block away from a mosque on Chicago's far South Side, studying the situation. "This mosque," Richard explains, "is their major headquarters for Chicago. Aga usually heads here when he's in town, with a few of his cohorts. But we had to check the safe house first to know for sure, and it was easier to deal with this location if they had all been there. The mosque is a bit dicier."

Once they are out of the vehicle and in position, Richard employs hand signals to direct his agents to the front and back of the mosque. He signals for Sam and Roger to remain back, and Sam follows Richard's instruction, having gained confidence in his ability from the previous house incursion.

As Richard and his agents enter the mosque, Sam and Roger once again hear the sound of silencers and muffled gunfire.

Sam and Roger carefully enter the mosque minutes later and view several Arabs in robes and headscarves around their necks lying dead on the floor. The agents also have several other Arabs in custody and sitting in chairs with their hands tied behind their backs.

Sitting on a chair in the kitchen, also with his hands tied behind his back and a gag in his mouth, is Aga.

Aga looks up just as Sam and Roger enter the room. His eyes widen in shock as he first views Richard. Aga then wets himself when Sam points his .45 between his eyes and removes the gag in Aga's mouth.

"Richard? Thank Allah. These men, they captured me and Amy. They . . ."

Cutting off Aga's incessant mumbling, Richard asks him, "Jig's up, Aga! Now tell me, where is Amy? Tell me now, while you still breathe."

Panicked, bordering on mental collapse from fear, realizing the real threat to him is Sam, Aga begs, "Richard,

Richard you must keep him away from me. Please. Please, Richard."

The NSA agents begin removing the dead and wounded from the room, taking them to the van, realizing they cannot explode a bomb in the mosque, even in the South Side of Chicago. Sam stands over Aga, as dead and wounded are carried by, and Sam looks down into Aga's eyes and tells him, "You are going to tell me where Amy is, Aga. And the quicker you tell me, the better and quicker your death will be. Believe me, you don't want to waste any of my time at this point."

From the other side of the room, a bound man on his knees scrapes his gag off against a countertop and immediately calls out to Aga in Arabic. One of the Arab-speaking agents turns to Richard. "He just called Aga 'brother.'"

Sam and Roger both hear the agent.

"Bring Aga's friend to me," Sam commands, with the corners of his mouth turned up in the beginning a smile.

Richard motions for his agents to comply with Sam's request and the agents drag the bound, bearded, crying Arab to his feet and pull him over to Sam as the man screams in terror, calling out to Aga over and over again.

Aga remains silent, ignoring the man's pleas as Sam forces the man into a chair in the corner of the room and ties his hands behind his back. To quiet the screams, Sam places a gag deep into the man's mouth, nearly choking him in the process. He then anchors the cloth gag in place, which requires circling the man's head with a scarf.

Having secured the gag, Sam pulls out a very large knife from a sheath on his belt and proceeds to cut away with one slice the man's pants and underwear, exposing his genitals. Standing over the man, Sam commands Aga to tell him where Amy can be found.

"Where is she, Aga? Where?" Sam screams.

Aga looks away, but Sam instructs Roger to hold Aga's head, forcing him to watch what is about to happen. Roger moves behind Aga and holds his head, forcing him to watch, as Sam, with no hesitation, without even looking down at the man but instead staring into Aga's eyes, slices off the man's testicles and penis, then throwing them in Aga's face.

The man's muffled screams can be heard outside, and agents rush inside to quiet him.

Moments later, with blood drenching Aga's pants, Richard cuts the screaming man's throat from behind, silencing him. Giving Aga a reasonable amount of time to assess what will likely happen next, Sam steps next to Aga and cuts away his piss-stained pants. Now with a smile on his face, Sam says to Aga, "I guess with no balls, Aga, the virgins you are soon to meet in the afterlife won't have much to worry about. Last chance to die without pain, Aga. Where is she?"

Aga begins screaming, crying, "All right, all right. She's at a warehouse at Cicero and 65th, near Midway Airport. I told you. Enough of this. She is there. Amy is fine. She is unharmed."

Sam looks to Richard, directing, "They have to bring her here. It's the only way we can be sure they won't just kill her. A warehouse is too big. If we break in over there they will have time to kill her. "

Understanding what has to be done, an agent hands a phone to Richard, who instructs Aga, "You will call and tell them the meeting has been changed till daybreak, and for them to bring the girl here. No questions, Aga. If you do it, and you help us make this happen, I will keep Sam away from you. I promise. You can save your own life, and your manhood. Do you understand me, Aga?"

Aga, unable to speak out of fear, shakes his head to indicate yes. He takes a moment to compose himself, which is difficult with Sam waving his knife in a slicing motion in front of him.

Richard hands the phone to the Arab-speaking agent, who puts it to Aga's ear. The agent speaks to Aga in Arabic with final instructions.

Sam moves inches from Aga's face, watching up close as tears of fear stream down Aga's cheeks, and in a whisper, Sam tells him, "You say one word out of line, Aga, one word, and I will immediately severe your best friends, one at a time. And we won't cut your throat, because we need your mouth to put your balls in!" Sam's smile leaves little doubt in Aga's mind that he will follow through with his threat.

When the call is answered, Aga speaks in Arabic, amazingly calm in his tone given the circumstances, and when the short conversation ends, the agent nods to Richard that the conversation went well.

"He did as he was told," the agent informs Richard. Then speaking in Arabic, the agent congratulates Aga.

Sam and Richard move away from Aga. "You know," Sam explains, this will turn messy before it's over. This bunch will be suspicious when they arrive. We are going to have to act quickly."

Richard makes no attempt to hide his frustration with Sam, confirming his leadership position by saying, "Look, Sam! I've given you a lot of slack thus far, but it ends now! This is our case, and Amy is going to have to be debriefed; she'll be in our custody for a time. That's just part of the plan, if it goes well when they get here."

Sam is angry, but holds his temper with Richard, rhetorically questioning, "Really? Debriefed? As planned? Whose plan is that, Richard?"

Richard is frustrated but knows he has to deal with Sam, keep him calm or eliminate him and Roger from the scene, which he knows would be difficult. Richard speaks in a level voice to Sam, "Look, Sam, we need you to assure us that we will have all the papers. That's the deal. We get you Amy, and we get them all, and I mean all of the boxes, papers, notes, whatever. I will do the best I can to clean up this mess. I'll get you and Roger back to Austin tonight and Amy in a few days."

Sam does not appear to be buying what Richard is selling, leading to his question, "You think we can go back, Richard? Are you serious? How are you going to protect us from the Arabs in the future, not to mention our own government?"

Sam walks back to Aga but Richard steps between them. Sam looks at Aga's wet, fear-puffed face and tells him, "If we get Amy back you will live, and you won't have to piss sitting down, like a woman. But fuck this up, and pissing will be the least of your worries!"

Richard steps away and begins speaking to his agents. Roger approaches Aga, pulls up a chair and sits, looking eye to eye with Aga. "Sam suggested you and I talk, Aga. So tell me, why? Why, Aga? Why?"

Aga laughs. "Oh, Roger. You would never understand, but Amy was never supposed to have become involved in this; that was just a last-minute necessity. We needed a bargaining chip once Sam got his hands on the papers."

"Did you harm her?" Roger asks.

"I did not. She was not harmed the last time I saw her. She never even knew that I was involved. She was drugged."

Roger picks up the bloody knife that Sam had used to carve up Aga's dead relative.

"Believe me, Aga. What Sam did to him will be mild compared to what I will do to you if she has come to any harm. Now, I want you to explain to me what this is all about. Why are you so interested in the papers? And speak slowly, Aga, as I know you don't believe I'm an intelligent man."

Aga responds in an attempt to control the situation. "It's about what it is always about, Roger. It's about power, how to get it and how to keep it. Don't you understand this after three years of graduate study? Shit, I knew more than you when I was eight years old."

Roger doesn't look away, but continues staring into Aga's eyes. "You know, Aga, I've gotten much smarter over the past few days. I know that your idea of power is one of a tyrant over the weak, of a bully over a small child. How does it feel to be about ready to be a soprano, if only for a few moments?"

"Richard promised me," Aga begs. "He said I would be free, unharmed if I helped get Amy back."

Roger smiles, looks at Sam and then back at Aga. "Yeah, Richard probably would, but I don't know about Sam."

Chapter Forty-Four

Sam, Roger, Richard, and his crew stand ready. They have cleared out any evidence of their earlier surprise mission. While Sam and Roger stand in the back of the large greeting area of the mosque, Richard and his agents are on both sides of the entry door, while Aga sits, handcuffed and gagged, in a chair just out of view.

The first signs of morning light are on the horizon as two men arrive in a car with Amy, who is tied and gagged in the backseat, with a cover over her head. They park near the front of the mosque, still in early-morning shadow, and walk toward the front entry.

Unavoidable telltale signs of their earlier action linger in the mosque, such as the harsh stench of bleach used to cover Kuwaiti blood and excrement on the floor. But for Sam, the most obvious smell of action cannot so easily be removed, never having left his senses and memory from his early days in the Marine Corps. He fearfully anticipates that the lingering smell of cordite in the air and filling his nostrils could give away the surprise aspect of their mission.

Amy's captors, one on each of her arms, walk her to the front of the mosque. Richard has anticipated multiple actions and has also posted one of his agents at both the rear and side entries. As her two captors reach the front, one of them remains holding her arm while the other opens the front door, steps in and calls out, "Aga, it's Mohammed."

The front door opens slowly, cautiously. Suddenly, simultaneous silenced gunfire, along with two unsilenced shots of a .45, takes out both of Amy's captors while other muffled shots can be heard on the side of the mosque where another two of Amy's kidnappers, apparently suspicious as to the change in plans, had attempted entry.

Moments later, one of Richard's agents arrives and advises him of having dispatched two other kidnappers.

Disregarding any potential danger, Roger rushes to Amy, who has fallen to the ground, as Richard's agents quickly pull the bodies of the two that had been dispatched by their multiple gunfire away from the entry and further into the mosque.

Roger scoops Amy into his arms and quickly carries her safely inside. Removing the cover from her head, he anxiously asks, "Amy! Amy, are you all right?"

Recognizing Roger as he unties her hands and removes the duct tape from her mouth, Amy laughs softly and begins to sob hysterically.

Before she can speak a word, Roger says to her, "Oh, baby, you are a sight for sore eyes, as beautiful as ever . . . and not a hint of makeup."

Amy breaks a smile, then laughs as Roger kisses her on the cheek, on her forehead and lips, and pulls her tightly to him.

Sam reaches down to Amy, pulls her to her feet, and they also embrace. Feeling safe in her grandfather's arms, she asks, "How did you find me, how did you know where they were taking me, to here, wherever the hell this is?"

Sam continues hugging his granddaughter, his eyes closed, his memory going back to the promise he had made to his dying daughter, temporarily halting Amy's ability to ask questions.

"Sam!" Richard explains, "Amy needs medical attention. We have prepared rooms for you at the Drake. So take her there. I'll send a doctor from Northwestern to attend to her. He's one of our guys, so it will go unnoticed. You don't have to worry." But Sam does worry as he notices a change in Richard's voice, a more militaristic character, sounding more like an order than the offer of help or a suggestion, and Sam's inner alarm continues as Richard completes his instructions to him with "But stay there, Sam. Stay there! You understand?"

Richard does not wait for Sam to respond but immediately turns and directs his agent to pull the Suburban to the front of the mosque, while another of their vehicles, which had been hidden and waiting a block away, is sent to the back of the mosque. Richard instructs them, sounding more like movie dialogue bravado than the command from an actual event, "Clean up the little mess we have created here this morning, boys."

Richard directs another of his men to give the Suburban keys to Sam, while telling him, "Take the Suburban, Sam. I'd better wait here until the local clean-up boys are done."

Sam shakes hands with Richard and in a relaxed, even, controlled voice, he smiles and says, "Okay, Richard. Just need a word with Aga, officially ending our professor-student relationship."

Thinking that Sam's anger has subsided, Richard agrees, answering, "Sure, just make it quick." Sam smiles, indicating he will do just that and signals for Roger to take Amy to the van.

Roger and Amy move toward the Suburban and out of hearing range as Sam reenters the room where Aga is still tied to the chair. Moments later a blood curdling scream fills the mosque. Sam walks out, cleaning blood off his hands, wiping it away with a towel, and explains to Richard as he passes, "Aga tried to escape. He came at me with a hidden weapon, can you believe it?"

Richard looks from where he and Sam stand back inside the mosque, as Aga's agonizing screams trail off and then disappear. One of Richard's agents gives him a hand-across-the-throat sign, indicating that Aga is dead.

"Any problem, Richard?" Sam asks.

Richard, knowing he can do nothing, as he is still desperate to recover the files Sam controls, smiles and with a touch of irony responds, "Are you kidding, Sam? But, Sam, you need to leave the files with me. I can't let you take them."

Roger walks up to Sam and Richard, holding the two file boxes under his left arm while Amy waits in the Suburban, with his .45 in his other hand.

"Like you instructed, Richard," Sam explains, with clear, early-morning light cascading over the rooftops, "we'll go to the Drake and get cleaned up. We'll get Amy some medical attention. But you need to make some more arrangements for us, besides the Drake."

"Like?" Richard asks Sam, frustration obvious in his tone.

"Like, we need new identities," Sam explains. "And money, and a new start in life. One million for each should do it, should help each of us begin our new lives. Hell, these papers," he continues, pointing to the boxes Roger holds, a smirk on his face, "are worth hundreds of millions, if not billions. And," Sam halts his explanation for effect, "you do need to make sure you have them all."

Richard is unsure what to do with the new wrinkle Sam has thrown him, one that he had been hoping could be avoided.

Sam continues, "I know it'll take you a little time to arrange that, so let's meet for a nice traditional afternoon tea in the Palm Court at the Drake later today, just to touch base, so you'll know we're cooperating, that we're still in town, that we have the files and a description to where the others are."

Richard realizes he cannot take the box forcibly, knowing it would expose him to repercussions that would follow post haste, and understanding that Sam likely has copies in other locations, and also understanding, as Sam had explained, that they will have to start new lives because their lives, at least the lives they have known are over. He also understood the true value of the files, as Sam had described. So, for Richard, the easiest way to solve his current problem was to appear to do as Sam wanted. And, understanding all this, Richard nods to Sam, smiling, appearing in a most sincere manner to accept Sam's terms, and following verbally with, "Will do, Sam. Will do!"

Sam and Roger walk to the Suburban to join Amy. Sam climbs into the driver's seat and after waiting for Roger to be settled in the front passenger seat hands Roger the files, Amy sits, smiling at them from the backseat, handling the events of the past

12 hours far better than Sam or Roger could ever have imagined, which causes them both to give her a simultaneous second look as she sits, smiling widely at the two of them, from her comfortable position in the backseat, a blanket wrapped around her.

Richard walks up just as they start to pull away, the sun breaking over the slums of the South Side. He hands Roger a duffel bag and his briefcase, which he passes to Amy in the backseat.

"Go straight to the Drake, Sam," Richard instructs. "Two rooms are ready for you in the name of R. M. MacIntosh. They won't ask for an ID." Richard pauses, then continues, "You know that you'll be followed, Sam, so don't take any detours. The doctor should ring your room in three or four hours. Get some rest. So I'll see you for a late brunch, or tea, this afternoon. Right?"

Sam starts the vehicle. "This afternoon," Sam responds to Richard, and adds, "Keep calm and stay strong."

Richard smiles a response to Sam's confidence, demeanor, and World War II English reference.

"You know you will all be safer in our hands, Sam," Richard tells him, as he places his hand on the open widow of the vehicle, stopping Sam from departing.

"Yeah, thanks for that, Richard," Sam responds, "but we'll feel safer just taking care of ourselves."

Richard reaches out his hand to Sam and they shake hands, sharing a little of Aga's blood spatter as they do so, and with Richard reflecting, "You know, Sam. We're not the bad guys."

Sam laughs as he releases Richard's hand. "Well, Richard, these Muslim pricks are bad guys, but it's not them I fear now. It's our own people, who share with our Middle East pals a ruthlessness, barbarous manifestation, driven by desire for power and control over other people and commodities. The difference is the Muslims do it but don't lie about their intentions. Our folks, on the other hand, will do it and lie to your face about their motives. I guess that's because we're supposed to be a democracy." Looking

Richard directly in the eye, Sam concludes, "Maybe you should keep your eye on our own government, Richard. So keep that in mind, will you, Marine?"

Inside the van, as they pull away, Sam and Roger share a glance, and Roger watches as Sam continues wiping blood from his hands and pants, reflecting on what Roger assumes to have just taken place with regard to Aga.

For the remainder of the trip downtown to the Drake, both Sam and Roger avoid any conversation or questioning in fear of frightening Amy. They had her back, safe and sound, and that's all that really mattered to either of them for the moment.

Traffic seems light as the sun rises to showcase Chicago's skyline against a clear blue morning sky and Sam navigates around the morning flow of commuters into the city.

As Roger reflects on what has happened, and his new found awareness of life's priorities, he enjoys the hard-won luxury of considering the next stage of his life, of his and Amy's lives, of their life together, he hopes. And perhaps, he can only dream, that all the baggage between them is gone. And that possibility brings the hint of a small smile to his face. But wait, he suddenly thinks, just take one step at a time. First, Amy needs a much-needed rest, then we must evaluate what direction we should go, individually or together. Hopefully, he prays, and God willing, Amy will want to be with him. And, hopefully, and God willing, Sam will allow that to happen.

Chapter Forty-Five

The Suburban arrives at the East Walton Place entrance of the Drake Hotel. Roger helps Amy out of the vehicle while Sam retrieves the files, briefcase, and small, black duffel bag, which conceals weapons.

Sam hands the bag and briefcase to Roger but maintains control of the files.

"Check in for us," Sam tells Roger. "And remember, the reservations are in Rufus's name. So pick up one key and go to the room and get some rest. I'll pick up my key at the desk later. The doctor should be here in a few hours," Sam instructs Roger.

Sam looks down the street toward the lake, then back toward Michigan Avenue as they begin to exit the Suburban at the Drake. "We were followed coming here. It was probably Richard's guys but we can't be sure, so be careful!" Sam warns Roger and Amy as they start walking into the building. "I'll park the truck and be up soon," he tells them and adds, "I need to pick up a few things from storage, drop something off, and make a few arrangements."

Both Roger and Amy are confused but confident that Sam has a plan. They continue into the hotel as Sam pulls away. He starts out driving the large SUV slowly but speeds up at the light and turns left even though the light has turned red, leaving several cars behind him and others honking their horns furiously, especially the cab drivers.

Once in their room, Roger and Amy fall, exhausted, onto the bed and both are asleep within a minute. Roger glances at the clock on the bedside an hour later and asks Amy, "Honey, are you asleep?" When she doesn't answer he allows his head to fall back on the pillow, but, only a moment later she tells him, apparently in a la-la land, "I want to go to the University of Chicago. I promised myself that the next time I was in Chicago I would go there. I want to see where Rufus and Saul Alinsky went to school, where they became friends, studied, worked, came up with their ideas." But as Amy's words trail off into a whisper, Roger tells her, "Honey, you have to sleep. Please, just rest now. Try to sleep."

Seemingly on a different wavelength than Roger, Amy continues, "I know. Yes, I know, but how could Rufus have gotten it all so wrong? How did he lose his way, develop such horrible and destructive tendencies? I believed so strongly in our policies, our programs. I have always been so proud to be progressive, liberal. But now, now that I discover, because of Rufus's papers, that all of it was a power grab, that evil men manipulated and tricked so many into believing them. Now what to believe?"

Amy's words finally fade into a mumble and Roger watches her sleep for a moment, then lays his head down and is again asleep within minutes.

Two hours later Roger awakens to a ringing phone. He answers it. It is Sam.

"Roger, listen carefully," Sam explains to a half-awake Roger. "Grab Amy now! Take the elevator to the second floor, then walk down the back staircase. You following this?"

Roger rubs his eyes, reaches over and shakes Amy.

"Yeah, yeah, I'm listening, Sam."

"Go to the door on the second floor that connects to the private Drake residences. Go all the way through to the East Lakeshore Drive entrance. If anyone tries to stop you, act sick, or, if you have to, use your weapon. Shoot 'em if you have to Roger, but get the hell out of there, and make sure you protect Amy. Now get out of there!"

For a moment, Roger tries to question Sam. "Sam, I . . ."

"No time!" Roger. "If you love Amy, if you want her to be safe and alive in the next 30 minutes, then do as I say!"

"Okay, Sam."

Sam provides Roger with a few more details to assure Roger of the necessity of getting out of the hotel immediately.

"Once you are outside," Sam explains, "walk east, toward the lake. I'll meet you as you walk but make sure you are not followed. Now, Roger, if I'm not there within a few minutes, grab a cab and go to Manny's Deli, it's on the South Side, just off Roosevelt Road and Jefferson. All cabbies know it."

Amy is awake and signals Roger that she wants to talk to her grandfather. Roger confirms for Sam that he understands his instructions, but adds, "Sam, Amy wants to talk to you. She just woke up. We went to sleep in our clothes. We didn't even take our shoes off we were so tired."

Sam cuts Roger off. "Not now, Roger! There are backup instructions in the duffel bag and $15,000 in cash I brought with me from Austin. Take the duffel bag and the briefcase. I will have someone meet you at Manny's if I can't make it there myself."

Roger is surprised when the phone abruptly goes dead. He turns to Amy, emphatically explaining, "We gotta go, Amy! Sam's orders, and there's no time to explain!"

Amy, groggy, in desperate need of sleep, realizes she needs to be alert, and asks, "Can I at least wash my face?"

"Honey, I'm sorry" Roger answers as he grabs the bags. "Sam's instructions were to get out of here now! I know you're exhausted, with all you've been through, but this is not the time for rest. We have to go, and we have to go now!" he adds, in a serious and rising voice Amy has never before heard.

Amy jumps to her feet, Roger grabs the bags, and they are out the door in less than a minute.

Chapter Forty-Six

Cars of people arriving and departing are backed up in front of the Drake Hotel. Well-dressed, happy people come and go, unaware of one another, caring only about their own personal comings and goings. It is a perfect fall morning in Chicago as the doorman opens the door of a limo for a couple arriving from the airport, their Louis Vuitton luggage being taken out of the trunk and piled on a cart for check-in. Another couple laugh, repeating lines they heard at Second City the night before, still awake after an all-night party, and now anxious to enjoy the Drake's famous brunch.

The doorman rushes about, accepting generous tips from each of the people he serves, but bumping into the anxious and frightened Roger and Amy as they make their escape from the hotel.

Amy and Roger exit the Drake residences and walk east toward Lake Michigan, Roger nervously looking over his shoulder as he supports an exhausted Amy, who holds tightly on to him around his waist.

As they nervously put distance between themselves and the hotel, they walk about two blocks when there are sudden flashes of light and the sound of automatic gunfire a block away. Roger immediately recognizes the sound of Sam's .45 and wonders if he should run toward the sound of gunfire to help Sam, or if he should run away to protect Amy.

As they flee, with Roger carrying the bags while attempting to support Amy, and with Amy running as well as she can but making it difficult for Roger, he says to her, "Amy, honey, you gotta pull it together. Hurry! I won't leave you. Sam made it clear, we gotta get away from here. And we do it together. Whatever happens, we stay together, and I'd rather be alive."

Amy smiles up at Roger, his words obviously providing her strength.

Suddenly, a black limousine pulls up beside them and brakes to a stop. Roger pulls his hand gun from the belt in his back, and he and Amy begin running away from the stopped limo, which quickly catches up to them, pulling ahead and stopping their escape.

The passenger window of the limo lowers in back and Roger steps in front of Amy to protect her, aiming his pistol at the open window.

"Sam!" Amy yells, and Roger lowers his weapon. Sam is seated in the back seat with an Uzi submachine pistol resting on his lap, his trusty .45 in his right hand.

Sam appears anxious, glancing quickly down the street behind them. "Get in! Get in!" Sam shouts as Roger and Amy jump into the back seat and the limo speeds away from the curb.

"Grandpa!" Amy says, hugging Sam, while he smiles, warmly and thankfully returning her hug, all the while keeping his eyes on the street behind them.

"Where are we going, Sam?" Roger asks. "I thought we were going to meet with Richard this afternoon?"

Shaking his head, Sam explains, "It was all just too easy. When Richard let me kill Aga and take the files, I realized how desperately they want all of the files, all the copies, before they reach any real deal with us. They won't do us harm until they have all the files, are confident they have all the copies. At the very least they want to know exactly how many copies there are, and where they are."

"So the hotel?" Roger questions Sam.

"Yeah, just a set-up," Sam explains. "They planned to let us get comfortable, fall asleep, then they would have separated us, questioned us, until they felt comfortable they had the information they needed in regard to the files. They were setting us up, but this time it was our own country's guys instead of another version of Aga's gang."

Amy sits up, wide awake for the first time since morning. "So Richard is behind all this?" she questions.

Sam continues glancing out the back window and down side streets at each intersection while attempting to answer her questions, "I don't know Richard's true involvement in all this, Amy. I'm not sure what his involvement really is. But he is definitely involved, and not in a good way as far as we're concerned, I'm afraid. He's got his orders, and who knows who is giving them."

Sam laughs. "Can't really differentiate the good guys from the bad guys it would seem."

"That's nothing new, is it?" Roger contributes.

Without looking away as he concentrates on what is going on around them, Sam responds to Roger's assessment. "Sadly, not since Vietnam, Roger. Since then the guys in black and the guys in white pretty much became one and the same."

"So Richard must be a bad guy?" Amy questions. But Sam hesitates, not wanting to worry her, realizing there was little sense in any longer keeping the truth from her.

"He helped us, Amy. I'll say that for him. He did help us."

Roger asks Sam about the gunfire they heard leaving the hotel.

"Yeah," Sam responds, "A government car had been following me, along with another car, Arabs I would guess. The Arabs must have been following the feds, or vice versa, but neither of them had any intel on where we were headed. My guess is the feds were FBI. I don't know for sure who it was, but when they slowed the feds down with that gunfire, it gave us the chance to slip away. I gave them something else to worry about, and at least one of their group was headed to the hospital."

As Roger digests this information, Sam adds, "I had this limo, and my old friend Rick waiting for me after I ditched their car. If needed, this was going to be our escape option."

Sam points to his friend, Rick, who is driving the limo. Rick appears about the same age as Sam, except with a few more wrinkles, likely due to the cigarette he had hanging out of his mouth. Rick, like Sam, also looks like someone capable of taking care of himself, at least when he was younger.

Sam pats Rick on the shoulder, adding, "Rick and I go way back. We served together in the Marines." The two men glance at one another, acknowledging their history.

Sam gives Amy a long look as she slides down into the comfortable limo seats and, only moments later, she is asleep.

"She's all in," Sam comments to Roger.

Sam leans forward and gives Rick directions, but Roger cannot make them out.

Minutes later Sam turns to Roger and instructs him to wake Amy. When she seems to be cognizant, Sam says, "You two have important decisions to make, and unfortunately, very little time to make them. I'm sorry, but that's just how it is. You're going to have to decide on your future, right now. Your lives as you knew them are over."

Amy sits up, now wide awake. She places her hand in Roger's, waiting for her grandfather to speak.

"We all know what an idiot I've been," Roger explains as he looks at Sam and then at Amy, and continues, "But that's done, over. I want a life with Amy, if she'll have me."

Amy smiles widely, leaving no need for a response on her part.

"Okay, good," Sam expresses himself, with a heart-felt smile. "I've spent a lifetime believing I made a positive difference in this world. But what I've learned is that my type of caring has been an emotional linchpin politicians use to sell themselves and their policies and, in my case, dependency abuse that is ruining America."

Sam looks again out the back window, then continues, "Their ends have nothing to do with genuine caring, sacrifice, and honest contributions many of my friends and colleagues have made. The fact is, we were manipulated. Those in charge were only concerned with their own personal gain, the power they could acquire and maintain. I hope the two of you can learn from an old man's lifetime of error and regret."

Sam, appearing physically and emotionally exhausted, looks to Amy, not knowing whether or not to continue.

Amy places her hand on Sam's shoulder, attempting to defend his many contributions. "But also, Grandpa, you had a life well spent and lived well, with honor and dignity and the respect for others that brought loyalty and integrity to your many, wonderful contributions. Your caring was used against you. Maybe that's the trait they look for in selecting their cohorts."

Sam smiles at his granddaughter, thinking how accurate her assessment was. He marvels at how beautiful she has become, even after a night with no sleep, and under terrible pressure and threats from horrible men. He promises himself he will make amends, God willing.

"Well," Sam responds to her compliments and diagnosis of the susceptibility shared by many others in the Democratic Party, "we're going to enter a new period now. It's going to be a different game, a game of 'Who do you trust?' And we're going to have to make up new rules as we go along."

Rick drives for several minutes, then pulls under an overpass on Hubbard between Wabash and State Street.

"Shaw's Crab House is a safe place for us," Rick explains as they pull up to the well-known restaurant. "The valet will let us keep the car out front, out of sight; we're covered by the streets above and the side streets that intersect, also making it easier for us to get away if we need to."

"Are they open?" Amy asks, looking into the restaurant through its revolving doors.

"They don't open until 11:30 a.m.," Rick explains. "But they know me, so they'll let you in. I'll step inside with you and then return to the car. I will sit out here with the engine running."

"Good," Sam responds. "We need more coffee, and some food."

"They'll bring a phone to the table for you," Rick tells Sam. "In fact, they'll bring as many phones as you ask for," he continues explaining, with an Irish tinge of humor in his voice.

"Good. Good," Sam responds.

Moments later they arrive, and Sam, Amy, and Roger follow Rick into the restaurant. Rick speaks briefly with the maître d', his shirt open and his jacket on a chair, and then returns to the limo.

Sam, Amy, and Roger are immediately seated at a table in the oyster bar, near the kitchen entrance and back door exit. They order coffee and sit, relaxing, for several minutes, enjoying the quiet, peaceful atmosphere.

"Okay," Sam begins, "time to create our retirement plan."

"What?" Roger questions, with a combination of curiosity and humor.

"Retirement," Sam continues. "Money! We're all going to be taking some government sponsored vacation time. And it requires money."

"So I assume you mean we're going into hiding?" Amy asks.

"Yes," Sam confirms, "for a time, a time."

"Are we talking years, Grandpa?"

Sam smiles at Amy, confirming her fears with a slight nod of his head, responding, "Yes honey, and with new identities."

Roger appears perplexed. "How the hell we gonna do that, Sam? I mean, we have no time, no connections to make something like that happen."

"We're going to play one against the other," Sam explains. "Richard and the NSA are going to give us new identities and guarantee to leave us alone. But we will have to disappear. The Arabs will not be so forgiving, especially as they won't be getting the papers they want so desperately, not to mention the untimely demise of two of the royal family."

A waiter brings a phone to the table.

"Rick asked me to bring this to you," the waiter explains, then turns and walks away.

"Who are you calling, Grandpa?"

Sam casually sips his coffee and answers, "Rick's son, Bobby. He will call Richard and the NSA, a contact for the Arabs, the FBI and, finally, my old friends at the DNC."

Amy comes back with "Can I ask you why, Grandpa?"

Sam smiles and casually explains, "Each of them are going to contribute a million dollars to our retirement funds. Nice of them, don't you think?"

"But why?" Amy questions.

"For the documents, Rufus's papers, honey. Those documents may save our lives and our country, my dear. They will expose the Democratic Party, which needs to be done. And each of our four contributing parties thinks they are receiving all the copies of the papers for their contribution and that they will have complete control of the information in those files." Amy is obviously concerned, upset, not convinced Sam is doing the right thing or that this will really work. "They'll be furious when they discover what you have done. We won't be able to hide from all of them."

Sam laughs. "If we have the money we have a good chance of staying hidden. I will make this work. My dear friends at the FBI and now the NSA hate one another, never share information and purposely try to mislead one another. The DNC, believe it or not, is the most secretive organization in Washington, and the Arabs have no one to talk to, except the Black Panthers, who really have little interest in developing any long-term relationship with them. So with enough money we can disappear from their radar."

Amy looks across the table to Sam and asks, "How will Bobby know who to contact for the Kuwaitis?"

Sam shoots her as sinister a smile as he is able.

Roger answers, "Sam suggested I have a little talk with Aga earlier this morning. He shared a contact name with me, his top contact here in Chicago."

Amy is confused. "I don't understand how this is going to work."

"Each party," Sam explains, "will transfer their share to a private numbered account on the Isle of Man, an account Rufus set up years ago for the party, but which we have never used. We kept our private retirement money in there, all of which were "nontaxable gifts," which have now become available for our private use. I was always curious why Rufus held back with us having this joint account. Now I know."

The waiter interrupts to serve them lunch and asks, "Can I get another drink for any of you?"

"I'll have a Schlitz," Sam says. "After all, I'm not calling anyone. Bobby is making all the calls. He will make the scheduled calls, give them their instructions, and call me with confirmation that all deposits have been made to the Isle of Man."

Amy cannot suppress her curiosity.

"Grandpa, when did you set all this up, get all of these other numbers to call?"

"Honey, things like this have gone on for years. This is the way business is done in the shadow world. I just had to organize it for our use today, logistically. Rufus and I had this all planned out years and years ago, part of his and LBJ's secret back-alley stuff, I guess. I wasn't in on all their dealings, but I was in on and aware of enough so that I knew, if we ever needed to, we would be able to move quickly, if necessary. It was just our retirement fund."

"And you really believe that Rick's son can be trusted?" Roger asks.

Sam takes a long drink of Schlitz.

"He's an attorney," Sam explains. "A very successful attorney here in Chicago. He's doing it to help his dad, actually, because the money he is raising will be split four ways, between the three of us and Rick, Bobby's dad. I will send him his share."

For several minutes they sit silently, enjoying the calm, digesting their late breakfast, and the scenario Sam has set in motion.

Thirty minutes later, Bobby enters the final phone booth, across from McCormack Place.

"Hello, yes. I'd like to speak with Mr. Jenkins; he's the head guy there, in your building, at the DNC. I believe you will find he's expecting my call. Tell him I'm a friend of Dr. Sam Brown and Dr. Rufus MacIntosh. Sure, I'll be happy to hold."

Sam turns to Amy and Roger. "You both understand why we will have to disappear, right?"

In unison they respond, "Yes."

Sam reaches into his black duffel bag and pulls out a small package. "This is $175,000. It's yours. It's a wedding present to help you get started."

Amy is dumbfounded. "Grandpa, where did you . . ."

Sam cuts her off midsentence. "I saved it, honey. It's my money and I want you to have it. Look, the two of you will be able to pursue your academic careers again, in a year or two. I'll set it up, once you are both established with your new identities. But you need to live in the meantime. The money in our international accounts will be there, but it would be best for you to take no chances and just use the money I'm giving you today for the foreseeable future. Here's the codes to get to the account."

Neither Amy nor Roger can think of a response, too surprised by the money Sam has just presented them, let alone the millions they have access to.

Amy asks, "So, what's our next step, Grandpa?"

"We'll let the Dems and the Arabs fight it out for a time. The Arabs have been good friends with our government for a while now. So let 'em stew a bit. Let 'em play their games on one another."

The waiter arrives at their table with a large, gallon bottle of red liquid, and the check. The phone rings and Sam answers it. He listens for a moment and hangs up.

"That was Bobby. All the wire transfers have been confirmed as deposited in our account."

Roger cannot take his eyes off the gallon bottle sitting next to Sam.

Sam observes Roger. "It's pig's blood," Sam explains to Roger. "I'm going to put some bogus files in it for the Kuwaiti's and will leave it for them at a designated drop spot, just off Halstead and Larrabee, next to Cabrini Green."

Amy laughs. "You've got this all figured out, don't you Grandpa? And you're enjoying it!"

Sam smiles, pays the check with cash, leaving the waiter the largest tip he would probably ever receive.

"After we drop off the bogus files for the Kuwaitis we're headed for the Knute Rockne rest stop, just outside of South Bend, Indiana, about an hour from here. We'll meet Richard or one of his cohorts there and make the final transfer of documents, with a listing and the locations of all backup documents and files."

Sam winks at Amy. She laughs, delighted suddenly with their great adventure. They walk out of Shaw's Crab House, get into the waiting limo, and Rick pulls casually and confidently away from the curb.

Chapter Forty-Seven

Sam, Amy, and Roger sit in the back of the limo drinking coffee from a thermos Rick has provided. After an hour's drive on the Indiana Toll Road, Rick pulls into the Knute Rockne rest stop just outside of South Bend, Indiana. It is just after one o'clock as the three exit the back of the limo and Sam hands an envelope to Rick, who at first refuses it with a "you gotta be kiddin' me" smile.

Sam acknowledges his friend's gesture with a familiar laugh and a pat on his shoulder but places the envelope into Rick's jacket pocket.

"Don't need this, Sam. I'll get my share from Bobby, like we set up," Rick explains. But Sam insists, and the three stand in the parking lot, waving goodbye as Rick pulls away, back onto the toll road, headed back to Chicago.

Sam tosses his duffel bag over his shoulder and stuffs the files under his left arm, to permit easy access to his .45 on his right hip.

Roger supports Amy as she holds on to his right arm, and the three walk side by side, into the brightly lit rest stop that sports a McDonald's, a Dairy Queen, and a convenience store inside the facility. They enter and sit at a table in the eating area, near the front entrance, as it has a full view of the front parking lot, and part of the rear parking lot can be viewed through the windows and glass doors.

Sam directs them to a table and continues walking to the McDonald's counter and orders three coffees.

Sam delivers the coffees to the table and then excuses himself and heads for the restroom, taking the file boxes with him.

"Be right back," he says.

Roger and Amy sit at the table, alone for the first time since early that morning, lying on the bed at the Drake.

"This has all been more than a little hard to believe," Amy says, a small smile on her face, a lighthearted, playful, and yet unbelieving tone in her voice.

Roger smiles back. "Sam has certainly provided us an education, as well as with the means to support ourselves for a long time, maybe the rest of our lives."

Amy reaches across the table and squeezes Roger's hand.

"It's a future we will enjoy together," she says, with sincerity and love so true and obvious in her voice that it brings Roger to tears.

"I will never let you down again, Amy," Roger tells her. "I promise you that I will always be there for you, that I will always want to be there . . . that I will never falter!"

Sam returns and places the boxes on the empty chair between him and Amy, along with a large envelope.

"What is in the envelope?" a curious and observant Amy asks.

"A friend left it in the men's room for me," Sam explains. "Along with a car out back for you two."

Sam places a set of keys on the table.

"Your car is a blue Chevy. The notarized title and your new identity papers are in the trunk, along with some clothing and a briefcase, with additional important documents."

Amy is overwhelmed.

"My God, Grandpa! How did you do all this?"

Slightly embarrassed, Sam offers a short, concise, but generally truthful response to his granddaughter's question.

"I know. I never realized how good I am at this stuff until today. But there is a lifetime of relationships and connections that go into putting these things together."

"You are something else, Sam. Who could have ever guessed?" Roger acknowledges.

Sam laughs, comfortable for the first time that day.

"You two will be fine now. Study your new life histories carefully, then destroy them. I understand that there is a very impressive academic record for you, Amy. A little less impressive for you, Roger."

Roger laughs. "Well, that's appropriate, isn't it?"

Amy leans over and hugs Sam.

"I don't know how you could have done all this. But thank you."

Sam obviously appreciates and treasures the gratitude Amy displays for him.

"One of my old Washington pals helped. I've still got a few connections. Good Americans, loyal. I like to keep in touch with them."

Roger leans forward and touches Sam's shoulder.

"What about you, Sam? What are you going to do? Where you gonna go?"

Sam replies confidently, "I also have a new identity. Right in here." he explains, pointing to another envelope.

"You're not coming with us?" Amy asks.

"No, honey. I have my own car coming in the front lot. We need to leave separately. But I know where you'll be and I'll contact you as soon as I can."

Sam turns his full attention to Roger.

"I want you two to take good care of one another."

A black Chevy Suburban and a Ford sedan arrive in the front lot. The Suburban flashes its headlights twice. A man gets out of the Ford and into the Suburban.

"I've got to go," Sam explains. "That's my new car, but you two also have to go."

Roger stands and emotionally hugs Sam.

"Thanks, Sam. For everything."

Sam hugs Amy and then shakes hands with Roger.

"I love you, Grandpa."

Amy's words bring tears to Sam's eyes, and he struggles to hold them back.

"Oh, honey, you two are going to make this old Marine tear up and cry. Now go out back, your blue Chevy is waiting for you. When I see you pull away, I'll go out front and have an exchange with the boys out there. I'll give 'em what they want. Then I'll be gone too."

Amy and Roger start for the back door. Amy turns and waves to Sam.

"Go now, honey. And don't come back. No matter what. Understand? I'll find you. I know who to look for."

Sam points to Roger, indicating he expects him to care for Amy and to follow the instructions Sam has laid out for them in the trunk of the Chevy.

"You got it straight?" Sam yells to Roger.

Roger stops, sets down the bag and performs a perfect military salute, then turns and disappears out the back door with Amy.

Chapter Forty-Eight

Roger and Amy approach the blue Chevy in the back parking lot of the Rockne rest stop adjacent to the parking area for the 18-wheelers, many with their parking lights on as their drivers sleep.

They deposit their bags in the trunk. Roger stands in place, looking for Sam but unable to see him in the restaurant. After a minute or so he turns and gets behind the wheel of the Chevy. Amy is already in the car, looking at another envelope Sam left for them.

"There was a memo in this envelope Sam left us," Amy tells Roger. "It explains that, included in this envelope, there is a notarized car title, driver's licenses, college transcripts, life histories, all with our new names, with birth certificates and social security cards. I'm Sandra and you're Anthony."

The two look at one another and laugh.

"This says we've both been accepted at the PhD program at . . . you won't believe where."

Roger, happier than he can ever remember being, smiles with confidence and a new sense of self. Amy radiates happiness, sliding over to sit next to Roger.

"Sam is amazing. How in the world could he have done so much in so short a time?" she says. "It's as if he and Rufus had been anticipating all this for years." She is fully aware that Sam did this without any previous planning.

Sam waits in the front entry until he sees the blue Chevy pull onto the toll road on ramp. Then he takes a long sip of coffee and walks out the front door with the file box and an envelope with details inside identifying all the locations where additional files can be found.

Sam walks up to the black Suburban. The door opens, Sam hands the combined file boxes and envelope to the waiting hands of the man inside. The man hands Sam a set of keys for the Ford sedan, and Sam backs away, turns, and walks to the car.

Minutes later, Roger has just entered onto the highway a mile or so from the rest stop when a huge fireball explodes back at the rest stop. Remembering Sam's specific instructions, Roger keeps driving, ignoring Amy's pleas to go back to the rest stop.

"No, Amy," Roger explains. "We promised Sam. Remember? We promised! He made us promise."

Roger continues driving but touches Amy on the shoulder as she weeps, and she touches his hand, accepting that he has done the right thing, knowing that it would be unsafe and foolish for them to return.

As Amy looks back at the huge fireball, she smiles. "I know he's all right," she explains to Roger. "He wouldn't let me down now, just when he is going to be a great-grandfather in about eight months."

Roger almost stops the car, but continues driving. A tear rolls down his cheek, and he knows he is unable to speak at the moment.

"Don't worry, Roger." Amy tells him. "You'll be a great dad!"

Chapter Forty-Nine

Twenty-Five years later, a sign on an easel outside the ballroom at the Waldorf Astoria Hotel in New York City announces the 2005 American Sociology Association Conference.

Over four hundred people are in attendance as Roger and Amy make their way through the crowd, Roger shaking hands as they go to the head table. Roger looks over the audience, thinking it's been one hell of a ride from nothing to being a serious academic. He laughs to himself, Who woulda thunk it?

Amy is dressed in a long black skirt with a gray long-sleeve sweater adorned with a turquoise necklace. Her shoulder-length hair is jet black, which it has been for the last 25 years, with not one gray hair to be seen. Roger is wearing black boot-cut Wranglers with black Tony Lama cowboy boots, a white button-down shirt and a tan leather coat. His western look is set off by a short beard, receding hairline and a ponytail of about six inches.

As they eat their desserts, Amy chats with a nearby couple, and Roger looks around the room, on the alert for anything or anybody out of the ordinary. This is his very first time at such a national conference and is actually the first time he has every attended any type of formal academic meeting. He thinks, "It's been 25 years; that's time enough."

As the dishes are being cleared after dinner, Roger thinks he may recognize someone from his past in the very back of the room, though it takes a moment for him to accept that he is actually seeing her. He has always been worried that this would someday happen.

But there she is, he realizes, Ms. Pyramid, from all those years ago, returning to her seat. And Roger's mind wanders back, remembering her, their time together at UT and in his last class. She with the same hair, the same incredible body, and she sits next to a man, a man Roger hopes is her husband. But what in the world is she doing here now? Will she recognize me? Will she approach me? If so, what will I say? How can I explain my disappearance from UT? My new name? More importantly, have I been discovered?

An older gentleman approaches the microphone and clicks a glass on the table to draw the attention of the audience. "Ladies and gentlemen," the older gentleman explains, "as the outgoing president of the American Sociology Association, it is with great honor that I introduce someone whose scholarly work we all know and respect. Professor Anthony Madison has an incredible academic record, publishing 47 scholarly papers and 4 very significant books over the last 20 years. He has been the most referenced scholar in our field in each of the last eight years. Although his work is well known, unbelievably this is the first time he has ever attended one of annual our meetings. Hard to believe this University of Wyoming cowboy professor will be our next ASA president. I guess coming across the country by stagecoach from Laramie takes quite a while."

There is loud laughter and applause from the audience, and then he continues.

"Many of these works he coauthored with his beautiful and equally academically successful wife, Sandra. It is my true pleasure to pass the gavel to our incoming president, Dr. Anthony Madison."

Roger shakes the outgoing president's hand and accepts the gavel to a standing ovation. He pulls a single sheet of paper out of his jacket pocket and begins his speech. "Professor Seymour told me the custom is that I can only read my acceptance speech if it is on a single sheet of paper."

Roger holds up the single sheet to light laughter and applause. He avoids looking at the back of the room, where his former identity, he fears, could be known.

"Of course, this is a great honor for my wife and me to be here tonight. I am truly humbled by your having named me as your incoming president. This is an exceptional honor for two reasons. First, that you would consider a cowpoke," there is some laughter, he continues "and second that you would select anyone who came up with a seemingly crazy notion to establish a separate division of the American Sociology Association for Political Sociology."

There is a solid round of applause.

"At the age of 52, I have witnessed in my lifetime the ever-increasing importance of sociology to the development of political strategy. I think we all have.

"Why? Because of the fundamental truth that one's social, societal environment is the lens through which an individual views the world. Politicians have come to realize this simple truth, and have leveraged it to their own political and, all too frequently, to their very personal self-interest. What a surprise."

There is light laughter. Roger is unsure if his political reference will trigger a UT memory from his former student.

Roger continues, "This strategy, put ever so simply, is to foster the politics of dependency so voters will elect whoever promises the greatest personal benefit. The net of this process, unfortunately, destroys politics as a tool for helping to solve societal problems. The reality is, it actually creates more of them."

There is uneasiness, rustling in the audience, indicative that many are, or could be, uncomfortable with what Roger has just said. But he turns over his single piece of paper, smiles to himself and to Amy, once again holds the paper in the air and continues, "Professor Seymour was not specific in limiting me to one side of the paper."

This is followed by genuine laughter from the audience.

"As you know from my writings, this overreaching dependency-creation strategy is manifested in two very specific ways. One, it creates a culture whose sole focus is on material things, without the requisite realization that one's commitment to work is what provides opportunity. This has been operationalized, so to speak, through ever-increasing government funding of necessities, like food and shelter. In the short term this is caring. Perpetuated in the long term, this is manipulation, solely for

269

political reasons. And two, the by-product of this is that it destroys the culture of family by establishing accepted behavioral norms, not only due to not working but also extends to having children out of wedlock, which is also reinforced by government subsidies."

Roger pauses, looking out at the audience, realizing that he has their full attention but also knowing that many, if not most, of his fellow academics will react negatively to the fundamental premise he just postured.

"The end result of the creation and reinforcement of the material culture is that the sociology of debt becomes the norm, versus saving for one's future and for the future of others. The new norm is that self becomes more important than family and family values, and material goods come to represent the only path to happiness. The problem in this, of course, is that work is not part of the equation."

He pauses, looks at Amy, gains confidence from her expression and continues. "So, where is our society headed if we continue to follow this path of dependency on government?"

Roger looks up, knowing his next words will carry the weight of his argument but also the risk of dividing the room, likely more to the alternative point of view. "The logical sociological conclusion: the bankruptcy of our society, both moral and financial, both individual and collective." He pauses to let his words sink in, then continues, "And I must ask you to think of how such a scholarly society as this will be able to provide the necessary analytical focus to stop this cycle of dependency before our unique American society reaches its tipping point, beyond which there can be no return."

Tears of pride roll down Amy's cheeks as Roger receives a standing ovation from almost half of the audience, while the other half looks away in confusion, unsure how to respond, but having been challenged by Roger's remarks. Those not standing are clearly fidgeting in their seats, with many shaking their heads.

Roger's worst fear is realized; the woman he recognizes remains standing as the rest of the audience sits back down. And she continues applauding until others are compelled to once again stand and to begin applauding again. It is Ms. Pyramid. He asks himself, "Is it my words, what I said, or does she recognize me?"

Roger waves his hands, gesturing for those standing to take their seats, and says "Thank you. Thanks for listening." He is relieved when she sits back down and the rest of the audience follows her lead. He knows, though, either way, she will make her way up to speak to him.

The audience begins to leave their seats. Roger is bracing for something, unsure what it is. He looks down at Amy and recognizes the true joy in Amy's eyes and knows nothing can ever separate them again. He looks skyward, raises his hands as if in prayer and says, "This speech was for you, Sam. Now get me the hell out of here!"

NOT THE END

About the Author

Dr. Thomas J. Reynolds has been educated in three diverse disciplines (philosophy, mathematical statistics and psychology) providing him a unique foundation for his distinguished academic career in the field of decision theory and research methodologies. While serving on the faculties of the University of California and the University of Texas, Tom authored scores of scholarly articles and several books, as well as more recently some choice-related patents, with the commonality being understanding and quantifying facets of the decision-making process. More recently, Tom co-authored two political decision articles: one related to the relative effectiveness of negative political advertising (Journal of Consumer Research, 2008) and the second regarding how to optimize political strategy based upon a decision segmentation approach (European Journal of Marketing, 2010).